SOUL
VOYAGE

NOVELS BY
CAMERON ROYCE JESS

BEARER OF THE CHOSEN SEED, 2003

SOUL VOYAGE, 2004

SOUL VOYAGE

BY CAMERON ROYCE JESS

INSCAPE PUBLICATIONS
PORT WILLIAMS, NOVA SCOTIA
2004

Printed and bound in Canada by AGMV Marquis
Cover Design and Typesetting by Olivier Lasser

National Library of Canada Cataloguing in Publication.

Jess, Cameron Royce, 1943 –
Soul voyage/ Cameron Royce Jess

ISBN 0-9732414-1-1

I. Title

PS8569.E74S68 2004 C813'.6 C2004-904160-6

Inscape Publications
P.O. Box 401
Port Williams, Nova Scotia
B0P 1T0
www.inscapepublications.com

Publisher: Chris Alders
Shipper-Receiver: David Beach
Distributor: Derrick Boone
Communications: Paul Fitzgerald
Special Events/Bookkeeper: Elizabeth Fleury
Webmaster: Kathy Leighton
Cover Illustrator: Caitilin W. Pelletier
Editor: Larry Powell

ACKNOWLEDGEMENTS

This is a testament to people in my life whose encouragement and support have made the writing and publication of this novel possible.

Jacqueline & Bassam Nassar, friends who are always there

Morley Ward, my cousin and oldest friend for seeing me through many things

Chris Alders, a publisher who never says die

Linda, a partner still enthusiastic after copy editing the manuscript for the fourth time

Ron Corbett, a bosom pal who keeps me sane through it all

Malcolm and Sally, brother and sister-in-law for putting up with a writer in the family

Elizabeth Jess, my mother for cradling the desire to write

Joshua, a navigator whose example is a Pole Star to steer by.

*This book is dedicated to Ann & Peter Goddard,
whose enthusiasm for preserving the saga of
Joshua Slocum inspired the writing of this book*

PUBLISHER'S FOREWORD

"In the fair land of Nova Scotia, a Maritime Province, there is a ridge called North Mountain overlooking the Bay of Fundy...I was born (there) on a cold February 20, though I am a citizen of the United States, a naturalized Yankee, if it may be said that Nova Scotians are not Yankees in the truest sense of the word."

So begins *Sailing Alone Around the World,* an account of the first solo circumnavigation. Joshua Slocum began life on a subsistence farm at Mount Hanley, Nova Scotia, in 1844. His impoverished family was soon forced to move to Brier Island, Nova Scotia, where he grew up apprenticed to his father as a boot-maker, malnourished and virtually bereft of formal education. Despite this, his invalid mother's love of books stayed with him all his life.

Running away from home for good at the age of six-teen, Slocum commenced one of the most intimate relationships with the sea any person has ever lived. Fighting his way up from lowly deckhand on British merchant ships to captain of an American sailing ship at the age of twenty-five, Slocum set sail for Sydney, Australia.

Here he met Virginia Walker and began an extraordinary nautical marriage. Born of American gold-rush parents who kept going west till they reached Australia, Virginia claimed Amerindian blood and was an excellent

I

horsewoman and crack shot. A more appropriate mate for the adventurous Bluenose can hardly be imagined. She would remain by his side through typhoon and mutiny for the rest of her life. Theirs is one of the great star-crossed love stories of all time.

Life on the sea began inauspiciously with a voyage to Alaska, newly purchased from the Russians by the Americans. The *Washington* sank on an uncharted reef, but not before Slocum managed to save his wife and a profitable cargo of salmon which he landed in San Francisco, "a feat of self-reliance bordering on genius."

Slocum was soon at sea again as captain of the *Constitution*, a San Francisco to Honolulu packet. Virginia gave birth to their first child, Victor, aboard this ship in 1872. Restless for more adventure, Slocum soon became captain of the *B. Aymar*, a square-rigger bound for Asia. Their second son Benjamin Aymar was born aboard this ship as was their first daughter, Jessie, in Philippine waters in 1875.

Here Slocum took time out from the sea to tackle his second profession: shipbuilding. He set up a primitive boatyard on Subic Bay and lived with his family in a nipa-thatched hut while building the steam vessel *Tagadito*. When the purchasers reneged on their contract, he traded the *Tagadito* for the schooner *Pato*, moved his family aboard and set sail for Hong Kong. In 1877 he set sail for the Sea off Okhotsk, where they "began to take in fish" when Virginia's twins were four days old.

The voyage was a commercial success, thanks to Slocum's ability to trade for salt to process their bonanza catch. The *Pato* landed the first cargo of salt cod in Oregon, but the twins soon died. Slocum completed the 8,000-mile voyage by sailing the *Pato* back to Honolulu.

Selling *Pato*, the Slocums traveled to San Francisco and bought the 350-ton *Amethyst,* an ancient but full-rigged ship. Virtually the entire Slocum clan was soon employed aboard the *Amethyst* on her regular sweeps across the Pacific. Virginia taught the children, sang and played the piano. She also hunted sharks with her revolver.

March of 1881 found them in Hong Kong. Here, their last child was born, and Slocum fell in love with *Northern Light*, an 1800-ton windjammer and one of the greatest ships of her kind to ever sail the sea. Slocum, not yet forty, was soon her proud owner.

Moving his family aboard the windjammer, Slocum set sail from Manila with a cargo of sugar for New York via Cape Horn. At the zenith of his career, Slocum invited his father, to visit him in New York. Then they were off to Yokohama with a cargo of case oil.

The disastrous voyage signaled a long decline in Slocum's fortunes. It began with a bloody mutiny from which Virginia saved her husband with a pistol in either hand. Making a bad decision to sail onward with a mutinous crew, Slocum rescued a party of boat-wrecked Gilbert islanders before discharging his cargo in Yokohama. Then on to Manila to load sugar and hemp for Liverpool, passing Krakatoa days before the volcano exploded in the greatest eruption in history. The cargo was lost off the Cape of Good Hope and Slocum was forced to imprison a mutinous officer for the duration of the voyage.

The voyage was a financial disaster. The imprisoned officer successfully prosecuted Slocum, damaging his reputation. Forced to sell *Northern Light*, he bought a bark, the *Aquidneck*, and set sail for Brazil, then on to Buenos Aires. Here Virginia took ill and died – and the great love affair ended.

Slocum never recovered from loss of Virginia; the slow decline in his fortunes grew precipitous. After two years, he entered a marriage of convenience with his cousin, Hettie. Their voyage to South America ended in the loss of *Aquidneck* and financial ruin. While living in the wreckage he built the *Liberdade*, "an ocean-going canoe." Embarking his family aboard in 1888, he navigated five thousand nautical miles to Washington, D.C. – one of the truly extraordinary events in nautical history.

His bad luck continued. Hettie was left to look after his children while Slocum drifted ever downward. On the verge of becoming a derelict, a practical joke took him to Fairhaven in 1893 – and to *Spray.*

Slocum completely rebuilt the oyster sloop he found abandoned in a Massachusetts pasture – and started rebuilding himself in the process. When he set sail for Nova Scotia, he had actually embarked on the first leg of his now-famous voyage around the world – a voyage which most people said couldn't be done.

Gathering strength and confidence in Nova Scotia, the fifty-one-year-old sailed via the Azores for Gibraltar. Persuaded there by the British navy to turn round and head the other way, he re-crossed the Atlantic. Surmounting truly impossible odds, he passed the Straits of Magellan and voyaged across the Pacific, visiting Fernando Po and Samoa along the way. From Australia he crossed the Indian Ocean via the Keeling Cocos Islands to Durban. Then he sailed around the Cape of Good Hope and diagonally across the South Atlantic via St. Helena and Barbados back to Newport.

Little noticed and still unable to find employment, he was forced to write *Sailing Alone Around the World,* detailing his epic voyage. The book proved unexpectedly successful, for it is more than a chronicle of a sea voyage.

Success as an author enabled Slocum at long last to satisfy his family's need for a home, but he and Hettie were never happy together. More and more, Slocum spent his time sailing *Spray* until 1909, when his true mistress, the sea, mysteriously claimed them both.

IV

One of the most consummate masters of the sea who ever sailed, Slocum's legacy is not only his oft-emulated feat of sailing alone around the world; *Sailing Alone Around the World,* the work of a boy who received little if any formal education, established a literary genre and remains the outstanding work of its kind. He stands as a shining example of what the human spirit can accomplish in the face of adversity.

Now that we have established the contextual basis with which to proceed, Inscape Publications is proud to present the award-winning novel *Soul Voyage* by Cameron Royce Jess.

Chris Alders
Publisher
Port Williams, Nova Scotia
September, 2004

V

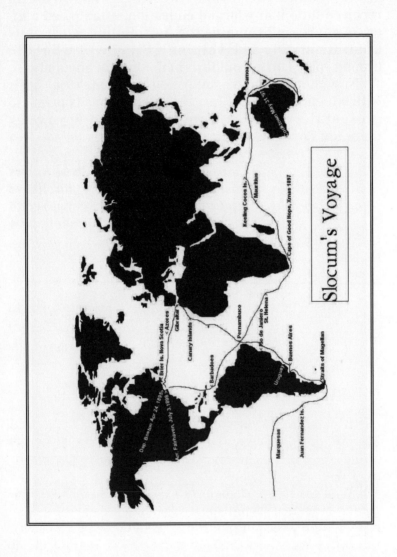

PROLOGUE

A feeling of awe crept over me. My memory worked with startling power. The ominous, the insignificant, the great, the small, the wonderful, the commonplace – all appeared before my vision in magical succession. Pages of my history appeared to me which had been so long forgotten that they seemed to belong to a previous exis- tence. I heard all the voices of the past laughing, crying, telling what I had heard them tell in many corners of the earth.

– From *Sailing Alone Around the World*
by Joshua Slocum

Boston: April 23, 1895

'It's right good of you to come see me off like this, Miss Wagnalls. I don't know how I would have got along without all the encouragement you've given me over the past two years.'

'Whatever do you mean, Captain Slocum? It's not as if men of your intrepid spirit need encouragement from a poor weak woman like me. Oh, some people are say- ing one man alone can't do what you're setting out to do. I've even heard some say that you're a fool to try it in this cockleshell of a boat, but like my father Adam

1

always says: the people who don't dream of doing worthy things are the real fools in this life. God willing, I'll be here to greet you when you come back.'

'As for that, Miss Wagnalls, I'll only promise you one thing: *Spray* and I, we'll not be turning back from this voyage around the world. It's not as though a pair of old derelicts like us have anything left to lose by "damning the torpedoes".'

'Why, my dear Captain, you make it sound as though you've nothing to come home for!'

'Well, ain't that the God's truth, ma'am? It comes to me that I'm a lot like that favorite Biblical character of yours.'

'Now don't blaspheme, Joshua Slocum! You're not the least bit like Job! You still have some true friends to come back to.'

'Just you, my dear lady, and maybe there's another true friend way off on an island in the Pacific I might call upon – if I were ever to make it that far, that is. Seems like my other friends all went down with my ships and my money.'

'Aren't you forgetting some things, my good Captain? You've a wife and four children who love you dearly!'

'No need to humor me, Mabel Wagnalls! I'm not that far gone yet. You know Hettie and the children are passing strangers to me now. Besides, they've all got their work cut out for them just surviving in this hard old world – what with no husband or father to look after them. God knows I forfeited my right to their love a long time ago.'

'And God also knows that real love doesn't stand on its rights, Joshua Slocum. You of all people should have learnt that by now. And look what a trim little vessel God has provided you! Look how she sits there in the water, waiting so proudly to carry you across the seven seas! The *Spray* will return! You may take it from me! I know it as certain as I know we're standing here on this dock.'

Aye, my dear Spray, Captain Eben Pierce was having his little joke when he gifted you to me, but now we've turned the joke back on him, haven't we? 'Well, Slocum, come up to Fairhaven and I'll give you a ship,' *says he, as church-charitable as you please.* 'She's an old oyster sloop from Chesapeake Bay. Mind you, she'll be needin' some repairs.'

A drowning man clutching at straws, that's what I had become somewhere along the way. So I took the old rascal of a Bluenose at his word and hied myself up to Massachusetts.

You had been moldering in that orchard for seven long years and more. You lay there propped up on spindly poles and covered with an old sail. Aye, you looked more like a beached whale than a man-made vessel. My spade-bearded guide, an old Gloucester sailor, gave your rotten rudderpost a gratuitous kick. 'Breakin' her up fer scrap, I s'pose?'

Tears came to my eyes. You had once been a proud and useful craft, plying your trade and enjoying the respect of the world, but time had passed you by and laid you low. And now you were good for nothing but to be broken up for scrap and firewood. Just as I had become good for nothing but to drown in rum and vomit on Skid Row or else eke out a few more years in some old sailor's home.

'Breakin' her up? Why no, sir, I'm going to rebuild her from stem to stern. Might as well rename her while I'm at it, I suppose. How does "Spray" sound to you, sir?'

'Spray?' *My guide hawked and spat his quid of tobacco before turning to stare at me as though I were a mad man.* 'Rebuild her? My Gawd, Slocum! Will she pay you for your trouble?'

'Why certainly she will pay, sir! You're looking at the very boat I am going to sail around the world!'

CHAPTER I

PORT OF CALL

It is known that a Briar Islander, fish or no fish on his hook, never flinches from a sea.

– From *Sailing Alone Around the World*
by Joshua Slocum

Brier Island, June, 1895

Well thar she blows at last! Pardon my Queen's English, old girl, but if this ain't one whale of a sight, then I don't know what is. And look at us! Here we are a 'scudding in through Grand Passage with a bone in our teeth and the fog lifting off the water. Aye, 'tis a moment like this that gives a man a feeling that life's worth living. I mean, isn't this just about as grand as it ever gets? Almost makes that long and dreary crossing up from Massachusetts seem worth all the tacking and heaving, don't it? And if it's frosting on your cake you be wanting, girl, why just take a gander at what's waiting for us up ahead!

Not that I'm saying little old Westport is worthy of the setting God gave her. Even after all these years, she still don't have a proper false front to her at all. Reminds me of a woman that's missing her whalebone stays and whatever else fine ladies wear these days to set themselves off. All gray and weathered and sort of strewn along the shore as if she'd been cobbled together from drift timbers and logs cast up by the Fundy tides. Oh, she's a far cry all right from those raw and bustling Yankee towns down south where the hammering and sawing never ends.

Aye, it's most as if someone framed the village like a painting and hung it up on a wall to dry. Reminds me of them seascapes Virginia used to clutter up Aquidneck's bulkheads with. Mind you, I don't see nearly so many masts foresting the Narrows as there used to be. Not so many brigs and topsail schooners bellying up to the docks either, but say now, that could just be old age fogging up my boyhood memories. You know how it is, *Spray*, when you coast back into some snug little roadstead where you ain't dropped anchor since the native oak in your hull was still sappy green. Everything and everyone that comes along looks and feels like a pair of cotton long johns that's all shrunk up from hanging on the clothesline.

Now don't go getting me wrong, old girl. I no more want this little backwater to ever go Yankee than I'd think of trading you up for one of the ships I used to skipper. Heck, it gives a seafaring man kind of a warm feeling to come back home every few years and find nothing's changed, like the place got stuck in time. Oh I know what you're thinking, that it ill behooves an old salt like me to wind up blubbering into my beard like this.

For I'm damned if I can remember ever feeling anything but miserable while living here as a lad. All right, maybe that's stretching the truth just a bit. I admit I've a few good memories tucked away, like that time I sneaked off with my mates in a dory on a sailing lark around the island, even if I did pay for it later with a thrashing. And how could I ever forget my dear old

Grandfather Southern helping me build my model ship up from scratch like he did?

Aye, Grandpa, there's the sunlight glinting off your mirrors and lenses way down there at the point. You've been gone now must be forty year and more, but I expect you'd be mighty glad to see the old lighthouse still going strong. And your lovely young daughter, as you always used to call her, she's been laid to rest beside Grandma most as long as you have. It must give you some sense of peace that all her misery and suffering are over at last.

Aye, Mother dear, here's your prodigal son come sailing back bold as brass into Westport harbor. He's come home one last time to pay his respects. It was at least partly because of him that you kept your face turned to the bedroom wall all those miserable years, was it not? You never reproached him to his face, but he's learned a skinful about life over the years. He's learned that it takes a heap more than just a hard and mean husband to make a woman give up on living for the sake of her natural children.

Aye, Father, here's your old cobbler's shop coming up fast on our starboard beam. It looks about ready to keel right over into the drink. Reminds me of a keel-broken vessel going down for the last time. That's the roof you'd never leave us mend, saying it was good enough to last out this evil old world. Lord, when I think of all the bad days you made me spend stirring the tanning vats inside that reeking hellhole! Why it's almost enough to make me come about and head *Spray* back down the Bay.

If you were to pop up wearing wings on the coach roof before me this very instant, I swear I'd brace you to tell me whether you ever got anything out of this life worth the living of it. Your heavenly reward for bearing and causing so much misery on Earth, has it been all that you were hoping for? Somehow I doubt it, though I'd not begrudge you something for your trouble. Whatever was the unspoken promise we Slocums brought to this land, I don't think you made much of a stab at keeping it. But who am I to preach to you about the keeping of promises? We always steered for opposite points of the compass, you and I. Strange that in the end we should have scuttled ourselves on the very same reef.

'Ahoy there, boy! Aye, you there on the dock with the peaked cap and the patched britches!'

'You talkin' to me, sir?'

'Aye, I'm talking to you, lad. Grab ahold of this line and warp me in! Step lively now and don't gawk about as if ye've never seen a sailing sloop come in to dock before. Where's your Bluenose manners anyway? You didn't grow up way down south on a Mississippi raft by any chance, did you? There, that's got it! Now take a turn round that bollard and put your shoulders into it like you was a grown man. I'll be along to help you tie her up as soon as I finish dousing this mains'l.'

'From the foreign way you talk, sir, I'm guessin' you're after being a Yankee.'

'You'd not be guessin' wrong, lad, though I originally hail from these parts. My name be Captain Joshua Slocum – you ever hear of such a man?'

'Slocum? I don' know of any Slocums here in Westport, Captain.'

'There be plenty of Slocums in your cemetery, lad.'

'I don't ever go up there, but the rest of the tribe, them that's living, they must have got up and left just like you did, Captain. Me mother, she says everybody's leaving the Neck and Islands these days. They're all a headin' out west a lookin' for gold or for greener pastures down in the Boston states.'

'Well, boy, I'm the living proof not everybody's dead or leaving. I've been the better part of a fortnight sailing to get back here from down Gloucester way.'

8

'You sailed this little sloop all the way here from Gloucester, Captain? Then why ain't your crew up here on deck helping you put her to bed?'

'Crew? What crew you talkin' 'boat, lad? I can't be bothered ferrying a crew around with me. Don't rightly need a crew nohow.'

'Not even to stand watches, Captain?'

'Listen, boy, I sail alone and see my vessel through whatever comes our way night or day, come gale or high water. Avast there, just what do you think you're doing with that dock-line? Didn't your father ever teach you how to rig a proper spring-line?'

'Do you do it like this, Captain?'

'No, by thunder, you do it like this! You want her to fall over on her beam's end at low tide? What in tarnation are you young folks coming to these days?'

'Sorry, Captain. Would you like me to come aboard and stow your mains'l for you?'

'No thank ye! I'd be a month of Sundays just getting the creases out. Better you just finish up with those stern-lines. And by the by, that clove hitch you're working on won't do for any vessel of mine. Make sure you tie off fit and proper around those bollards with a bowline.'

'A bowline, Captain?'

'Now don't go telling me that father of yours ain't taught you how to tie a bowline!'

'I ain't got me a pa, Captain.'

'What, you ain't got no father?'

'Not one to speak of, Captain.'

'Then you'd best watch my hands, son. See, you lay the rope's end over its standing part like so to form a loop. And then you work the end around behind the standing part like so and out through the loop again. Now there's a fair bowline that will see you through the devil's own storm if need be. Now you try it.'

'Like this?'

9

'Aye, the varmint comes out of its hole and goes around the tree and then back into its hole again. That's not too bad for a first effort, but you need to keep working at it, son. The tying of a good knot ain't like riding a bicycle. You leave off tying knots long enough, your fingers get all knotted up themselves.'

'Thank ye for showing me that trick about the varmint, Captain Slocum. I will remember that.'

'Did I hear you say you ain't got no pa, son? How come that to be?'

'My real pa, he got his self drownded fishing off George's Bank in the big storm of '92.'

'Did he now? I'm mighty sorry to hear that, son. It must be particular hard on your poor mother not having a husband and all.'

'Oh, you don't need to worry none about me ma. It didn't take her long to get herself another man.'

'Ahuh! What's your name, son?'

'Fred. It's still Fred Little, but my new pa, he wants me to change my last name to his'n.'

'Well, don't you ever even think of doing that, Fred Little. Whatever comes to us in this life, a man needs to keep his father's name about him. A good name is all a man leaves behind him for other men to remember him by. Here's a nickel for your trouble, son.'

'What, a whole nickel just for me? Captain Slocum, you want I should take you home to meet me mother? My new pa, he's been gone over to Portland quite a spell, you see, so there's room at our table and a spare bed out in the shed. Me ma, she's a good enough cook when she puts her mind to it, and I know she'd be some happy to take on a boarder right about now.'

'I can't afford to sleep anywhere but right here on my sloop, son. And I make my own meals down in her cabin, such as they are, but right about now I could use a speck of human company. Tell you what, I might find another nickel for you to take home to your ma if you'd care to tag along.'

'Tag along where, Captain?'

'Just up to the cemetery while there's still some daylight left for us to see our way around. I've got some kin up there I'm long overdue visiting, son.'

'Well, Captain, for another whole nickel, I'll go even up there. Just so long as we come back down to the village afore it gets too dark.'

Aye, Elizabeth, here's your wayward brother come casting his long shadow over you one last time. This slab of granite I had them set up for you as a marker, it's tilting over a bit, but otherwise you seem to be keeping yourself in proper trim. So here's a bouquet of lady's slippers I had young Fred Little pick specially for you along the way up here. I've already given some daisies and daffodils to Mother and the others, but there's some special things I need to say to you alone.

My dear Elizabeth, I do hope you're not feeling too short-changed that it's you lying up here cold and dead so young, 'cause I'm here to tell you right now that staying alive till you're old isn't all it's cracked up to be, either. As you can plainly see, I'm not flying high like I was the last time I visited you. Lost my money, lost my ship, lost the respect of the men I most respect....

Heck, I've even lost my new wife, assuming she was ever mine to lose in the first place. I married your young cousin Hettie in a weak moment, you know, but that's another story. Anyhow, she took off on me about two years ago with Virginia's children in tow, can you believe it? What may strike you as even more unbelievable, there wasn't anyone, myself included, who could blame her for going. Oh, being my sister, you might say she'd made her bed and ought to lie in it, but when there's no roof over that bed, nor even a bare cupboard, and the children are crying for hunger, well I ask you, Elizabeth: what's a good woman supposed to do?

Now Elizabeth, don't you go turning over in your grave because of me. It's not like I didn't give Hettie and

11

the children all I had to give. It's just that there isn't nothing left inside me since Virginia died. You know I was never one to be afraid to get my hands dirty. Why I even got down on my sorry knees and tried my hand at being a shipwright, but it sure didn't get me too far. It's like everything I turned my hand to melted into butter. And you know what a fussy cuss I am when it comes to choosing the ships I skipper. I cannot abide those new-fangled stinkpots with their grease and smoke and racket. Why I even fell so low as to try skippering one of them, but that didn't work out worth a damn, either. As for the sailing rigs, they're fast vanishing from the seas. It seems like there's nothing left in this world for an old-fashioned sailorman like me to grab on to.

Aye, Liz, the long and the short of it is that your brother's all washed up. He won't be ever coming back this way again. That's just as sure gospel as that God made those little green apples hanging from that bough over your head.

Do you remember how I was always showing off and making myself the center of attention? A lying braggart, that's what our father called me each time he thrashed me for my sin of pride. Our dear mother, she was more genteel. "Now, now, John, he's just putting his best foot forward," she'd say. "Lord knows, that's what he'll have to do if he's going to get ahead at all in this hard old world."

I lived for her kind words, Liz. At times, I swear they were the only things that kept me going.

Trouble is, it's plain now for all to see that our father knew your brother a whole lot better than our mother ever did. Heck, even the old man would be surprised how his son outdid himself this time around. You see, Liz, I've gone and shouted to the rooftops about how I'm going to sail my little oyster sloop all the way around this hard old world alone.

Now don't you go giving me that patented girl-look of yours, the one that much as says: you've gone and taken final leave of your senses, Josh Slocum. Don't you think I know as well as anyone alive that sailing alone around the world can't be done? So the thing I want you to try and understand, Elizabeth, is that I'm not fixing to finish this last voyage of mine. This world has narrowed down for me to the dagger-point of no return. So my good sloop, Spray and I, we'll sail off alone across this storm-racked North Atlantic. I don't expect we'll get too far, to the Azores maybe, if we're lucky. And then, after that, I hope to be seeing you, if the good Lord can find it in his heart to forgive me for being so reckless. Aye, Liz, I know what you're thinking: that being reckless is the least of my sins in need of forgiveness.

A strange thing happened on the way up here from the harbor today. I stopped off at the village store to buy the boy here a twist of licorice. Remember how you and me, we used to go down to the store and divvy up a penny worth between us? You'd always accuse me of chewing off the bigger piece for myself.

Anyway, today there was a newspaper fresh in from Portland with a front-page spread about my favorite writer, Robert Louis Stevenson. I do believe I once sent you his Treasure Island for a birthday gift, Elizabeth. Did I ever tell you that Virginia and I, we once ran across him out in San Francisco?

It was years later that I read about how his wife Fanny took him way off to the island of Samoa to try and keep him from dying of consumption. Seems like a long way to go just to take the cure, doesn't it? But you have to give her credit. Her idea won him the time he needed to turn out a few more good books afore he passed on.

Aye, Elizabeth. Robert Louis Stevenson, he up and died a few months ago way off on that island in the

South Pacific. Now you would think that would have made me feel real low, him being one of the few people I still count as a friend, but somehow it didn't strike me that way at all. Instead, the news came over me like a light opening in the gray sky ahead, which it shouldn't do at all. A mighty strange feeling it's left inside me, I can tell you.

So I'm going to have to do some hard figuring on what it all means. Maybe I'm just getting mean and hard like Father did, but then again, maybe I'm on the verge of discovering there's something more to this life than meets the eye. Whatever I come across before I reach the end of my rope, Liz, I look forward to sharing it with you just like in the old days. And this time I promise you'll get lady's first choice of the booty. So just keep on steering as best you can till you see Spray's sails spreading over the horizon.

CHAPTER II

BACALHAO

It was the season for fruit when I arrived at the Azores, and there was soon more of all kinds of it put on board than I knew what to do with.

– From *Sailing Alone Around the World*
by Joshua Slocum

The Azores: July 21, 1895

Sunlight glinting off Horta's harbor as *Spray* comes gliding in among the fishing-smacks. Work-gnarled hands proffering plums and cheese as I pick up a mooring. So many smiling faces bidding me welcome! One young boatwoman signs the cross over my head while standing upright in her battered dory. 'Senhor capitán, you sail here alone all the way from Boston, no?'

'Among other places, senhorita.'

Dark-browed and full-lipped, she lets go the sculling oar and grabs hold of *Spray's* taffrail in a flash of white teeth. She's really still a girl, but her ringless fingers are work-worn and hook-scarred. 'They tell me you are sailing this little *batel* around the world! Is this true?'

'Aye, senhorita. At least that is what I always tell people who make it their business to know mine.' I feel buck-naked hiding behind such threadbare words, but there's something about this young woman that holds me back from spinning her my usual web of lies.

She tosses long black ringlets at me ever so knowingly. 'Please take me with you, senhor capitán.'

'Take you with me, senhorita? I only wish I could, but whither I go a man must travel alone.'

'Who steers while you sleep, senhor?' She flares her nostrils and sniffs the salt air, lashing her painter to *Spray's* aft bollard. She tenders me her hand like a queen in coming aboard. 'A man like you ought to know better than to go off sailing without a good woman to cook and sew for him.'

'Can you cook flying fish, senhorita?' A better man than I would cast off this callused palm, would steer clear of these almond eyes.

'My specialty is dressing *bacalhao*. But you can teach me to cook flying fish for you, senhor capitán. I pick up such new things very quickly.'

'I'm sure you do, senhorita! What is your name?'

'Emilia Inéz Luisa de Sousa Maria, but I am called Inéz.'

'Inéz? Tis a rather delicate-sounding name for such a fine strappin' lass. Who taught you such good English, Inéz?'

'Another Yankee sailor from Boston. He was shipwrecked here last winter.' Is that a tear I see glinting in the far corner of her eye? 'Know you my John Wilson, senhor capitán?'

'There are many John Wilsons in a city so big as Boston, senhorita.'

'Boston is bigger than Horta, senhor capitán?'

'Aye, Inéz, much bigger.'

'But not so big as Lisbon, I think. You need only take me with you so far as Lisbon, senhor capitán.'

16

'So it's Lisbon you want to go to, eh? I am sorry, Inéz, but I am not heading that way.'

'How can you possibly hope to circle the world without passing through its navel, senhor capitán?'

'Lisbon may be the navel of the world, senhorita, but it lies much too far north of my chosen route. I sail direct for Gibraltar, and I have sworn to go every sea-mile of the way alone.'

She tosses her hair about her face as though to hide her chagrin. 'Have you sworn so heavy an oath by the Virgin herself?'

Long glossy hair whipping in the wind as Virginia takes the air upon the quarterdeck of the Morning Light. Nimble fingers matching the ivory keys as she sings for me some new-fangled tune in the windjammer's wood-paneled saloon. Coal-dark eyes blazing, a Smith & Wesson at the ready as she drags me free from an under-tow of murderous mutineers.

'Aye, senhorita, 'tis something heavy like that.'

'Then I shall pray for Her to watch over you, senhor capitán.' She stretches out over Spray's taffrail, lithe as an unfettered tigress reaching for her skulling oar. Old man that I am, the coarse black smock is way too faded and thin to forestall my desire. The pearl in her ear catches the muted sigh that leaps forth inside me. 'Had you no woman to sail with you, senhor?'

'My woman, she is dead these seven years, senhorita.'

'*Deus é grande,* senhor capitán, we must all accept His will.' She crosses herself and squints her eyes at me again. 'Perhaps you did not pray to His Virgin Mother long and hard enough. Did your woman die bearing you a child?'

'Nay, senhorita. She died on a voyage to the Southern Seas after bringing seven children of mine into this world.'

'What? Seven children! What a good man you must be, senhor capitán! But tell me, who looks after your little ones while you go off sailing round the world?'

'I took me a second wife, senhorita.' I do not bother telling her that my children are no longer little.

'Ah!' Her eyes open wide, chasing my thoughts back to Hettie sewing dresses and shirts to feed Virginia's children. Virginia's children and mine. Hettie writing me for money to help her bear my burden. 'Did your new senhora not wish to go sailing around the world with you, senhor capitán?'

'Joshua, I've had my v'yage.' Holding Virginia's daughter by the hand, the stepmother walks quickly away, not able to bear the sight of the ghost drifting at my side.

'My new senhora loves not the sea, Inéz.'

'Ah-h, the sea, she can be a bitch, no? A mere woman cannot help being jealous of her, for the lovers she takes never truly come back to the land.' Hands on wondrous hips, she turns her back on me, a splendid sigh uplifting her heavy bosom. 'The sea, I think she took you away from women of the land a long time ago, senhor capitán.'

I say nothing, content to smell the breeze riffling through her hair.

'Let me tell you my special secret, senhor capitán!' She looks around the bright and noisy harbor as though afraid of being overheard. *'Pai nosso* have mercy on me, but I am a true woman of the sea. Indeed, sometimes I dream I am the sea.'

I know her dream will run true, but a proper helmsman would turn aside from this course she sets me. Lord, how she frightens me as she tows me down the companionway! I've steered through full force typhoons with less binding in my guts than I take below. Shadow-striped, the sea-tigress crouches down on the cabin sole beside my berth. 'What is this book you are reading, senhor capitán?'

'The Life of Christopher Columbus. He and his crew keep me good company on my voyage. What in God's

name are you doing, senhorita?'

'It is too dark and close down here for the reading of books, senhor capitán. So let us imagine I am your lost senhora of the sea. Come!'

'Ah-h, senhorita, you will be the death of me!'

'Oh no, senhor capitán, I will be the life of you!'

'Look at me, Inéz! Look at me! I am fast becoming an old man!'

'That is why you need Inéz just now. She will breathe life into you again! Come!'

'Look, Joshua, the moon is full. Come, let us make a son tonight.' Virginia's smooth ivory body tightening around me.

'A man should not go forth to face death alone upon the sea with no woman to comfort him, senhor.'

CHAPTER III

STOWAWAY

*A sailorly chap, who understood how matters were ...
jumped on board ... and with a friendly hand helped me
set up the rigging. This incident gave the turn in my
favor. My story was then clear to all. I have found this
the way of the world. Let one be without a friend, and
see what will happen.*

– From *Sailing Alone Around the World*
by Joshua Slocum

North Atlantic: July 25, 1895

Perhaps you only dreamt that some Azorean boatwoman boarded you like a crew of fierce Barbary
pirates. Can it be only four days since she first told you
her name was Inéz? Is it possible only a few hours have
passed since she signed the cross on your naked chest
for the last time? Perhaps you only imagine that you
still smell her wild fragrance oozing from your pores,
still feel her heavy salt-laden curls trickling down your
neck. Well then, take it as some small consolation that
you need never wash away the spoor of her from your
leathery old skin.

She warned you not to eat too much of the plums
and the Pico cheese, but you were too drunk on the

wine of her to listen. Aye, you drank and you feasted till it was time to go. And now your gathering sickness goads the sea into a frenzy about you. Bestir yourself, man, bestir yourself while you still can.

But why should I lift a finger to forestall what must be? I always knew it would end thus. Virginia foresaw it all as she lay dying.

I'll be waiting for you, Joshua. When you are finally ready to take leave of the sea, I'll be waiting there on Heaven's dock for you.

Well then, fair enough, my dearest friend! I would not keep you waiting any longer, though I much fear old Saint Peter will not let me land. Twill be good to have done with this miserable world. Twill be more than good to be with you again, even if we find ourselves nothing more than shades caught fast in some fire-shadowed labyrinth of Hades.

Joshua, that heavy sky to the sou'west bodes ill. Whatever made you turn out those reefs? You must turn them in again somehow or perish!

Dear God, how these cramps seize upon my vitals! I cannot even rear myself off my hands and knees. If Hettie could only see me now! How she would shake her head and roll her eyes at me!

'Didn't I tell you so, Joshua? Didn't I tell you going back to sea would be the death of you?'

Bah! You never understood me at all, woman! Oh you tried, Lord knows, but you never understood what it means to be a man!

'Give up the sea before it's too late, Joshua. If you don't think enough of me to do it, then think of Virginia's children. We need a place on dry land. A snug little farm on Martha's Vineyard would suit us all just fine.'

Hah, a little farm on Martha's Vineyard! O God, the pain of it all!

There, Joshua, it draws back just a bit. Lets you breathe again. Better get that mainsail down while you still can. Haul out the earrings and tie away point by point in the double reef.

No, I mustn't lose my nerve this late in the game! Leave off chiding me, whoever you are! I'll not reset the sails for love nor money! I've spread every stitch she'll carry. It all comes down the same in the end. Far better to go down like a proper seaman than fizzle out as a rustic squire on Martha's Vineyard.

Here, son, what do you think you're doing? You know better than this! Why would you be swaying up more sail in such a gale? Don't play the fool! Even reefed, she's carrying way too much canvas for such heavy weather.

Aye, now I make out who you are. Well I remember your hardscrabble farm and your cobbler shop back in Nova Scotia. Better to be dead than live your life through again, Father. So I'll belay the sheets double fast lest *Spray* undo what I have done. This oyster sloop's a far better sailor than I am. If I were to make all snug and go below, there's just a chance she'd make it through the night. So I'll give her the double-reefed mains'l and the whole jib and set her on her course. I'll drive her down before the storm, by God. I'll drive her down into the deep if only just to spite you, Father.

Here comes that pain again. The devil's own claws rending my entrails. I'd best get me below.

Wait, man from the valley of sloe plums[1], at least have the guts to face the end at the helm like a proper Christian!

Don't cavil with me, Father! I'm way too sick to go down fighting. Besides, I've a way with the old girl. She might best the storm if I help her make it through the night. I'll just lash the wheel and let her go. Now I must get me below!

---

1. Apparently the name Slocum derives from the 'valley of the sloe plums'.

Aye, lie face down on the cabin sole where lingers the warm fragrance of that loose boatwoman you picked up. Lie there and dream of all the wicked women you have known till the sea closes over you. I heard that fancy wife of yours promise you she'd be waiting, but you won't find her at the gates of Heaven.

Ah Virginia, the world is spinning....

Miss Walker, see yon full-rigged ship moored there in the roads of Botany Bay? She's the American Merchant Vessel Washington, no less. A good ship in her day though a bit long in the tooth just now. I captained her here all the way from San Francisco just to find you. Not that I knew what I had come seeking till I saw your face. I only thought to go ashore and marry a suitable woman in Sydney Town. Yet the taking of a wife be the farthest thing from my mind when I look at you now. So what do you say, Virginia Walker? There is a whole new world out there for us to sail and see. Let us rather be friends for life and sail away from here, if it pleases you.

What's that? Do I hear someone singing? In Spanish, no less! Or maybe Portuguese. A stowaway come aboard from the Azores, perhaps? Inéz? Not possible for so much woman as she is to hide from a man such as me on so slight a vessel as this. I would smell her out instantly. The bilges are sloshing full, soaking me, but how passing strange the *Spray* still lives at all! She should have foundered by now. Gone delving deep into Davy Jones' locker. But wait, maybe she has! And we are both transported somewhere else. No, 'tis mere wishful thinking. She still plunges through a heavy sea, and neither angel nor demon ever sang so badly as this one.

'Avast there! Who are you, sir?' Why do I bother brandishing this old Martini-Henry at this brave creature? If he runs me through with that wicked cutlass at his side, is it any more than I yearn for? How tall he is! And in what foreign country did he come by a garish rig like that? 'Speak up, sirrah, or I swear I shall shoot you down like the dog you doubtless are!'

'Señor capitán, I have come to do you no harm. That harquebus you point at me, she is a wicked-looking devil of a weapon. I do not remember ever having seen her like before.'

Aye, smile when you say that! You do well to doff that big red hat. I swear, haberdashers haven't cock-billed heads that way these hundred years and more. Your shaggy black whiskers bode me no good. Well, if you do mean to cut my throat, by God, I'm just mulish enough to make it go hard for you. 'Sir, what do you mean steering my vessel without so much as a by-your-leave? Are you a pirate come aboard to cut my throat, sir?'

'Señor, I have come to do you no harm, I beg you believe me. I am no pirate. I have sailed free, but I was never worse than a *contrabandista*.'

'May I take it that you are Spanish, sir?'

'You insult me with so loose a phrase, señor capitán. My two brothers and I are Andalusians pure. I have the honor to be the pilot of the *Pinta*. Francisco Martin Pinzón, at your service.'

'What's that you say? You claim to be the pilot of the *Pinta?*'

'Why do you look so surprised, señor? Her Most Catholic Majesty, Isabella of Castile, did she not send all three of us Pinzón brothers to duenna that mad Genovese, Don Cristóbal Colón? Who do you think it was found the Indies for him? Alas, on our voyage home we have been becalmed out here these many days, more like years it seems to me now, but mark you well my words, señor capitán: you shall hear great things of us Pinzóns when we heave in sight of fair Seville again.'

'Becalmed, did you say? Look around you! We're heading through a raging gale, sirrah! Aye, you do well to look dumbfounded. I may be delirious, you Spaniard, but I'm not such a fool as to believe such a cock and bull story as yours.'

'Si, señor, tempests arise quickly here on the edge of the world! Lie quiet, mi capitán, and I will pilot your ship tonight.'

'You will do no such thing, sirrah. Quit my vessel instanter if you value your life!'

'Quite impossible, mi capitán, to do as you command with this wild storm raging! You must have a *calentura* to even suggest such a mad course, but not to worry, you will be all right in the morning.' My God, the mast and stays strain to the breaking point! This Spaniard must be the very devil himself to carry so much sail. 'Look, señor capitán! Yonder is the *Pinta* ahead. We must overtake her. Give her sail! Give her sail, I say! *Vale, vale, muy vale!*'

'I see no ship. Are you trying to wreck and drown us, Spaniard? I'll shoot you down like a dog if you are! I've done such things before, by God!'

'You did wrong, señor capitán, to mix white cheese with plums. White cheese is never safe unless you know whence it comes. *Quien sabe,* cheese made from goat's milk easily become capricious.'

'Avast, there! I have no mind for your preaching, sir!'

'I was not preaching – I was but making a clever play on words, but I forget you do not speak Spanish. Capricorn and capricious, don't you get it? Lie down, señor capitán. Si, that's right. Spread your pallet as a good master should where you can best keep an eye on your pilot. Don Cristóbal Colón would have done better to keep a closer eye on us Pinzón brothers, ha ha! Madre di dios, but you've all the comforts of home here on this little ship of yours. Aboard the *Pinta*, an ordinary seaman only rates a hammock if he be sick.'

'Then I rate a hammock even aboard the *Pinta*, Francisco Martin Pinzón. Proof of that be your presence in my cockpit.'

'What's this? Do you take me for a demon of your delirium, señor capitán? Why must you condemn me so?'

'For one thing, you speak fairly passable English. I much doubt you ever heard it spoken in your life!'

'*Inglés*? *Inglés*? My tongue may not shape Castilian fit for Her Majesty's ears, but I speak good enough sea-Spanish for all that. So lie still, mi capitán, while I sing for you an old Andalusian chantey. Harken to my song!'

High are the waves, fierce, gleaming,

High is the tempest roar!

High is the sea-bird screaming!

High the Azore!

'Stop that infernal racket, sirrah! That's not Andalusian or whatever you claim to speak! I quite detest your jingle!'

'Jingle! Did you call my song a jingle? You should know that I once killed a man for a lesser insult than this! But you do have a calentura, señor. As I am a good Catholic, I will forgive you this time, for doubtless my song loses something in the translation. English is a barbarous tongue by all accounts. Ah, if you could only hear me sing in Spanish, it would melt your heart of stone.'

High are the waves, fierce, gleaming —'

'Just tie a rope-yarn on it, sirrah. I suffer bad enough without your singing.'

'I've only seven more stanzas to go, señor capitán!'

'Watch out! There's a fine-weather sea set to poop us! Hard to port, pilot of the *Pinta!*'

'What, señor capitán? You presume to teach an old sea-dog of a pilot how to steer? Why, I could helm us through a worse storm than this blind drunk. *Ave Maria*, this is the mother of all waves breasting us, is it not? Oh, is there anything to equal moments like this, waiting forever down here in the trough to see if she will rise up again? This wave, she is drenching us, but at least she is warm! Si, she rides up like good Andalusian cork, this little ship of yours! Now tell me, did I not handle that better than you could do it yourself?'

'I can tell you've helmed a boat or two in your time, Señor Pinzón. Just keep your mind on the job, sirrah, that's all I ask.'

'Then go to sleep, señor capitán. We shall talk in the morning when you are feeling better. You may rest assured your vessel will make it through this night with Francisco Martin Pinzón at the helm.'

'Sir, I must in all fairness tell you that it was not my purpose to survive this night!'

'Why think you I have been sent aboard to relieve you, señor? Rest now, and we shall talk more in the morning.'

'Come morning, I trust you'll be long gone, Francisco Martin Pinzón.'

'Don't think to get rid of me so easily, Don Jèsu Slocum. We've a long voyage ahead of us, you and I!'

CHAPTER IV

SECOND CHANCE

The loneliness of my state wore off when the gale was high and I found much work to do. When fine weather returned, there came the sense of solitude, which I could not shake off. I used my voice often, at first giving some order about the affair of the ship, for I had been told that from disuse I should lose my speech.

– From *Sailing Alone Around the World*
by Joshua Slocum

North Atlantic: July 26, 1895

Dear God, leave off all this pain and have done with it! Damn those fool draymen up there on the pier, pelting us with puncheons off their wagons. *Spray,* where in hell are your fenders? Gird thy loins, I say. 'Ahoy there! You'll smash your brandy casks for naught, you damned fools! You can't hurt the *Spray*. Oh no, she's way too strong for the likes of you!'

'...Stop pounding on my cabin, you fools!'

'...Mabel, I fear you'll wait in vain for Spray's return. But I've been no worse than my word to you. At least *Spray* and I did not turn back.'

'...Inéz, I am so cold and wet. Don't let go of me! Make them stop pounding my poor head! I know, I should have minded you and left the Pico cheese and plums alone....'

'...Hettie, was there ever a wife more dutiful than you? Will you ever find it in your heart to forgive me what I've done? Very well then, God knows that I don't blame you. I commit Virginia's little ones to your prudence and mercy.'

'...Ah, is it really you, Virginia? My lover and soul mate, please wait for me, for I am following after you as fast as I can.'

Give praise to God, my son: the pain in your guts is easing! Get yourself on deck and see to your vessel!

There's no one at the helm! How is it, *Spray,* you survived all this long night without me? Aye, survived in spite of me if God's truth be told! Leaving you at the mercy of your sails the way I did. Your deck washed white as shark's teeth. Swept clean of everything not nailed down, I see.

And still easting like a runaway racehorse, by God! At this rate you must have come thirty league if you've come a mile. Grand Admiral Colón himself could not have done any better with his fancy *Santa Maria.* So you should thank your lucky stars for old Francisco Martin Pinzón coming aboard to pilot you, eh? Never mind that he let your jib blow itself to ribbons. Damned old pirate, didn't I tell him he'd jump ship by morning?

So just keep on truckin' while I haul my ass out of these wet clothes. I'll hang them from your shrouds to blow dry in the sun....

A meridian altitude, that's what I need most right now. Thank God I did not leave my sextant in its deck bracket, else I should have to make do with dead reckoning the rest of my voyage, just like old Cristóbal and that deadbeat pilot of his. Stop shaking, old hand of mine, or much good it will do us to shoot the sun. You and I together, we've picked off a whole Milky Way of stars in our time, have we not? At least the gale is slacking off and veering round. Now, if only bashful Sol will stand clear of the clouds a moment for to have his tintype taken. Ah-h! By Jove, I do believe we've got it! As pretty a sun sight as we've ever shot, I do swear. And now it's straight for the navigation tables. Holding faith in them is much like holding faith in the Bible – one must take both with a grain of salt – but unlike the good book, the Admiralty math's simple enough that I can fathom it out in my head. *Spray*, I make your longitude nineteen degrees, thirty minutes west. How did a thirty-five footer ever come this far so fast?

Just for luck, I'd better pull in the patent log and have a gander at what it reads.

Tis a wonder its line didn't break loose in the storm like everything else. Look down there, a pair of fat dolphin following it up! Ahoy there, you ought to be a mighty smart fish sporting such a brainy forehead as that. Aye, handsome sir rainbow, if only I'd thought to rig this log with a baited hook, I'd be eating you for my dinner, and your lovely bride would be a grieving widow by now. Dolphin widows do grieve for their husbands, don't they?

Hah! Can hardly believe it! The counter's gone crazy. One hundred and twenty one nautical miles logged since I set it last. *Spray,* you must have been surfing out of the water to make it so far! Dear God, I'm shaking so! Best lay down here in the sun and rest. 'So tell me, old girl, how did you ever do it? You ran true as an express train for more than twenty-four hours with no steersman at the helm!'

'You know better than that, señor capitán!'

'What, sirrah, are you back again to plague me? Do you actually have the gall to face me down in broad daylight?'

'You were expecting someone else in the middle of the Western Ocean, señor? Did we not agree to gam each other this morning? First though, I'd advise you to reset that jib and turn out the reefs in the mains'l.'

'I'm still weak from the calentura, sir. Perhaps you'd be so kind as to do the honors for me.'

'Oh, so you think to test me, mi capitán! I've come aboard to pilot your ship along, not to do your deck work for you!'

'Why do you wink at me so? Tis not you but my own senses I be testing, sir. It would seem that I'm an even sicker man than I thought.'

'Yet not so sick as you wish me to think you, señor capitán.'

'Truly I am going mad, sir! Why I can even pick up your foul scent when I shift downwind of you!'

'Tis no great wonder, señor capitán, for bathing is a pastime the company of the *Pinta* avoid like the plague.'

'What, no bathing at all? Why so dirty, sirrah?'

'First of all, we have neither room nor time for such trivial pursuits aboard so tiny a caravel. Airing our clothes in the sun once in a blue moon, just as you are doing now, is the best we can possibly manage in so crowded a space. And besides, 'tis common knowledge one can catch one's death by washing more than once a year. So you see, señor capitán, there's really no need to cover your privates while your outfit dries! God knows I've seen my full share of naked men before, and you may rest assured I find the sight none too pleasing even at the loneliest of times. Nor do I demand that you partake of my bread and wine either, as the saying goes. I shall rest content with your company so long as you do me the honor of paying heed to my good nautical judgment and piloting advice.'

'Tis hardly a bankable offer you make, Señor Pinzón! Tell you what though, I'll suspend judgment on whether you are real if you'll be so kind as to take yourself off my deck and promise never to return. There now, sir, is that not a square enough Yankee deal even for an Andalusian?'

'Rave on all you like, señor capitán, but it will do you no good to huff and puff so. I shall often be with you on this voyage of yours less you do yourself an injury. There, there, it will do you no good to curse at me. You would need to speak Spanish to do it with effect. You may console yourself that I'm rated pretty fair company aboard a seafaring ship.'

'Pretty fair company, sirrah? Then why do you pester me so by stowing yourself aboard my ship?'

'For the sheer love of adventure, señor capitán! For the sheer love of adventure I first came aboard, that and nothing more! But I confess to you that I've developed a definite soft spot in my heart for you and your little ship. So let me suggest that you toss those Azorean plums and the Pico cheese overboard while you still can.'

'First sensible thing I've heard you say so far, Francisco Martin Pinzón! There, are you quite satisfied? A capital feed for the fishes bobbling along way out here. Imagine dolphins and tuna nibbling at plums and cheese hundreds of leagues from the nearest shore. I only hope that the eating of them brings them better luck at steering clear of bloodthirsty pirates than I have had. Now, sir, for the last time, will you kindly take yourself off my ship and leave me be?'

'You know deep in your heart you wish me to stay, señor capitán. You are still quite ill. You need me to pilot your vessel while you get yourself some rest. Si, you'll be needing all your strength whither we are going.'

'I'm going to Gibraltar, sir. And I fervently hope you'll soon be Seville-bound in Columbus's scullery, where you doubtless belong, though it comes to me the devil's own kitchen be your true home.'

'Columbus's scullery? Alack, señor, your insults will get you nowhere. I fear the Grand Admiral of the Indies has gone on without me. God himself is my witness the

Genovese was never a patient man. As for the Devil, you need me at your side more than he does, good Catholic that I am. Someone to steer while you sleep, mi capitán. But first you must put your dry clothes back on or you'll catch yourself another *calentura*. In your wasted condition, it would surely be the death of you.'

'You forget yourself, sir! Aboard this vessel, I am Grand Admiral of all the Seven Seas! I take orders from no man!'

'Yet even an admiral ignores his pilot's advice at his own risk, si? So I wish you a good siesta filled with sweet dreams of dusky maidens. Buenos noches, señor capitán.'

Potatoes boiled and mashed to mush. Their stench reeking up from the outhouse. That is what I best remember along with gnawing hunger, for even the potatoes were in short supply. And Mother forever lying sick in bed. Her husband, John Slocum, my father, a dark brooding presence shadowing her small guttering candle of light. 'We are sending you to spend the summer in Hall's Harbour, Joshua. The fisher folk there are more prosperous than the farmers here in Mount Hanley. As you are my son, be sure to be a good boy for your Aunt Mildred.'

I wept a few tears, I'm ashamed to say, more for want of a parting kiss than at the dread prospect of boarding that coastal trading schooner. How sweetly she did lay offloading flour and salt at the rickety old fishing dock in Port George. In secret I already dreamed of going to sea in the likes of her. Oh, but how I did revel in that ripping sail along that bluff-bound shore! Great sea-spumes breaking on broken pillars and crags of rock. I knew, even as I puked out my guts into the swells, that I had found my true home, that I had only to bide my time till I grew big enough to break free of the hard-natured land. I've never once been seasick since.

No one was there to meet me on the great wharf at Hall's Harbour. After quiet Port George, I feared I might get lost in so bustling a place, although I doubt the fishing village could have mustered five hundred souls all told. The place did boast an inn, several stores and even a tidal boatyard for building big schooners such as the one that bore me there.

The kindly skipper hallooed an urchin tossing stones at gulls and asked him to guide me home to my aunt. This strange boy and I looked each other up and down as we made our way up the steep hill past the big whitewashed houses. I wanted to ask him whether these stately homes belonged to rich sea-captains and their dainty wives.

'What's that you got there?' The urchin snatched my mother's moth-eaten carpetbag right out of my hand.

All it contained were some flour-sack clothes and a few agates tumbled so smooth by the sea they could pass for marbles. I must have been born knowing what had to be done in such cases.

The boy sat up in the ditch and rubbed his jaw admiringly. 'Hey, you throw a pretty fair left for so scrawny a lad.'

'I get in some practice each time I go to Port George.' I gave him a hand up from the ditch as I slung my bag back over my shoulder. After all, I still needed him to guide me home to my aunt.

In a trice he kicked my feet out from under me and rolled me into the ditch.

'Just so you don't go thinkin' us Hall's Harbour boys are a bunch of pantywaisted girls.' He flashed me a freckled grin as he straddled me. 'We'd rather wrassle than fight with our fists, thass all. But hey, maybe I could get you to teach me boxin'. What's yer name?'

'Joshua, Joshua Slocum. I kin hardly breathe down here. Get off me quick else I'll knock you down agin!'

'I might just do that if you say 'uncle' nicely, Joshua Slocum. My own name will be Captain Ransford

35

Dodsworth Bucknam someday when I get to be a grown man. I'm gonna go to sea and sail ships round the world like my father did afore me.[2]

'Hey, get yourself off me, you blowhard! The likes of you sail ships round the world? I don't hardly think so!'

'And why not?'

'Cause that's what I'm going to do!'

'Now, is that a fact? Well then, maybe I've got somethin' fer to show you, Josh Slocum.' Ransford Dodsworth Bucknam let go of my shoulders and plucked something from under his big floppy cap, quite forgetting to make me say 'uncle'. I saw my chance and heaved him off me. Then as good as my word, I brought up my dukes to knock him down again, but instead of squaring off for a fight, he was holding out something for me to see. 'Careful now! You break it, Joshua Slocum, and I'll do more than just sit on you.'

'Why, it's the spitting image of a pretty little three-masted topsail schooner! Did you steal it?'

'No, but an old whaler with a patch over one eye gave it to me, which is just about as good as pirating it, I should think. Ole Billy Bass, he boarded at my house till my mother died last winter. Then he had to shove on, I'm sad to say. He used to say that he could plainly tell I'd be at least an admiral someday.'

I scoffed at him. 'You have to be an Englishman or at least a Yankee for to get made an admiral. What's your little schooner made of? I've never seen it's like before, not even back in Port George where we've got most anything you can think of.'

'Ole Billy carved it from a little piece of whalebone after the Rummy Maid.'

'I'll give you three agate marbles for it.'

---

2. In fact Ransford becomes a Yankee sea-captain, who went on to be created Bucknam Pasha, Grand Admiral of the Ottoman Empire's Navy.

'I should think not, but let's see them anyway.'

I half-talked Ransford into trading for four of my agate marbles, but he thought better of it before we got to the top of the hill. Not that I could blame him for welshing. In all my years of sailing round the world, I've not seen so fine a scrimshaw piece as the one he kept under his hat. We were jolly bosom pals by the time we reached my aunt's house. 'Well, I'll just take my leave of you right here, Josh. Your Aunt Mildred, she don't like boys much, especially ones like me.'

I was scared enough of bracing my aunt without Ransford Bucknam telling me that. I stood there in front of the whitewashed fisherman's cottage, just staring at the stretch of freshly painted picket fence and the hanging rocker on the porch and thinking: these relatives of ours must be a whole lot richer than I was told!

Just then a shadow darkened the doorway and a face peered out at me through the burlap screening. 'You Sarah's boy come up from Mount Hanley?'

'That I am, ma'am. Would you be my Aunt Mildred by any chance?'

'That depends on you, boy. You willing and able to work for your board?'

'Well, my father says I cut seed potatoes and rick hay most as good as a grown man, if that's what you mean.'

'Then most likely you can be learned how to filet pollock and hang 'em to dry. I guess you can come on in, boy.'

The screen door screeched on its hinges like a scalded cat. I got a full view of my Aunt Mildred for the first time: a wizened-up mite of a creature armed with a long filleting knife. I remember thinking that women must either get hard as nails like her, or else stay soft and take to their beds like her younger sister did. 'You'll be sleepin' there under the stairs. You can fill a tick from the straw out in the barn. What Christian name did your mother give you, boy?'

'Joshua, ma'am.'

'Joshua? Why, Pastor Baines was preachin' just the other Sunday that Joshua is Latin for our savior's name. Now that's what I call a prideful name to be giving a mere boy! I suspect that's my sister's doing. I've always said that she's a foolish woman, but that's no excuse for it, your father being a deacon of the church an' all. He should have had more sense than to let you be set up with such a temptation to sin.'

Aunt Mildred was a god-fearing Baptist, which meant Fred got to take her to church on Sundays. Fred being her big shambling hulk of a husband. He spent every day he could of that summer fishing out on the bay from dawn to dusk. Even when the weather was blowing up a gale or raining, he'd row out through the breakers and run up his little sail. A body didn't have to be too smart to figure out why he was so devoted to his fishing.

Still, I did like helping him hitch up the old mare to the little trap. Hanging on behind for dear life as she trotted along wasn't so bad either. Every Sunday we paraded Aunt Mildred down around the harbor and up the other steep side. Wearing her bonnet tied tight under her chin, she never failed of reminding me that the church had been built at a distance from the village just so that sinful people wouldn't get the idea that making it to heaven was going to be too easy.

Certainly Pastor Baines didn't leave us in any doubt about the need to make it to heaven, no matter how narrow and winding the road might be. He was a fire-breathing preacher who prayed for eternal hellfire and damnation to fall upon anyone who danced or swore or played cards or just generally did anything worth living for. Grown men would come out of that church still shivering and quaking. The children would be crying and one or another of the village women would usually require smelling salts. Not my Aunt Mildred though. She'd look certain members of the congregation straight in the eye

and say, 'didn't I tell you just what's in store for you, Cora
Bentley! Samuel Bucknam, you're going straight to hell if
you don't mend your smuggling ways.'

Yet in a strange kind of way, I think everybody kind of
enjoyed all that Sunday hellraisin. You'd hear people talk-
ing about the last service throughout the week, wondering
how Parson Baines was ever going to top it with his next
sermon. His was indeed a hard act to follow, but his
Sunday customers always seem to come away satisfied.

But what I liked better than going to church was
going out fishing on smooth-sailing days with Fred. He
taught me to sail the fishing-dory he'd sloop-rigged with-
out so much as a centerboard to steady her. Out on that
tricky Bay of Fundy day after day with the tide racing
and the wind blowing half a gale as likely as not, it's a
wonder he didn't drown long before he finally did. I'd bait
the hooks with herring while he took us out where the
gulls circled. He never said one word to me, although he
could talk well enough whenever Aunt Mildred asked him
a question. He'd just beckon for me to take over the helm
while he hand lined cod and halibut. Dear Lord, how I
loved the feel of the tiller in my hand and the wind filling
the sail as we coasted along fishing!

Some days Fred nearly swamped that little boat with
slithering fish.

Which meant I'd have to spend the next day helping
Aunt Mildred. She'd keep me busy slicing mackerel or pol-
lack and racking their fillets in the sun. She'd box my ears
for leaving too much flesh on the bone or hanging the fil-
lets too close on the rack. 'Don't waste the Lord's prove-
nance' and 'let the wind and sun get through, sister's son!'
She quite refused to call me by my proper Christian name
because she decided that would be taking the Lord's name
in vain. He's my witness how hard I worked for her, and
sometimes I even half-managed to please her, but it sure
wasn't easy doing that.

The best part of that Hall's Harbour summer were the long evenings after Fred came home for his supper and Aunt Mildred took him firmly in hand. That's when I would slip away from the cubbyhole under the stairs to go off playing with Ransford. We'd dory out into the cove and go aboard the Rummy Maid where she lay tugging at her mooring. Ransford showed me the plugged bullet holes in the topsail schooner's pilothouse from the time Yankee revenuers had come that close to making a complete orphan out of him. Standing there behind the spoked oak wheel, it wasn't too hard pretending we were daredevil rum-runners, just like Samuel Bucknam himself.

Yet try hard as we might, we could never get the fishermen of the village to tell us stories about the rum-running, which was kind of disappointing considering that several of them made the better part of their living crewing for Bucknam. Several times a season, he'd sail the Rummy Maid up to the French Isles and pick up a cargo of Martinique rum or maybe even some real French brandy. Then he'd slip down along the Boston States and rendezvous with Yankee smugglers. That would have been the really dangerous part of the whole business.

Aside from having to worry about being picked up by revenuers, Ransford explained how there was always the chance that the bootleggers would refuse to pay for the smuggled booze. Which meant someone stood a good chance of getting shot. On one occasion Samuel Bucknam stranded a crew of Yankees in their dinghy after sinking their steam launch for trying to hijack his cargo. It amounted to self-defense, Ransford maintained, but I figured the story signified a lot more than that. It made me look up to his rum-runner of a father as a pirate in good standing.

Sometimes I caught myself wishing my own six-foot father were a rum-runner instead of a dirt-poor farmer! I'd feel ashamed of thinking like that, him being a church deacon and all, but my shame didn't run deep enough to keep me from dreaming of growing up to be a man just like Samuel Bucknam, all five-foot-seven of him. He was a man who let nobody walk over him, no sirree, a man who shaped the world around him into the shape he wanted it to take.

It comes to me now that Ransford's father only forbid us playing aboard the Rummy Maid because that made it a lot more fun for us boys. Certainly he seemed to always wink and look the other way. Can't imagine my own father wanting things to be fun like that. One thing for sure, Ransford never seemed to be too worried about us getting caught.

Not that much ever seemed to worry that boy. Even way back then, I could tell that my new friend was going to amount to something when he grew up. I figured he couldn't help it with Samuel Bucknam for a father.

Aye, it was downright depressing thinking on what my own father held in store for me back in Mount Hanley. Such thoughts only made me more bound and determined to break away. I was going to make something more out of my life than just scrabbling out a living from a rock-poor farm.

Early in September, I left Hall's Harbour on the same big-bellied trading schooner that had brought me there. Aunt Mildred was busy up at the house racking a mess of cod, and Uncle Fred had gone out on the Bay fishing before daylight. For all I know, that may have been the very day he drowned, what with him being used to having someone along to handle the tiller and all.

Ransford was there on the dock to see me off, just as he'd been waiting there back in June to welcome me. He took off his cap and handed me the scrimshaw as a parting gift.

I held the Rummy Maid in the palm of my hand and thought about his mother dying and ole Billy Bass shoving along. I wanted to give his treasure back to him, but I knew I didn't dare. So I gave him a grin and folded it up inside my slouch hat for safekeeping till I could give it to my sister Elizabeth. I think we both knew that we'd not be seeing each other ever again.

CHAPTER V

fRANCISCO

I awoke much refreshed, and with the feeling that I had been in the presence of a friend and a seaman of vast experience.

– From *Sailing Alone Around the World*
by Joshua Slocum

North Atlantic: July 28, 1895

Good morning, my dear *Spray!* Aye, here you are still bounding east like you were an express train with your engineer dead at the throttle! Not that I've any call to complain about your shenanigans, mind you. It's no thanks to yours truly that you're still afloat. I know, old girl, I know! Your skipper let a ghost helm you right through that savage storm. If you'll forgive me, I'll promise on a stack of Holy Bibles never to let Old Nick catch hold of me again! Then maybe that damned Spanish minion of his will take himself off and leave us alone.

Still giving me a cold shoulder, are you? It's no wonder, *Spray,* we sailors think of ships and boats as being women. Well, the heck with trying to placate you! I'm starving, which means I must be coming to myself again! So while you sulk yourself out, I'll go stew up those ripe pears. Here's hoping they sit better on my stomach than the Azorean plums did. A gallon or two of coffee, that's what I need right now! Just so I remember to reserve some sugar and cream for the pears.

First things first, I'd better stick some real man-food to my ribs. And hello, what's this littering my deck? Flying fish! Aye, one, two, three, no four of the little beauties! You are manna fallen from heaven, my hearties. Probably last night you were winging along with your mates before some great monster of a fish. Thinking yourself free and clear skipping from wave-crest to wave-crest. Till you smacked aboard *Spray*, that is. Sad, but your rare bad luck is my crowning fortune of the day. You're enough to fry up a good batch of fish cakes in case the pilot of the *Pinta* should come back to me hungry. Aye, what a few of you wouldn't have done for the potato hash that was the staple fare back at the Slocum homestead in Mount Hanley!

Elizabeth, gray-eyed and gangly in her flour sack frock, already worn thin-chested from trying so hard to look after her siblings. Our mother just lying there with her face turned to the wall. Our father out ploughing the stones, the reins hanging round his neck like a noose.

Best you not think about that, senhor capitán. There's enough pain to go around in this world as it is without us reliving what's bygone. Here, O man of the sea, stew this big onion over the double lamp while you're frying up the fishcakes.

It's not your *bacalho*, Inez, but still a repast fit for a queen. Ah, if only I'd ferried you to Lisbon! How pleasant and harmless to think of impossible things that might have been. We'd dine together on fishcakes, and then, perhaps, you'd kindly oblige your *senhor capitán* down here on the cabin sole.

Enough! It's thinking such lewd thoughts that drive a man crazy, like a boy who plays with himself, according to the Gospel of John Slocum, that is! God rest his unforgiving soul.

Virginia at least would forgive me. Aye, if ever there was a woman who understood what it is to be born a man, it was she. If she could do it, then *Spray*, my dear, surely you can also find it in your heart of wood to forgive me for being what I am. Aye, here I am able and ready to man your helm once more if you'll have me back. Your tiller still cold and wooden to my touch. If I were to jump overboard right now, why I do believe you wouldn't luff so much as your jib. You'd steer away from me and sail straight on to Gibraltar all by yourself!

Nothing but azure sea out there as far as the eye can see in all directions. Swells still heavy, *Spray*, my love, but there's just enough wind to keep you ghosting along. Nothing out here but us castaway sea rovers... Do forgive me for abandoning you last night!

Ahoy there, straight ahead! What's that speck dancing on the waves? Driftwood? A whale perchance? A raft full of bones perhaps ... a passel of shipwrecked sailors who ate one another raw. One might still be left whole in that case. Unless the poor wretch threw himself overboard in the horror of it all.

You're still feverish, Slocum. How about you break out the spyglass and take a closer look?

It's a sea turtle, by God! A full-sized monster by the look of him. Asleep in the sun. And lulled by his bigness into thinking himself safe. He didn't count on a marauding predator wandering out here in the middle of the ocean. Too bad for him but awfully good for me. First fried flying fish and now turtle soup. Nose over just a point to starboard, *Spray*. Easy does it, my dear. And hush your rigging. We wouldn't want to startle him awake and make him dive deep, now would we?

Now gently unsheathe your harpoon and lay it ready on the deck. This be a whole lot easier than sticking whales despite the shells.

Now where did you ever have occasion to do either, Slocum?

Way back in the Sea of Okhotsk, was it not?

Thrashing ahead after humpbacks just for a lark. Virginia behind me shouldering the rifle, twinning the carved Siren I added to Pato's rig in Hong Kong, except she wouldn't bare her breasts to the wind, despite all my entreaties. 'None of your tomfoolery, Joshua. I must need stand prepared to put you out of your misery if the whale should break your foolish back,' she shouted back at me with a mock-indignant smile. The harpoon sinking in straight and true. The red blood spurting....

Got you, my friend. Forgive me.

Quick, let go the sheets!

Forgive me, old man turtle! You didn't feel a thing. As good as a High Lord Executioner, I am. But what am I to do with you, what with all this blood spreading on the sea? Got to get you aboard before the sharks come, that's for sure. You're to be my feast, not theirs. Dear God, Turtle, I swear you're as big as a Boston tug! Perhaps I could winch you in with the anchor rode.

'Caramba, what are you doing, Inglés!'

'Avast there, you papist Spaniard. I've work to do.'

'It is precisely because I am a God-fearing Catholic, señor capitán, that I am here to tell you that you cannot hoist that turtle aboard *Spray*. You might just as well try to hoist this boat aboard the turtle!'

'Francisco, I mean to have turtle steak for supper, come hell or high water. What would the Admiral of the Indies do in such a case, think you?'

'Don Cristóbal Colón? Why, he would lower the mains'l and hook onto a flipper with the throat-halyards, of course. But do not forget, señor, that lazy Genovese, he has a full crew of Andalusians heaving and pulling at his beck and call.'

'Aye, but your idea might just do the trick, Francisco! We could work the shell up onto the stern, which should keep *Spray* from heeling over on us. Then all we need do is let these following seas poop our turtle aboard for want of your Andalusian crew. Here, belay that jib sheet, will you? We must run before the wind.'

'Caramba! The seas will wash aboard with the turtle! You will swamp us for sure, señor capitán!'

'Nothing the pumps can't handle, Francisco. Hard a lee!'

'You need a burton to do such a thing, señor capitán!'

'Capital idea, Francisco! Remind me to rig a proper burton up for next time we need it. Here, lend a hand, will you?'

'Señor capitán, already she is shipping too much water!'

'The better to ship this turtle aboard, sirrah. Here, pull, damn you!'

'Señor capitán, you are mad!'

'Francisco, we are both mad, you and I, else why would we both be sailing right off the edge of the world?'

'Señor, God fashioned this world without an edge. How else could you be thinking of sailing around it? We Pinzons proved as much on our voyage to the Indies.'

'Heave, you lazy Spaniard, heave! That was no Indies your Genovese admiral discovered.'

'Do you call me a liar and insult me to my face, señor? And must I tell you again I am Andalusian? Caramba, your turtle is shipped aboard, but we are sinking! Are you satisfied, you crazy Inglés?'

'I am a naturalized Yankee, sirrah, not a damned Englishman. Here, man the helm and cut her hard into the wind while I work the pumps. Move your bleeding guts, damn you!'

'I must protest the discourtesy you show me, señor capitán! I hold special commission from Queen Isabella of Castile as one of Her Majesty's Pilots of this Western Ocean.'

'Well, Pilot of the Western Ocean you may be, but Queen Isabella, she may also be damned to hell for aught I care! Her Majesty was a Castilian landlubber of the first water from all accounts I've read. Bring her about, sirrah!'

'Señor capitán, you have shown discourtesy to a great queen. I shall require satisfaction of you when we reach land.'

'Haven't time to jaw with you right now, Francisco. I must pump my heart out else we'll be swamped for sure!'

'Si, pump your heart out, capitán! Si!'

Quick, pump the soaking vats full of brine, Joshua. Quick, Father will soon be coming. These foul fumes give me a splitting headache.

Aye, that is what I best remember of that time after John Slocum shook the Mount Hanley dirt off his boots and took us all to Brier Island to be a cobbler – of all things. Refusing to mind that he had been born with the sea in his blood. Condemned by his own stubborn will to eke out a bare living by the sweat of his brow. Aye, he was born to follow the sea if ever a man was. Didn't I come by my salt-lust naturally from him? 'You are ten years old now, Joshua. Time to stop mooning after all these sailing ships that come into port. Time to earn your own living as an apprentice cobbler. As for more schooling, that would only lead you into sin, my son.'

What sin? What sin could survive this narrow cell, I wondered, looking out through the cracked, cobwebbed window of the boot shop. From its loft, I had a good view of Westport and most of Brier Island. I could see the tip of Grandfather Southern's lighthouse down at Southwest Point, of Grand Passage and the moored fleet of small fore-and-afters that fished Saint Mary's Bay. Which only made it a whole lot worse being trapped inside that cheerless hellhole day after day. Through the long hours I stretched reeking cowhides over the cobbler's last, stitching them into uppers and pegging on their soles. Worst of all I hated tending that foul soaking-vat brew. Father might as well have asked me to cut my throat as command me not to dream of slipping away on one of the small brigs moored just beyond my reach.

The winter I turned twelve, I began fashioning a model of a topsail schooner. To my eye, the most beautiful things ever shaped by the hand of man are sailing ships – more beautiful even than the great Yankee bridges or the soaring cathedrals of Europe. Mine never became so perfect as Ole Billy's scrimshaw, but it was a labor of love nonetheless that I wrought in furtive moments snatched away from Father's vigilance.

The keel and stem I shaped from a single piece of tamarack tackle found floating in the harbor. The knees I carved from native oak twigs, carefully matching them in pairs. The planking I shaved out with my case knife from spruce scrap saved from the sawdust burner at the village mill. These pieces I steamed one by one over the kitchen kettle, scalding my fingers sometimes, then raced down to the dark cellar with an oil lantern. There I pierced each one with my cobbler's awl to receive the miniature oak pegs I also whittled from twigs. Those pegs I drove home with the same cobbler's hammer I used to make fishermen's boots, but oh! What different feelings it summoned up in me to work on my own ship!

But how my heart sank when I finally exposed my work to the light of day. For what a monstrous offspring I had begot!

My secret dream of building a beautiful sailing ship would have died there stillborn if not for the old lighthouse keeper at Southwest Point. My grandfather had no wish to spite his pious son-in-law and cause his daughter grief, but what was left of the old British tar could not turn his back on my poor wreck of a model. John Southern was missing several fingers, and those remaining were too gnarled by arthritis to form a good right hand, but he walked with me in the snow and fog among the piles of lumber and half-built dories and fishing sloops littering the waterfront. He taught me how

Nova Scotian shipwrights fashion out of raw spruce some of the finest vessels to ever sail the Seven Seas. Great ships, many of them, well able to carry our people round the world in search of trade and profit, of prizes and spoils. 'I'm an Englishman born and bred to the sea, but these Bluenoses are born with seawater in their veins,' he'd say.

We worked at my little schooner in the great beacon atop the lighthouse on those rare days when Father had gone away or was too ill to work. 'A ship is only so good as the life-blood men pour into her,' Grandfather Southern told me as we draped scraps of muslin from her match-stick yards.

Back in my cellar, I sanded and rubbed my little Bluenose schooner with loving care. She was no great frigate like the one Grandfather had served upon, but I painted H.M.S. Bellerophon across her stern in honor of the ship that carried Napoleon on his final voyage to St. Helena.

I was filled with a vision of Bellerophon circumnavigating Grandfather's great rotating beacon as I burst up through the cellar doors that fateful day. My father stood there, towering above me like some huge genie. Thus it was that I tried to dispel his anger by rubbing the little vessel I held in my hands as though it were Aladdin's lamp. 'What's that you got there, Joshua?'

'Only a ship's model, Father. I made it as a gift for Grandfather Southern.'

'Give it to me!'

I knew better than to surrender Bellerophon to the genie, but what else was I to do? He turned her end over end, amazed I think at what this boy of his had wrought, but his amazement quickly turned to anger. 'You are a thief, Joshua! Not only do you steal from me, but you steal from the Lord!'

His open hand smote the side of my head like a bolt from the blue. I lay on the frozen ground, dazedly looking up at him. My first thought was that he was quite right, that I would surely go straight to hell for working on the Lord's Day. And there were all the other days which belonged to him when I had sinned, building the model when I should have been cutting seed potatoes or stacking wood. He struck me again, harder this time. I sat up, the better to receive my due punishment.

He must have read in my eyes that there was only one way to truly hurt me. I saw him relish his triumph as he crumpled Bellerophon in his strong hands, then dashed her to the ground and stomped her rigging and hull into rags and kindling. But I would not let him win so easily. I laughed in his face. I can still hear, as if it were yesterday, the measured tones of my piping voice, but I think perhaps I was screaming at him. 'You are a coward and a bully, John Slocum!'

I do not remember more of that beating, but my father lost a son that day.

There was a time back in Mount Hanley when Mother often held me in her lap and read to me, but that was long before we came to Brier Island. Cooped up among the chickens just outside the very wall to which she turned her face, I gritted my teeth to stop the convulsive sobs, but she did not call out to me. In truth, she was long past taking a hand in anything. If I had not still been able to see the masts of sailing ships from where I lay, I believe I would have hanged myself that night.

'Josh, you all right? Pa told me I might unlock the chicken coop. Oh, your poor face is all covered in bruises!'

'Go way, Lizzie!' Muscles I didn't know I had ached. My misery was too sweet to share with anyone, even Elizabeth.

'Josh, you come out of there now! It's too cold to spend the night out here. Father's gone down to the boot shop.'

'I hope he drowns himself in the soaking vat!'

'Don't say such terrible things, brother! What if it should happen? You would feel you had his blood on

51

your hands. Deep down, he's sorry for what he done to you, Josh. He just can't help himself when he gets so angry, is all, and you can't expect a big grown man to ever say he's sorry. He's mortal afraid you'll run away to sea.'

'Never you mind, Lizzie. I'll be gone in the morning.'

'Yere only twelve years old, Josh!'

'That's old enough to go fer a cabin boy.'

'Josh, bein' a cabin boy on some fishin' schooner ain't likely no better'n what you've got here.'

'At least I'll be at sea, Lizzie, and far from him. That's where I belong, not here in that boot shop of his.'

'Please don't go, Josh! Some day I know you will, but you know there's no way for me to ever leave this place. Stay here by me just for a while longer. As long as you're near me, I feel like I'm still alive. If you go, I'll be good as dead.'

'I'll send for you, Lizzie. That's why I have to go as soon as I can. Someday, when I'm captain of a ship, you'll come and live with me. We'll have a master's cabin with big windows at the stern, just the two of us, you'll see.'

'It's nice to dream on, Josh.' She gave a little cough as if to let me know it could never be. I kissed her cold trembling lips as though we were lovers.

'I'll make it happen, Elizabeth. You'll see.'

'I see a tall handsome woman on your great tall ship with you, Josh, but she doesn't look a bit like me.'

What? Lizzie's gone. Just a dream. But dear God, how real she was! Anyway, Joshua Slocum, you've been sleeping long enough. As if manning the pumps for a few hours were enough to tire a sailor worth his salt hoss. Better go see what Francisco is up to. Aye, you'd do well to keep an eye on that one.

The gale has broken. But not before it ripped my new jib to shreds. Oh well, bend this jumbo on the stay at the night-heads, and let go the jib. I'm in need of pot rags anyway.

That flight of birds heading for land just where I thought it would be. And those clouds making up over a point of land not far over the horizon. Cape Trafalgar, I presume.

'Those clouds shade my homeland, señor capitán.'

'Aye, Francisco, that they do.'

'Are we headed for Palos? How I should like to see it once more!'

'No, Francisco, we're bound straight for Gibraltar.'

'For the Rock of Jabal al Tarik, señor capitán? Caramba, there's nothing in that god-forsaken place but a swarm of Moorish corsairs! They'll cut our throats and steal your vessel for sure.'

'The Moors are long gone from the Rock, Francisco. English pirates have taken their place.'

'What? English pirates here in Spain, did you say? What are you English doing in Jabal al Tarik?'

'We captured it from your compadres long ago, Francisco. We have made it the greatest fortress in all the world.'

'That's all very well, but why haven't we ever taken it back, señor capitán?'

'Not for the lack of trying, my friend, but once we English stick our heads beneath your skin and start sucking, we're hard as ticks to get rid of.'

'What is that cylinder you're holding up to your eye, mi capitán?'

'An Italian invention, Francisco. It is properly called a telescope. It brings far away things close to the eye.'

'Ave Maria, Madre di Dios! It could well be the Devil's own magic you hold in your hands, señor capitán! I find it hard to believe that the Holy Office would have given their blessing to such a sinister device!'

'No need to cross yourself, Francisco. These days the Pope himself owns one of these contraptions. It's true the Inquisition did once condemn it, but those black-caped imps of Satan are long gone from this world.'

'Truly? That would indeed be a blessing. They burned my sister Juana in the great plaza at Cadiz, you know. I knew she was no witch, but it would have been more than my life is worth to say so at the time.'

'That was a long time ago, Francisco. No one burns witches anymore, not even Spaniards.'

'Caramba! Then the world must have filled up with witches!'

'Look, Francisco, see you that ship off to starboard there? She's an Italian bark by the cut of her jib. And a sister-ship follows in her wake.'

'You have the advantage of me with your magic cylinder, señor capitán. Can you tell whether those ships be Venetian or Genoese?'

'It matters not, Francisco. All Italy dances to the fiddle of a single king these days.'

'Surely you pull my leg, señor. Venetians and Genoans and Neapolitans all serving one king like they were Frenchmen or Spaniards? Not to mention Romans, Florentines and Milanese. What you say is quite inconceivable! Next you will try to tell me His Holiness the Pope has turned infidel.'

'These days many Christians do accuse him of that, my friend.'

'Then we would do well to confess our sins, mi capitán! The world, she is about to end.'

'You may be right, Francisco, but she looks solid enough through this spyglass for now. Here, take a gander for yourself!'

'I dare not touch that fiendish thing, señor capitán!'

'Just imagine how the Admiral of the Indies would laugh to hear you say that?'

'No man laughs at Francisco Martin Pinzón with impunity, señor, not even Cristóbal Colón. Here, give me your magic tube!'

'Hold it steady, Francisco! You need to gimbal out the sea-motion with your knees and elbows. Now tell me, what do you see?'

'Jabal al Tarik with the sun shining on her! Your cylinder is truly magical, señor capitán, though whether it be white or black magic, I am not priest enough to tell.'

'We shall soon be there, my friend. Twenty-nine days from Cape Sable – not bad! We seem to have beaten everything crossing over with us save the steamers.'

'Steamers, señor?'

'Aye, steamers. You'll see one soon enough, Francisco. Speak of the devil! Here, swing the telescope three points to starboard.'

'Madre di dios, what is this thing, señor?'

'That be your steamer, Francisco.'

'But I see no masts, señor capitán! How does she carry her sail or ship her oars?'

'She carries neither, my friend. From deep in her bowels, demons straight from hell drive her through the water faster than sails or oars ever could.'

'Holy Father in heaven, but this ship is a huge monster, indeed! Caramba, do my eyes deceive me? Her hull gleams as though she is made all of Toledo steel!'

'She's made of good Sheffield steel, Francisco.'

'A ship made all of steel? How is it they do not sink to the bottom like a stone?'

'Did the good friars not teach you the Principle of Archimedes in school?'

'I did not go to school, señor. I shipped to Rhodes on a galleass when I was ten. Are those cannon I see sticking up from her decks?'

'Aye, Francisco, she's a British naval ship. One such dreadnaught as this could sink all the galleys and galleasses that ever rove this Middle Sea. You see before you a ship of the greatest navy that ever was.'

'A very brutish ship indeed, señor capitán. I would rather go to sea on a caravel such as my *Pinta* any day.'

'And so would I, Francisco. So would I!'

CHAPTER VI

CORSAIRS

My course to Gibraltar had been taken with a view to proceed up the Mediterranean Sea, through the Suez Canal, down the Red Sea, and east about, instead of a western route, which I finally adopted. By officers of vast experience in navigating these seas, I was influenced to make the change.

– From *Sailing Alone Around the World*
by Joshua Slocum

Straits of Gibraltar: Monday, August 25, 1895

I know just how you feel, old girl, I know! Being steam-tugged out to sea like you were a derelict hulk, that isn't exactly my tot of rum either, but it would not do to offend such fine gentlemen. These Britishers berthed you up like a royal yacht so I could make you shipshape again. No end of paint and new sails for you and milk and fresh vegetables for me. Not like those damn Yankees back in Fairhaven. Aye, they called me a crazy old coot for raising you up from their orchard the way our Savior resurrected Lazarus from his tomb. But these Gibraltar captains and admirals didn't so much as ask whether you were worth my trouble. Even that fierce old Scotchman of a port doctor did us proud once I showed him he couldn't buffalo me with all his cant about quarantines and passports.

Aye, *Spray*, it was a nice change being treated like an English earl and all. Touring the galleries of the Rock with a master gunner for guide. Wining and dining with Admiral Bruce and his officers aboard his flagship. I swear, if you stretched all their gold braid end to end it would reach around the world. And the weight of the medals they were sporting, it was like to sink their great battleship.

And then there was lunching with the governor of Gibraltar himself and going off a'picnicking with their fine ladies. All lace and fans they were. I wonder what Virginia would make of such a lot. Aye, I'd almost forgotten the friendly grasp of manly hands and the smiling gaze of eyes that meet you straight on, with nary a look of pity or any sign that they wish you to take yourself off. Soon makes a man soft, that kind of royal treatment.

'I say, my good Captain Slocum, the bloody long shore pirates are thick as fleas from here down to Aden. Your way eastward is shut as tight as an Irish sailor. It's all a light naval rig can do to run such a gauntlet. Those heathens will snatch up your little vessel for sure!'

The lot of them ganged up on me after dinner, *Spray*. They trooped me into the Admiral's library and plied me with brandy and a cigar. Then they took turns assuring me that it was worth my life and vessel to sail up the Med, pass through the Ditch and try going down the Red Sea. Not that I would have cared one fig for running afoul of Moorish pirates before Inéz and Francisco came aboard. As well go one way as another, I said to myself at least once a day, but I could hardly ignore the courteous advice of such fine gentlemen of breeding, now could I? Besides, I think now that we have at last a fighting chance to make it around the world and come back again, you and I.

Aye, *Spray*, feel that steady breeze, we're clear of the Mount at last. How many sailors have gone out past these Pillars of Hercules since the Phoenicians first made it through, I wonder? Countless thousands of them never made it back in again, God knows!

There's the bosun's mate's signal to cast off. Let go the hawser and tip your hat to the Union Jack. Fare ye well, my British friends.

We're free again as the wind, *Spray!* Aye, free to go back the way we came with our tail twixt our legs, I hear you saying. Well, it's not quite so foul a case as you make it sound, for this time we follow the exact same course that Don Cristóbal and Don Francisco set for the Canaries. A mighty good omen this. Oh I know what you're thinking: that having already crossed an ocean we ought to have more to show for ourselves than just to be starting out on the first leg of our own voyage! Sad truth is, old girl, we've not even got back to square one yet. We must recross the whole wide Atlantic just to get back to where we started, circum-navigationally speaking, that is.

Yet still and all, I think us well enough paid for a mere two thousand leagues of straying off our course. For now we know we can do what we've set out to do. You're no longer a Chesapeake oyster sloop, dear friend; you're a proven blue-water cruiser. As for me, well, I still do not know what the heck I am, but one thing's dead certain now: I mean to find out many things before this voyage is ended.

So, *Spray* my love, we're bound for Cape Horn via the Canaries and Cape Verde with maybe a stop or two or even three at Pernambuco, Rio and Buenos Aires, if we're lucky. So let's up with your sails and catch this volant wind while we can. By the looks of that sky she'll be a furious Atlantic gale before we pass from sight of land. But say, I'd far rather run before a storm than sit becalmed on so unfriendly a shore.

'Aye, señor capitán, you'd do well not to forget that's the Barbary Coast hanging there like smoke upon the horizon.'

'Avast the doom and gloom, Francisco! Never go looking for trouble, that's always been my motto.'

'Never go looking for trouble? So what made you go off sailing alone around the world?'

I remember well my first storm at sea. I came to it straight from laying Mother to rest beside her own father. Grandfather Southern's grave not yet green-sodded. Father straightened his stiff back and walked away, tall and foreboding as a church steeple. Nothing Elizabeth could say would hold me back any longer. Coward that I am, I left her standing there on the boot shop wharf. Aye, I wanted only to run away from there to the ends of the Earth. Even that hulk of a deal droger bound for Liverpool looked good to me.

Crimps piled our crew aboard fresh from the fleshpots of roaring Saint John. Dead drunk to a man they were except for my new chum Cheny and me. Sixteen years apiece, we two stood turns at the helm as the green seas piled high around us, the wind cleaving their white peaks into sheets of spray and foam. The old man and his two mates knew there was no sense leathering the other hands till they sobered enough to pump. So the three of them worked the sails the best they could, while the ship settled deeper in her leaking bilges. 'Josh, she no longer answers the helm worth a damn. Did you ever think our first voyage out would be our last?'

'No fear, Cheny.' I roared back gaily through the driving spray, though I felt every bit as green as he looked. 'With a cargo of spruce deal aboard, we may not sail well, but we shall never sink.'

And amid that raging storm, I remember the sheer glee rising in my gorge at being at last afloat upon the sea.

'Señor capitán, did you not tell me the Moorish pirates were long gone from these waters?'

'Nay, Francisco, I only said the English had displaced them at Gibraltar.'

'Take your magic glass and look behind you, mi capitán. What do you see?'

'A lateen sail making out from that little Moroccan port. I expect she's some sort of fisherman.'

'She's an accursed felucca, señor. I remember that rig only too well. She's fast as the devil himself and crammed to her gunnels with bloodthirsty corsairs, of that you may be sure.'

'Corsairs, Francisco?'

'Si, corsairs, señor capitán. As a young man, I was taken by them and passed three years chained to the oars till my brothers ransomed me. These Moors are accounted the fiercest pirates in the world, señor capitán. Since the time of dread Barbarossa they have scourged these waters for a living. Some things never change, I think.'

'Then let us make them earn their booty, my friend! Be so good as to steer two points to starboard while I rig the foretopsail.'

'This full reach is your little sloop's best point of sailing, compadre, but not even so can she outrun that felucca. She is built long and narrow, the better to chase down her prey.'

'Aye, but she's too dainty built for such heavy seas as these, and she carries too much sail by half for this gale. Here, sir, belay that luff in the jib, if you please!'

'Si, mi capitán, but look, she changes course to follow us.'

'Aye, you were right! They are indeed corsairs hell-bent on pulling us down! Well, Francisco, at the very least this fine day, we shall teach them a thing or two about blue-water sailing.'

'Your little vessel, señor capitán, she will broach if we are not careful. We also carry too much sail.'

'Belay your fainthearted palaver, Francisco. I reshaped *Spray* for such heavy work as this with my own two hands, and I shall answer for her! Oh what a glorious race we are making of it, though I do not much like the stakes we're wagering just now.'

'Madre di Dios, here comes a great sea, señor capitán! I cannot hold her!'

'Hang on! God damn you, Spaniard! Brace those long bandy legs of yours and hang on for dear life! I tell you, sirrah, the open sea, she is all woman, and I've always had good luck from her.'

'At least, mi capitán, your mast, she still stands. Call it luck if you want, but I was not the pilot of the *Pinta* for nothing.'

'Aye, sir, I confess I could not have managed that wave better myself. Yet I fear you have the right of it, another such wave as that and we are done for. We must reef her or we shall be dismasted.'

'Si, señor capitán, lucky you may be, but you must reef her, pirate or no pirate! It was in just such high seas as this that our good little caravel thought to out-run such a felucca. I remember as though it were yesterday how we stretched every sail we had from the yards till we tempted God Himself. And so we were dismasted and forced to surrender without so much as a fight. They threw the old men and the sick overboard that day.'

'There, are you happier now, Francisco?'

'Si, señor, but the felucca, she is gaining fast. We are both too old to hope for oar-benches, and who would pay our ransom in any case? My brothers, they are gone back to Spain with that crazy Genovese.'

'You forget you've already passed over, Francisco, so you don't need to worry.'

'Si, señor capitán, but if your little vessel be taken and your throat be cut, I will likely drift about on this sea forever.'

'Then there's nothing for it but to outwit them, Francisco. There, even close-reefed *Spray* sails gloriously, does she not?'

'Si, gloriously for a little sloop, but look at yon felucca, señor capitán! They will not reef their sails for the very devil himself.'

'Good Lord, they come down on us like the wind! See the top-knots of hair flying loose on the heads of those grinning devils?'

'That is so Mohammed may the more easily yank them up to Paradise, mi capitán! Just look at those devils, will you! They are sprung from the loins of generations of pirates! Armed to the teeth and loaded with hashish. Look, that one with red hair, he's their rais! I'll wager you some of dread Barbarossa's own pirate blood flows in those veins. Look how he waves his scimitar at us and grins. They're getting set to board us, mi capitán!'

'Aye, Francisco, but we Yankees have tangled with Barbary pirates afore this. Reach inside the companionway, if you please, and hand me up my Martini-Henry.'

'Señor capitán, you would pose your lone harquebus and my cutlass against so many? Surely you jest!'

'They'll cut our throats in any case, my friend. So let us sell our lives dearly. Prepare to jibe. By God, we'll ram these villains!'

'Hold on, señor capitán! Abaft the felucca comes the mother of all waves!'

'Aye, Don Francisco, I see it, and they are too exultant at overhauling us to look. Aye! Steady as she goes, my friend. I must get myself ready to douse our own sails.'

'Señor capitán, the felucca, she is broaching on the crest of that wave! Madre mia! Look at her go!'

'Aye, Francisco. Did I not tell you, I am a lucky man? I would love to see their faces now!'

'Si señor, but that mother of waves, she is still coming straight for us!'

'Hold her steady, sir. I must douse the mains'l!'

'No time, mi capitán. No time! Hold on for your life.'

'Well, Francisco, we shall soon see whether the sea still loves me!'

'Ave Maria, Madre di dios, feel her shake! She is tearing apart, mi capitán!'

'The sheet-strop just snapped! Mind your head there, Francisco!'

'There goes the boom, señor! Father in heaven, she broke off just short of the rigging!'

'I must douse the jib or we are lost, Francisco! Put down the helm hard!'

'There's no time for that, señor, no time!'

'There, Francisco! She's coming up into the wind!'

'Caramba! Feel her bound, capitán, feel her bound! But the mains'l, she and the broken boom are overboard!'

'Hold her, you damned Spaniard! Hold her while I secure the rigging!'

'Hold her I shall, but you cannot manhandle that boom and sail all by yourself. Cut it free with your good axe, you stupid Ingles!'

'Did I not tell you I am Nova Scotian born? Hold her into the wind, damn you, sir!'

'I thought you said you were a Yankee, señor. Do New Scotsmen baptize their new-born in sea water like this? Look out for that tangled rigging, mi capitán, or it will drag you overboard. I tell you again, the task you set yourself is far too heavy for one man! Jésu have mercy on our souls!'

'There!'

'I know not how, but you have done it, señor capitán! Si, done it without so much as a rip or a tear!'

'How now the pirates! Are they upon us? Hand me up my good old Martini-Henry, Francisco. When the salt-spray clears from my eyes, I want to be sighting Barbarossa's red-bearded bastard over my gun-barrel!'

'That wave and squall utterly dismasted them, señor! All they can do is shake their fists at us and rail to heaven. May Allah further blacken their infidel faces!'

'Did I not tell you I'm a lucky man at sea, Francisco? The sea, she still loves me in spite of all. Here, I shall hoist the jib and foretopsail. Steer her away two points offshore while I fish the boom and furl these sails snug for the night.'

'How proud I am to sail under your command, Capitán Don Jèsu Slocum of the *Spray*!'

'And I thank whatever God there be that I have such a pilot as you at the helm, Pilot Don Francisco Martin Pinzón of the *Pinta!* Dear Lord, I have never been so tired in all my life!'

CHAPTER VII

GUANCHE

Columbus, in the Santa Maria, sailing these seas more than four hundred years ago, was not so happy as I, nor so sure of success in what he had undertaken. His first troubles at sea had already begun. His crew had managed, by foul play or otherwise, to break the ship's rudder while running before probably just such a gale as Spray had passed through; and there was dissension on the Santa Maria, something that was unknown in the Spray.

– From *Sailing Alone Around the World*
by Joshua Slocum

Fuerteventura Channel: September 2, 1895

God's blood, I shake all over! This old body's way too tired to sleep after that chase, but an extra dose of quinine will calm my excited nerves. Malaria's been lurking in my blood since a boy crossing the *South China Sea* on the old *Tanjore*. Lots of bloody-minded pirates out there as well. Those Chinese and Malays put these Moors to shame. Aye, we saw only too well what they could do.

The sweet stench of death hung like a shroud over that three-masted junk where she lay stranded on a reef.

Built all of Burma teak she was. As we came up, we could see her rudderpost was broken, but we wondered aloud why the slant-eyed devils hadn't bothered to tow off so fine a vessel. Our square topsails coming over the horizon must have been what stampeded them.

Aye, we were too late to save the poor wretches that sailed aboard that junk. Blood still trickling from her scuppers. They cut the throats of even the women and children, except for that one China girl.

I came down too sick after that to stand watch for the rest of the voyage. If the Tanjore hadn't been so short-handed and the captain so mortal afraid of pirates, I think he might have thrown me overboard. Quite out of my head I was by the time we made Batavia. How well indeed they named it 'Pesthole of the East'!

My shipmates marooned my bones in that wretched hospital down by the stone docks. The stink of human waste filling my nostrils. I would have given up the ghost there for sure if not for the old Dutchman.

Aye, if any man deserves of me the title of true father, it be the Dutchman. From the nightmare of the China girl nailed spread-eagled to the deck, I awoke to feel his pale blue eyes staring down at me. 'Here, son, drink up this herbal tea.'

'And who may you be, sir?'

'Captain Airy of the Soushay. I make it a point to check this hospital whenever I'm in port for sailors left here to die.'

The tea tasted so bitter that I almost retched. 'Am I going to die of this fever, Captain?'

'Oh you're way too stubborn a Yankee for that, Joshua Slocum. With a little luck, I'll have you standing watch in a week or two.'

'My ship!' I nearly passed out in sitting up. 'I have to get back to the Tanjore or she'll leave port without me!'

'She cleared customs three days ago, boy. Your captain gave you up for dead, but not to worry. That's how I come

by most of my crew. Able-bodied seamen are always in demand in such a hell-hole as this. A berth's yours for the asking aboard the Soushay.'

'The Soushay, Captain? But she's a steamship!'

'Ja, but she's a good ship for all that. Not your run-of-the-mill stinkpot by any means. We're bound for the Spice Isles tomorrow by way of Kubu and Flores if you'd care to sign on.'

I tried to rise up from my cot, but he pushed me back down. 'Save your strength, lad. A betjah will fetch you down to the Soushay first thing in the morning. I'll just take your kit along with me if you don't mind. This so-called hospital teems with thieves and beggars as thick as those cooties crawling on your collar. Here, drink some more of this quinine tea.'

Captain Airy proved as good as his word, even down to the matter of having me standing watch within a fort-night. We had fetched the island of Amboina by the time he began teaching me how to navigate. Long evenings we spent poring over his chart table with compass and tri-square in hand. The old man seemed quite taken aback at discovering my natural bent for mathematics. In truth, he was no more astounded than I was at finding I could solve a quadratic equation with my eyes closed. More to the point, I began to see how I might carve out for myself a place in the sun.

I found Ambon Town a far better place than Batavia all round. Gone were the beggars and pickpockets reaching out and clinging to your clothing. The healthful fragrance of nutmeg and cloves rolling down from the island's high mountains quite entranced me.

After we discharged our cargo of rice and salt, I took a stroll up from the waterfront among the little shops and stalls. Feeling thoroughly sick of shipboard fare, I wandered about in search of something safe to eat. I was what you might call fussy, for Captain Airy had taught me well to touch nothing in tropical places unless I saw it freshly boiled.

So it was that I happened upon an Amboinese maiden minding a stall there. Her dark eyes put me in mind of the China girl who haunted my dreams. Only this one hadn't been freshly violated and left to die in a pool of her own blood, thank God. I watched her ladling up sago pudding from her steaming pot. She surprised me by accosting me in passable English. 'Oh, you way too thin to pass for sailor, young man! You look like you not eat in weeks!'

Her pale-green offering looked utterly repulsive, but it was bubbling hot and her accent was delightful. I traded her a brass coin for a dollop of sago on a thin cassava crepe. The spicy mélange tasted far better than I had expected, though it might have been those searching shadow-filled eyes that led me to think so. 'Sailor, I see you come ashore from the Soushay, but you're too thin and small for a Dutchman. Where do you come from?'

'All the way from the far side of the world, missy.'

'Ah so, sailor, then I am right to take you for a Yankee!' Her beatific smile lit up the space around us.'The wife of our missionary from America, she teach me good to speak English, no?'

'Aye, she did a right good job of it.' Her white flashing teeth quite dazzled me. 'Tell me, what is a mission girl doing minding a sago stall here in the market?'

'Usually I am busy teaching the younger children in the mission school, sailor. Just now I tend this stall for my mother. She is giving birth, as we are hoping, to my first brother.'

'May her day prove as fortunate as mine.' I smiled back at my fair maiden through a mouthful of sago and cassava. It struck me then that she was a good deal younger than she looked, maybe even younger than me.

Birdlike, she removed the pot from its charcoal burner and darted her glance around the marketplace, as though making sure that no hungry patrons were in the offing. 'Come with me if you please, sailor. There is something I wish to show you.' She tripped off lightly from behind her high counter, wrapped brightly in batiked cotton from head to toe. That was the first time ever in my life that a young woman led me down the garden path, though never again has it been done with such sublimity. Conscious of my awkward sailor's gait, I strode along warily behind her lilting form.

Shrieking parrots and riotous shrubs as gorgeous in plumage as my guide thronged the way she led me under the palms and nutmeg trees. A bright green serpent slithered away through the underbrush. I had grown more than a little anxious by the time we came out on a bare outcrop thrusting high above the Banda Sea.

A three-masted clipper had just cleared port and was beating her way to windward. The great ship was heading off toward Sunda Strait and the Western World that waited far beyond. Feeling somewhat homesick, I gazed longingly after her white sails till the silence could no longer be borne. 'Why have you brought me up here, missy?'

Almond eyes flashing and heaving her bosom, she turned back upon me then. 'Because I read in your eyes that you are a man able to look beyond the surface of things. Never before do I see this in the eyes of an outlander.'

'What in heaven's name am I supposed to see? That ship out there?' I gulped a deep breath of the humid air rising off the sea, but I still felt myself slowly suffocating. Her cryptic words frightened me even more than our long hike through the exotic jungle had done.

Her great lustrous eyes would not release their hold on me. I had to fight hard to keep from screaming aloud. She clasped both my hands to her cheeks in trying to calm me, but her skin felt as dry to me as the tightening coils of a snake. 'Forgive me, sailor! I do wrong thing bringing you up here, for it comes to me clearly now that your time to find the light is not yet. But you must not despair of see-

71

ing, for truly, the power to see is buried deep within you. The time to go in search may still come before you take your leave of this world. If it should happen so, sailor, try to remember these words I say to you now.'

How I feared that I would lose myself in those glittering eyes! I broke away and ran back along the narrow path as though fleeing a devouring dragon. Horrid reptiles and screeching parrots scattered away from my hurrying feet. And the words already forming on her lips were forever lost to me.

'Full of regrets you are, my son. A repository of regrets, of opportunities missed, a pit of so much misery that were better avoided, that's what you have become. It would go better with you to repent your evil ways. Take a good look at yourself in the glass! It is still not too late to turn back from this suicidal voyage.'

Nothing do I see to fear or pity in my reflection! Get behind me, Father. Your son has always been a lucky man at sea, and his luck is holding still. Escaped the Barbary pirates against all odds he has, and this half-gale is blowing *Spray* back across the Atlantic at a furious clip.

Long rollers piling up out there, but down here in your cabin it's hard to realize that we're sailing on the rolling breast of a mighty ocean. Whoops a daisy, my dear, guess I spoke out of turn! That gust of wind knocked you right over on your beam's end. I'd better go take a turn on deck and see what old Francisco's up to.

'Santa Maria, this devil wind, she is rising fast. Quickly now, señor capitán, douse her foretopsail while you still can!'

'Avast there, Francisco! Mind the wheel, damn you! Are you forgetting who is master of the *Spray?*'

'You, of course, señor capitán! But perhaps you forget who is her pilot! See you not those land-clouds on the horizon?'

'What, have we fetched the Canaries already?'

'Si, señor capitán! And over there, see the harmattan blowing off the Sahara, and that's Fuerteventura lying off there to starboard.'

'Well, Francisco, you make good time for a bead-counting Spaniard. So I will indulge you this one time as a reward for good service rendered. Head her up into the wind for a moment, and I shall see what I can do to ease her sails.'

'Mucho gracias, you pig-headed Inglés. Must I remind you again that pure Andalusian blood flows in my veins?'

'It was from the ancient Vandals your beloved Andalusia took its name, did it not? It's likely much of your blood comes from them as well. Zounds, man, I'd far rather style myself a Spaniard than a Vandal.'

'Señor capitán, it was the true Spaniards, those death-sucking Castilians – not us life-loving Andalusians -who are to blame for what was done on these Islands of the Dogs. With such ill omens as were given me here, it's no wonder that I've wandered lost over the sea these last four centuries.'

'So now the truth comes out, sir! You never completed your voyage to the Indies, did you now?'

'No, señor capitán, I begin to remember how it went with me after passing through these accursed islands that lie ahead. Even after we came to the Indies, I still could not banish the faces of those wretched Guanche from my thoughts.'

'Guanche? Who in the devil are these Guanche you speak of? I don't recall ever hearing that word used before.'

'Your ignorance of them is no great wonder, señor capitán. Even at the time we visited these isles long ago, few of their original people yet survived. Perhaps today even their name is long forgotten for all I know. Yet I well remember the most reverend bishop of Las Palmas telling Don Cristóbal that the Guanche were cousins of the ancient Egyptians, an accursed Hamitic race of idol-ators that needed chastisement to break them of their heathen ways. I had to bite my tongue to keep from ask-ing: what excuse is that for Christians to be wiping a whole people off the face of the earth?'

'So, Francisco, I begin to catch a glimmer of your true story. These islands are where you believe your troubles began!'

'Si, Don Jèsu, the Guanche, 'tis no wonder they placed a curse on us all!'

'A curse, you say?'

'Si, I could feel within my bones that our three car-avels were carrying the curse onward with us to the Indies. Already we were doomed by the gold lust and bloodguilt we bore with us. Oh I may be just a simple Andalusian sailor, but Don Cristóbal – may God have mercy on his soul – he once told me that there beats within me the heart of a poet.'

'Tell me, Francisco, is that why you did not finish the voyage?'

'Si, señor capitán, I was drowning too deep in my own troubles to mind what was going on around me.'

'That's a fatal mistake for a seaman to make, my friend, let alone a ship's pilot.'

'Si, Don Jèsu. In the absence of a priest, I confess to you that I fell overboard while trying to sight the North Star. Oh I am too good a Catholic to ever think of suicide, but those few Guanche faces I saw haunted me ever after. There was this one young woman blind in one eye begging in the plaza. Madre di dios, how she reminded me of my sister Juana!'

'Do not weep, Francisco. This time we voyage together, and we shall help each other ward off the Guanche curse.'

'Si, mi capitán, it will be different for us this time, si?'

'Aye, my friend, this time we shall make a voyage such as no man has ever made before, that much I promise you.'

CHAPTER VIII

DOLPHIN

... I found myself once more sailing a lonely sea and in a solitude supreme all around. When I slept I dreamed that I was alone ... but, sleeping or waking, I always seemed to know the position of the sloop, and I saw my vessel moving across the chart, which became a picture before me.

– From *Sailing Alone Around the World*
by Joshua Slocum

Atlantic Ocean: September 3, 1895

'Ahoy there, me laddie! No need to be so shy with me! You've followed us a long way, so we're as good as shipmates, you and I. You're welcome enough to tag along with *Spray*, but tell me, where's your fair lady taken herself off to this morning? Aye, you're on your own now by the look of things. Can't say I rightly blame her for taking off on you like this; I swear you're just about the most peaked-looking dolphin I've ever laid eyes on.'

'Oh, I see how it is with you now! You've been in a scrap of some sort and come away the worst for wear! A close brush with some nasty shark if I may judge by the looks of those wounds! Is that how you lost your

lady friend? Very sad! And having trouble making ends
meet these days, aren't you? Your starboard flipper's
been damaged so you can't chase down smaller fishes
like God meant you to. But you've still got the forehead
of a great thinker, laddie, so maybe you'll make it
through your trouble with a little help from your
friends. Escort us all the way to Pernambuco if you've a
mind to. I'll help you get there all I can.'

'Here's a flying fish I don't need for my breakfast.
Catch! Very good! People back in Boston, they would
pay big bucks to see you pull off a trick like that. All the
colors of the rainbow flashing past their eyes! Sorry, no
more fish! Well all right, here's a stale biscuit for you
then. Hah! I see you've never been fed hard tack
before. I know, you were expecting fish, but us sea-beg-
gars can't be choosers, my friend. That's right, gobble it
down any which way you can.'

'You must have stuck with us right down through
the Canaries! Aye, that was some rousing great sail we
had down past Fuerteventura, wasn't it? A wild storm
coming at *Spray* from every point in the compass.
Hurricane from the south, harmattan from the east and
line squalls to north and west of us. Lord, but this old
girl did lift up her skirts and run. Francisco, he kept
yelling at me to reef the sails. Where did the old pirate
take himself off to this morning, anyway? He's supposed to be standing watch and minding the helm!'

'Do you always talk to fishes, señor?'

'Well, sirrah, it's no worse a habit than talking to
ghosts, now is it? When a man is sailing on his lonesome around the world, he must put up with whatever
company comes his way.'

'Soon we shall be served ill company indeed, mi
capitán.'

'Aye, the harmattan, she comes at us again! Tis not
her season yet, but she's been threatening us for days
now. So come she must.'

'She's the foulest wind in all the world, señor. Soon our sails will be caked with red-brown dust. Madre de dios, how she howls down on us! Look at her come! You best cover your nose and eyes, mi capitán.'

Perhaps I would have done better to stay in the East Indies. No harmattan there, just the occasional typhoon and plenty of fever of course, which was my excuse for needing to push on. To finish sailing around the world that first time. So I sailed before the mast back to Liverpool, but I was learning more than tying reefs and climbing rigging. I was learning to navigate by the stars.

I remember how small they made me feel on a running sea. Between books and imagination, it takes a seventeen-year-old mind to grasp the immensity of it all. Condemned to a life sentence on this planet, I swore to make the most of it. And it occurred to me then that those great burning infernos out there might serve no higher purpose than to guide my way. Gazing at them over my pig-yoke, chills passed up and down my spine. How far would those stars take me before I joined all those sailors gone down to the bottom of the sea?

Aye, eternally grateful I am to you, Captain Airy, not only for saving my life, but for all you taught me while bent over the charting table or standing on the bridge helping DeVries the first mate shoot his sunsights. Thank God I had a way with numbers, or you might have given up on that spider-thin Bluenose boy. No doubt, gentle sir, you are long gone from this world, but many besides me still mark your passing.

Back in Liverpool I soon got my officer's papers from the Board of Trade. There were junior officers' tickets to be had aplenty on the outgoing steamships, but I sprang for a focsle berth on a full-rigged ship bound for the Indies. All my life, I've wanted only to sail.

Someone else's misfortune favored me soon enough. A flailing tackle crippled the first mate for life before we

77

so much as cleared the Bay of Biscay. There was nothing
for it but to make port at La Coruña and send the poor
chap packing back to England. That got Cheevers pro-
moted to his place. In his turn, Sneed made second mate,
and Captain Gusman knew I had my papers.

How strange it felt packing my duff out of the focscle.
Roco and the other chaps gave me such mean looks. No
longer my chums. Already taking the measure of the new
third mate they were. Sneed warned me the moment I
moved aft with him, but it weren't needed. Seems I was
born knowing what had to be done.

The very next morning, I came upon Roco and two
more of them skulking idly among the deck cargo when
they should have been greasing anchor chocks. I was for
giving them the benefit of a doubt for old time's sake, but
one stuck out a leg to trip me. I almost went down. God
help me if I had.

Roco, scar-faced and grinning, lunging at me on his
bow legs, but I had stuck a belaying pin in my belt under
my pea jacket. He never saw it coming till it jabbed his
midriff. Wind exploding from his grizzled mouth and
nose. Then I laid it smartly alongside his white scar, and
he went down like a pig of iron. His mates thought to do
better, but my blood was up, and they never got past the
belaying pin. When I looked up from the heap of them,
Cheevers was grinning at me. 'Now that's what I call a
morning's good work, Mr. Slocum. I see you have the
making of a ship's officer, all right. Those lads must like
you, else they'd have gone for you with their case-knives.'

The old man seemed pleased as punch with me.
'You're mighty scrappy for a pint-sized Bluenose, Mr.
Slocum, and I thank you for having the sense not to dis-
able any of that riffraff. We're shorthanded as it is.
Methinks you'll get no more trouble from any of the
hands this voyage.' Treated me to a hot toddy and a foul
Cuban cigar he did. Even offered me the first mate's
berth the minute Cheever's back was turned, but I told

him I needed to bide my time as third mate yet a while.
He laughed and thumped me hard between the shoul-
ders. Once back in our cubbyhole, I passed the cigar
along to Sneed, but I kept my belaying pin tucked under
the tail of my shirt just for luck.

This dust's as bad as that cigar smoke was. Even the
sea's turning to mud. Night's coming on already thanks
to the harmattan. Hah, feel that? The wind's veering
around to the northwest. 'Steady as she goes, Francisco.
I'll trim the sails for you.'

'Gracias, señor capitán. By morning we should sail
clear of this accursed wind, God willing.'

'As clear as ever one can, compadre.'

September 4, 1895

'Good morning there! I thought we'd lost you in the
storm. But I see you've come back with friends. One,
two, three mademoiselles, no less. And still hungry as
all get out, I see. Well, you're in luck! I've two flying
fish for you this morning. We're getting tired of eating
them anyway, aren't we, Francisco? Here, catch this!
Tastes good, eh? But take it easy. Swallowing it whole
like that, how can you tell whether it's good or not?
Anyhow, I'm glad to see your rainbow is much brighter
this morning. Quite a dazzling fellow you are, really. I
think you're going to make it to Pernambuco, my
friend. No, no, let those yellowtails fend for themselves.
No need to share with them; they look able-bodied
enough. If we can keep you from starving, you'll make
a lot of dolphins a fine grandfather yet. What, don't you
want this last one?'

'Señor capitán, look! A great mako!'

'Aye, Francisco, I see him! I do believe he's coming
in after my friends!'

They're just fish to the mako, mi capitán. And so are
we if one of us should happen to fall overboard. Take it
from one who knows whereof he speaks. Look, see
how your little ones dash off in all four directions! At
least some may escape him that way.'

'I'll be damned if he shall have them! Here, hand
me that tin plate, will you?'

'That's no way to catch a shark, señor capitán. Fix
big hooks on your line or better still use your harpoon.'

'I've no mind to land the monster, Don Francisco.
Watch this!'

'Bueno! You've distracted him! That fool mako
thinks your flashing plate a fish in distress! Oh how
ugly they are when they turn like that! What are you
doing with your little harquebus, capitán?'

'What does a man usually do with a gun?'

'Caramba! What a noise it makes! You shot him
right through the head, señor! I've never seen such fine
shooting! Not even one of Her Majesty's own harque-
busiers could have done it better.'

'As for that, Don Francisco, I've seen it done much
better with just a popgun of a pistol.'

*There, on the poopdeck of the Washington bobbing to
her anchor. Manila, I think it was. Virginia, still a beautiful bride striding off her morning constitutional. She
bent over the taffrail to observe a young harbor porpoise
sheltering under our stern.*

*That was what the hunters came for. Three striped
torpedoes cruising in, dorsal fins skimming the surface.
The porpoise rose up from the water, gibbering in fear as
though she meant to climb the rudder with her flukes.
The tigers brushed past her, then turned to strike, their
flattened snouts breaking clear.*

*Virginia's right hand darting from her green shawl,
the .32 calibre Colt bared like the fangs of a serpent. It
spat its poison thrice, its hawking innocuous as the
cracking of a twig. The charge of the tigers broke in a*

great crescendo of spray that drenched her trim ging-
ham skirts. The porpoise still whistling and clasping the
rudder as though unable to believe she still lived. The
three tigers white-bellied and drifting on the tide. Ah
Virginia, my love, you could be so deadly at times!

'Ahoy, Don Jèsu, here comes another of your infernal steamships!'

'Aye, Francisco, a cattle droger by the look of her.
Up from the river Plate and wallowing like a drunken
Frisco whore. You'd think one of the steers she carries
was helming her from the way she yaws. Head for her.
She has the wind of us, but I mean to send her a signal.'

'Will she recognize your flags, mi capitán?'

'Aye, if she sees them. But judging from the look of
her decks and bridge, all aboard are drunk or dead.'

'Father in heaven! I believe you are right, señor
capitán. She's a ghost ship!'

'Worse than that, Francisco. Hear the cattle bellow,
poor devils! And no end in sight for them but the
slaughterhouse!'

'Madre de dios, I can smell them! Phew!'

'Aye, she's a ripe one for sure!'

'She much reminds me of the Moorish galley I once
slaved upon, señor. Are there many such horrors still to
be found in this world?'

'Aye, compadre, more horrors than you can shake a
stick at. I have my doubts that such things get better
with the passing of time.'

'Then let her go, mi capitán, let her go. Let us not
tarry in so dismal a place.'

September 10, 1895

'So you've come back to us, my friend! I thought
that foul-bottomed droger had tempted you away from

81

smooth-keeled *Spray* for good. No one served you flying fish on a silver platter over there, eh, so you repented your desertion of us? Well, I may have something for
you despite your fickleness. One of your fishy friends is
gone missing, I see. Life is precarious and fleeting at
the best of times. That's as true of my life as it is of
yours. For either of us to believe else is vanity, as the
scriptures say.'

'Landfall, señor capitán!'

'Aye, Francisco: There be Santo Antão, northwest
sentinel of the Cape Verde Islands. When you consider
no observations for longitude were taken, 'tis wonderful to see it there, right where I dead reckoned it to be.'

'Santo Antão, you say? What are those Portuguese
sons of whores doing way down here?'

'They came for slaves four centuries ago, and they
linger here still. They pass their time composing pious
hymns for good Catholics to sing, no doubt.'

'Reef her snug, mi capitán, reef her snug, and let us
be gone from such an accursed place. There's a devil of
a squall blustering up over that highland.'

'Aye, we must be arsehole and elbows over the horizon, as my old friend Cheny used to say. Very well, Don
Francisco, reef her snug I shall, and then I mean to
sleep till you leave those islands dead astern.'

'Sweet dreams, señor capitán. You may leave it to
me to pilot us safely away from this hell-hole.'

Dear *Spray*, your cabin air is oppressive this night.
Hark, that's thunder afar off. Hereabouts the *Alert* was
struck down by lightning. What wonderful good fortune
that her people were rescued from so dismal a place as
this. How now? What sound is that! Either I'm mad or
there are human voices alongside! Father in heaven!

'Francisco, what in the devil's going on up there?'

'A great white bark coming at us through the mist,
señor capitán! Her crew speak your lingo! I can see and

hear them bracing the yards! I must soon give way or she will ram us!'

'Listen!'

'Skipper, what's this little sloop doing way out here? Is she a derelict?'

'No, I see lights in her cabin. She must be a local fisherman. From out of Tarrafal on San Tiago, no doubt. Helmsman, hard a-lee, before we run her down!'

'Caramba, señor capitán! Her great wings brushed our mast!'

'Aye, she's a three-masted schooner. I felt her breath sliding past. This sea is not so big and empty as we thought, Francisco. We must stand a better lookout and keep our lantern lit for such as her.'

'You will get drenched with spray sitting there in the bow, señor capitán.'

'No matter that, my friend, no matter. I wish to think on passing ships and stars tonight. Our courses are much the same, I think.'

CHAPTER IX

BLACK MAGIC

My ship running now in the full swing of the trades left me days to myself for rest and recuperation. I employed the time in reading and writing, or in whatever I found to do about the rigging and the sails to keep them all in order. The cooking was always done quickly, and was a small matter, as the bill of fare consisted mostly of flying-fish, hot biscuits and butter, potatoes, coffee and cream.

– From *Sailing Alone Around the World*
by Joshua Slocum

South Atlantic: September 30, 1895

'Well, *Spray*, 'tis more than a month now we've been at sea. Am I tired? No, not one whit! But I do miss our friend's rainbow flashing clear of the water to catch a flying fish. Some shark must have got him in spite of all we could do. And how about you, old girl? Aye, you sail well enough in this fine weather, but methinks you carry too much mainsail for your own good. It'd balance your trim some to shorten this boom. What say you, we cut it down to right here where she broke when we bested the pirates? Aye then, I'll see to it when we fetch Pernambuco. Brazil isn't far off, I promise you.'

'Did you say Brazil, señor capitán? What kind of heathen-sounding place is Brazil?'

'Oh, Brazil is as good a Catholic country as Spain itself, Francisco – maybe better if I can believe half of what you tell me. Steady as she goes, I'm going to shoot the sun.'

'Shoot the sun, mi capitán? What manner of witchcraft is that? You'd be better off attending to the fish soup you left boiling on the stove.'

'That's not fish soup; that's my navigation clock, Francisco.'

'Your navigation clock, capitán? Is she a water-clock?

'Sort of. I have to boil it each time I need it to work so I can take a sight. Once it's been steamed, I just need to shake it like this. There, it's started working now. Hear it go tick-tock?'

'I thought only monks minded the hours.'

'Well, Francisco, I'm kind of a monk these days. But tell me, what does an old pirate like you know of monks?'

'I once sojourned at a Franciscan abbey in Estremadura, señor. The good monks cured me of a dropsy. For the purpose of purging me at regular intervals with an emetic, they employed a clepsydra which had a face on it very much like this water clock of yours.'

'Good man! Then I can rely on you to tell me what time it is!'

'What does it signify when this long arrow points straight up?'

'That it's high time for my next sun sight.'

'Capitán, as I am a pilot, what does a clock have to do with navigating a vessel at sea? And whatever is that dreadful thing you hold in your hand, señor? Yet another infernal device of the devil or the Inquisition?'

'It's a sextant, Francisco. You will see soon enough what it can do. Don Cristóbal and you Pinzon brothers should each have taken one of these on your voyage.'

'As I recall, we were all good Catholics and navigated very well without resorting to instruments of black magic.'

Black Magic? Aye, I remember her well. It was way back in '64 I signed on her as first mate in Bermuda. Captain Gusman of the Devon called me a damned fool and swore he'd blacklist me for deserting him, but I'd had my fill of his mean English ways. I'd still be waiting to skipper my first ship if I'd stayed second mate on that old tramp of his.Aye, Black Magic the quicksilver blockade-runner. Dear Lord, it's been years since I so much as thought of her. She was a proud Bluenose schooner with a stretched beam for fishing cod till Captain Braxton slipped the double-expansion steam engine and the twin-screw propeller-drive into her. It takes a real Philistine to so ruin such a beautiful sailing ship. Hah, he liked to warm her boiler with a little anthracite each time we ran the Yankee gauntlet off Cape Hatteras. Anthracite burns clean and doesn't send up a telltale column of smoke, but it cost so dear to buy in Hamilton that he'd not let the engine turn the screw till masts on the horizon absolutely forced him to it.

Aye, Black Magic, a blackened but still beautiful lady with her crew of escaped darkies from Georgia! Black-crewed and black-hulled and black-fueled and black-sailed she was for sneaking through black nights. Old Captain Braxton swore black sails were faster. Aye, his Black Magic was fast all right, but he kept a small Nordenfeldt mounted as a sternchaser just for luck. We never needed it till that night near the end of the war we were running to Wilmington with a full cargo of guncotton and quinine.

The wind quit on us about twelve mile from port. We sat becalmed for an hour or more feeling the Yankee blockaders swarming thick as fleas around us. I wanted to stoke up the engine for the final run. Braxton was against it on account of the noise we'd make, but when the moon slipped out from behind the clouds and that Yankee cutter rose up out of the darkness just a couple of cables off our port bow, it sure changed his tune. I had the engineers shoveling anthracite before the old man could spit his quid of tobacco.

Not that the engine stood a snowball's chance in hell of saving us by that time. We were still building a head of steam when some Yankee bawled out, 'stand by to be boarded, you Johnny-Rebs!' I don't mind saying I had trouble swallowing the lump in my throat. Being just nineteen years old, the thought of cooling my heels in a Union prison for the duration of their civil war didn't sit too well. Even so, it didn't sound to me like deliverance when ole Braxton opened up with the Nordenfeldt.

I don't think he hit anything, but my God, what a hellish racket that gun made! It sure changed the captain of the cutter's mind about boarding us. He held off long enough for the engineers to get the propeller churning the water, but we were still barely moving when the first return fire whooshed across our bows. I didn't see the shell light, but I heard it explode and caught a whiff of burning cordite. It wasn't hard to imagine what would happen if the next one punched through Black Magic's hull into all that gun cotton we were smuggling to the Confederates. So it came as the answer to my prayers when the moon slipped back behind the clouds.

A breeze rose up with the darkness, and I spun her wheel down. Then the darkies and I trimmed those black sails till they stretched above the deck as taut as drumheads. All I could see was the whites of their eyes and their teeth gleaming when they laughed. Oh, I was a lot more scared than they were. 'What have we got to lose, mastah? We is only runaway slaves!'

Damn the engine, I thought, we've got sail power to burn now. And ole Braxton, he was cursing steady and working his gob like his jaw was a steam engine. By this time, he'd jammed the Nordenfeldt because he didn't rightly know how to reload it in the dark. The old skin-flint always refused to let us practice with it, saying ammunition for it was way too expensive to be wasted.

A couple more shells whizzed overhead. We could see their fuses burning, but we knew the Yankees were just firing blind into the darkness. Just when we started feeling comfortable, they started sending up magnesium flares, which is what sensible men would have done in the first place, but they came too late to harm us. Black Magic's sails had caught a wind, and we were flying through those blockaders, the white bow-wave all one could see of her in the darkness. We were sailing so fast that we almost ran down the Confederate gunboat guarding the entrance to Wilmington harbor.

'The arrow points straight up, señor capitán.'

'Thank you, Francisco. Time for another sun-sight.'

'Be careful what you do with that infernal thing, señor capitán, I pray you!'

'There, that's got it good, Francisco! Hand me that almanac, will you?'

'By our lady, I will not touch your book of spells. Better far to lose my perishable body than my immortal soul!'

'I thought both were perished, my friend. Are you not a suicide condemned to dwell here in purgatory with me?'

'Si, señor, but we Catholics sojourning in purgatory still have some hope of redemption. After all, it was not so much suicide as sheer carelessness that cast me overboard. Mayhap I shall win early redemption if I can help you see the error of your heretic ways before it be too late.'

'Well, here's good luck to you on making that one come true! There! I make our longitude 29° 30' W, and we just crossed over the equator not more than a mile back, Francisco. In a few days we'll sail in sight of land.'

'If you say so, señor capitán.'

'Jumping Jehoshaphat, Francisco, a great swordfish swimming right alongside us there! A good omen, no?'

'Si, capitán, a good omen indeed. See what a tall black fin it has!'

'Aye, and they're good eating, too! Here, I'll just tickle it for you with my harpoon.'

'Señor capitán, one does not kill a good omen! Father in heaven have mercy on us, you made him strike his flag and dive!'

'Aye, you are right, my friend. I shouldn't have bothered such a magnificent beast. Old habits die hard, that's all.'

CHAPTER X

NEREID

Be the current against us, what matters it? Be it in our favor, we are carried thence, [but] to what place or for what purpose? Our plan of the whole voyage is so insignificant that it matters little ... whither we go, for the 'grace of a day' is the same! Is it not recognition of this which makes the old sailor happy, though in the storm; and hopeful even on a plank out in mid-ocean? Surely it is this! For the spiritual beauty of the sea, absorbing man's soul, permits of no infidels on its boundless expanse.

– From *The Voyage of the Liberdade*
by Joshua Slocum

South Atlantic: October 5, 1895

'Land ho, señor capitán!'

'Aye, Francisco! I've been spying it out with the devil's own instrument this past hour or more. See you those waves breaking on yon headland? May God help me, for I believe that's Olinda Point bearing straight ahead!'

'Caramba, Don Jèsu, how you disappoint me!'

'How so?'

'You should be leaping for joy at the prospect of going ashore. Here you have been forty long days at sea with naught but a lost and wandering soul for company. One expects more enthusiasm from a fellow blue water seaman after so long a voyage.'

'I know not why it should be so, my friend, but my luck always bottoms out the moment I sail into these waters. I feel the qualms roiling like waves in the pit of my stomach even now.'

'You speak as though you once lost a ship to this land, mi capitán?'

'Aye, Francisco, I did so, not one but two!'

'Santa Maria! To lose one ship is bad luck indeed, señor capitán, but to lose two speaks of more than mere bad luck. Now I know from first hand that you are an excellent seaman, so what could be the cause of so much misfortune? Some siren of the sea bewitched you, perhaps?'

'I have not so good an excuse as that, my friend. My last vessel before *Spray*, she went down not far south of here only a couple of years ago. I still mourn *Destroyer*, albeit I was no longer her master or even serving aboard her when her end came.'

'For the sake of the Virgin, Don Jèsu! Enough guilt piles up upon us in this vale of tears without we should go looking for more. If you were not the ship's master at the time she was lost, then it was not you who lost her, si? Not even Our Father in Heaven Himself may hold losing her against you! You would do better to beware lest He convict you of the mortal sin of pride for taking the weight of so foreign a thing upon your own shoulders.'

'Be that as it may, Francisco, I cannot help feeling it here in my heart that it was no other than me who abandoned her. I delivered her into the wretched hands of Brazilian naval officers who were not true seamen at all! She lies at the bottom of that bay because of me!'

'Don Jèsu, you should listen to your friend when he tells you that you tax yourself too heavily in this matter.'

'Ah, Francisco, so seasoned a mariner as you knows well how it is with the loss of a ship. You do not master a vessel across five thousand miles of open sea without some part of yourself going down with her into the deep.'

'What a beauty she must have been to bewitch you so, mi capitán!'

'Beauty? Why hardly that, sir! As for bewitching me, my poor old *Destroyer* was built all of heartless cold steel.'

'Cold steel? You mean, like those ugly English ships we berthed alongside at Jabal al Tariq?'

'Indeed, Francisco, she was even more ugly than they are, for she was among the firstborn of their deformed breed. What great submarine cannon and belching steam engines she had for such a little vessel! To think I should live to see such squat ugly monsters sweep the tall ships off the high seas! But for all that, she was mine, and I loved her, after my fashion.'

'Caramba! You are an odd duck to feel so, compadre! As for me, I give thanks to the Virgin Mother of God that she did not let me live long enough to see such works of the devil take hold of the world! But tell me, what was your Destroyer like to tack into the wind?'

'Tack into the wind? Why sir, she could not even run before the wind! She lacked even a proper mast, let alone a sail. As for her engines, they were on strike most of the time. Even if they did deign to work, she needed to be towed across any open stretch of blue water for want of adequate coal bunkers. Good Lord, but how she did love to shortcut through heavy seas! Each time she broached a wave and plunged down on her beam's end, she held you in suspense whether she'd ever rise up again.'

'You make her sound a veritable monster indeed, señor capitán! Yet you grew to love her all the same.'

'Why of course I loved her, Francisco! You have sailed enough to know that ships are to men much as women are.'

'Si, señor capitán, what you say is very fine and true. But I think of that as no great marvel, when all is said and done, for the sea herself is a woman and all ships are borne by her on her breasts.'

'Your old Genovese Admiral spoke the truth, Spaniard! You are indeed a poet of the first water. A boatwoman in the Azores, she said much the same thing to me just the other day. The sea is a mysterious woman indeed. I've been sailing on her breast most all my life, but she still mystifies me as greatly as ever.'

'As for that, Inglés, your dull awareness of the mystery of her is but the beginning of true wisdom. The best that a man can do is come to sense her rhythm and learn to roll with her. If we do not, she brings us to grief and wrecks us soon enough. Your very first ship, señor capitán, is not the memory of her as sweet as the memory of your very first woman?'

'Aye, Francisco, I remember her well.'

The three-masted bark Washington. Three hundred and thirty-two trim tons she was. Built from Douglas fir on Puget Sound with not a butt to be found in her planking from stem to stern. Rough and ready and grown green in the bilge, but a lovely ship all the same.

I was barely twenty-five years old at the time of winning her. Merrill & Bichard offered command of her to me not so much for my sea-experience as for my success as a fisherman on the Columbia. The gill-netter I had designed and built upon the great river proved just the ticket for fishing its waters, so they thought I might be their man for opening up the new Alaskan fishery. 'First, we'd like you to deliver a consignment of mining equipment to Australia, my dear Slocum, and then we'd have you stop off in Alaska and gill-net us a shipload of salmon on your voyage home.'

Christmas, 1870, I sailed the Washington out of San Francisco Bay bound for Botany Bay, near half a world away. It was already nine years since Mother had died, nine years since I ran away from my father and never looked back. Ah, if only the two of them could see me now, I thought. Here I am captain of my own blue water ship. Neither of them would have believed their son capable of coming so far in this tough old world.

So great waxed my youthful pride that I thought myself sole master of more than just a mere sailing ship. My fate stretched out as boundless as the azure Pacific rolling before me. Virgin riches beyond imagining lay waiting for those with the courage and stomach to reach out and take them. And I was determined nothing would stop me from grasping my share of the booty that now loomed within my reach. Aye, I could feel it in my callow bones that I was well on my way to ascending the highest summits this world had to offer.

I would have done better to remember the maiden I had met in the Spice Isles so many moons ago. If only I had stopped to listen to her, I might have bothered to ask the true name of the mountain I was bent on climbing. A lot of pain and suffering I might have spared those I hold most dear.

Fresh from reading Pilgrim's Progress, I headed for the isle of Tahiti, deeming it an appropriate place to test whether I had it within me to tread the straight and narrow path to success and salvation.

Sweltering resplendently on Washington's sun-drenched deck under my heavily braided captain's hat, I lowered my telescope from scanning Mount Orohena to view the gleaming beaches. I could see my pale-skinned crew cavorting on the white sand under the palm-trees with dusky grass-skirted wahines. Never has the devil so cleverly disguised his minions, I thought to myself. Yet it would have been to court certain mutiny to keep those rough and ready lads from sampling what they mistook for earthly paradise.

I ran my telescope over the native settlement straggling up the gentle slope from the beach to a steepled cross towering over what passed for a town square. I made out a cassocked figure moving about some sort of scaffolding erected there. Doubtless the resident missionary was keeping busy contending with the forces of evil that ringed us both all about. That thought gave rise to a vision of my father, and it struck me all of a sudden that it was he more than the true me who stood rooted in my boots upon the deck. I looked down into the clear water and caught a glimpse of him scowling back at me.

This painful discovery of John Slocum still lurking within induced me forthwith to hand over my ship to the sole care and keeping of Pin-Yin, our Chinese cook. He brandished his cleaver at the offending palm-trees. 'Not to worry, Skipper! Me chop-chop any savages who try to climb aboard while you are gone ashore. Beware of the devils who inhabit such a place as this!'

I cast off in anxious quest of I knew not what. So preoccupied was I by visions of carnal sin awaiting me ashore that I snagged the small ship's dinghy on a barely submerged coral head. Looking about me, I could see starfish and seashells littering the crystal-clear bottom of the lagoon. They seemed so close at hand that I thought of reaching down and plucking them up from the water.

Suddenly the church bell began tolling. In its musical intervals, melodic feminine shrieks carried to my ears across the harbor. The wahines were scattering into the palm-trees as though fearsome predators were descending upon them. It was a sore sight for eyes as long at sea as mine had been! I would need to hurry if I hoped to save my crew from rushing headlong into these snares of the devil.

Intending to push my stranded craft ashore, I shipped the oars, stood up and stepped manfully overboard as though I were stepping onto dry land. Instead I plunged down into at least two fathoms of clear warm water. Not for the last time in this life, I sincerely repented never having learned to swim.

A myriad of brightly colored fishes flitted around me. A bewildering forest of marine plants undulated in the gentle inshore current. Struggling to the surface in my heavy clothing, I gasped out a cry for help, but my vocal cords utterly failed me. So down I went again into the clear nether world of the lagoon.

I struggled toward the pink coral head, hoping to climb up and perch myself upon it, but a fierce eel-like creature lunged out of its hole at me. Twisting away from its gnashing teeth, my bursting lungs filled with water. I surfaced one more time, excruciatingly aware that I was drowning. I remember feeling the most profound regret that all my great plans should have been brought to naught so foolishly.

It was then that some grasping thing strong as a ship's hawser coiled around my neck. I sought to grapple with my attacker, but I was too far gone to offer up much of a struggle. I felt my boot heels bumping along the bottom of the lagoon as though the creature were dragging me down into its deep lair.

Its tentacles ripped open my collar. A tremendous weight heaved upon my chest. Water geysered from my lungs. Heavy blows smote me again and again. I coughed, struggling with the terrible pain, retching up Pin Yin's man-sized breakfast. I rolled onto my back, staring up at the racing white clouds and rippling palm-trees, trying not to let go of them.

One of Satan's own demons sat astride my chest. She stared down at me with the loveliest brown eyes I have ever seen. Her only adornment was some crimson water-flower tucked behind her right ear. For some odd reason

I remarked the absence of a crucifix around her neck. Indeed, the total absence of any chest covering at all persuaded me that she had not yet accepted Christ.

She wiped my nose and mouth clear with a thick skein of her long wet hair, her full pink-tipped breasts undulating all the while not quite in unison with the rest of her. If she be the work of the devil, I thought, the old trickster is an even greater master of deception than John Bunyan gives him credit for. I opened my mouth to speak, only to have more water and bile come gushing forth.

As though wishing to put all my fears to rest, the demoness leapt to her feet. In a wondrous flash of lissome thighs and curvaceous buttocks, she swan-dived into the lagoon. I sat up and watched her overtake my floating symbol of authority. She pulled it down over her long flowing locks and then quickly overhauled my drifting dinghy. Clamping its painter firmly between her flashing white teeth, she began towing it ashore, much as a faithful retriever might do, till finally she rose up like a newborn Aphrodite from the lapping waves. I finally was able to gasp out a few words appropriate to the occasion. 'Thank you for saving my life, wahini.'

Still wearing my hat, she seated herself cross-legged on the sand facing me. The act was done with consummate natural grace, but the immodest grass-skirt forced me to avert my gaze. The empty expanse of beach stretching to a distant headland induced me to wonder why this one alone of all the Tahitian women thronging the beach had remained behind to save me.

As though divining my thoughts, she held up both hands to me. Several of the finger-tips were missing to the first joint. 'You are the arii-nui of this big ship, yes?' She tossed her wet hair fearfully to where the Washington lay at anchor. 'You come Tahiti to take me away to Kalawao?'

My beautiful rescuer was a doomed leper!

The speed with which I recoiled did not seem at all to faze her. She handed me my hat and rose up from the sand in a lithe motion I dared not follow, but my downcast eyes noticed that both feet had been reduced to toeless clubs. Then as if wishing to relieve me of all distress, she smiled in farewell and went shuffling up the beach toward the looming headland of volcanic rock. Once she turned and called out to me. 'You need not go looking for the woman of the sea any more, monsieur le capitaine. I shall come draw you down to me soon enough.'

A dread far greater than that occasioned by the sensation of drowning swept over me. Had the doomed wretch infected me with her dread disease? I cast down my hat and went tearing off toward the steeple.

'Bonjour, monsieur le capitaine!' The young missionary glanced up from stirring a large earthen bowl of mush with a wooden spoon. He looked amazingly pink and fresh, standing there expectantly in his cocked cap in front of his rude little church. Indeed, it struck me that it was none other than myself he had been expecting. How he recognized me in my disarranged and hatless condition, I do not know, but he switched without more ado from speaking French into flawless English. 'Thank you for coming to see me so soon, Captain. You have saved me the trouble of rowing out to your ship. I need to speak to you upon urgent spiritual matters, but first let me welcome you in God's name to this island.'

'Spiritual matters, Father?'

'I would be a poor shepherd indeed if I failed to caution you about the trouble your crew is stirring up among our native people.'

'Surely that can wait, Father! I have just encountered a leper.'

'A leper, monsieur le capitaine?'

'Yes, a leper! She touched me when I was bathing in the water.' My hands flew to where the buttons had been ripped off my new jacket and shirt. 'What should I do to save myself, Father?'

'Oh, la leper!' The priest smiled apologetically and offered me a Gallic shrug. 'Oui, there is one such among the natives here. We send her away to Kalawao when – how do you say? – the leper ship comes. Malheureusement, the leper ship sometimes takes a year or more to get here.'

'Father, the leper, she touched me here and here! Will I catch her dread disease?'

'Who can say?' He shrugged, scanning my chest in open disapproval of finding no crucifix there. 'It is unlikely, but God works in mysterious ways. You and your crew would do well to stay away from these natives, Captain. We cannot expect such a simple people to resist the worldly temptations we Europeans bring among them. You place their very souls in jeopardy by just being here, I fear.'

As though to demonstrate his case, the young missionary drew my attention to the pillory standing in the center of the village. In my consternation, I had failed to notice the pair of middle-aged Tahitians held fast by their necks and wrists in its wooden stocks. The priest went up to them and gently offered the woman a dollop of the thick mush. She opened her mouth and gulped it down as though indeed very hungry.

'Father, what have these simple people of yours done to deserve such punishment?'

'They were taken in carnal sin.' The young missionary turned his spoon on the man. The Tahitian averted his clenched mouth, but the woman scolded him in a familiar fashion till he allowed himself to be fed.

'Are these two not man and wife, father?'

'Man and wife they are, monsieur le capitaine. I myself administered the marriage vows, but they were caught – how do you say it in English? – sacré à main, in their hut committing the carnal sin on the Sabbath.' The shallow-chested priest drew himself up like a genie into a likeness of my robust father. He seemed to lose all the vestiges of *youth before my eyes. I looked down, expecting to see the ruin of my schooner lying trampled beneath his feet.*

I turned without another word and trudged back down the beach, barely able to hold back from breaking into a run. There was still no sign of my crew, but my hat was waiting where I had dropped it. I picked it up and brushed off the wet sand. Placing it squarely on my head, I thought of my Amboinese maiden. Perhaps I was being given another chance to find that which I was seeking. I began dogtrotting toward the distant headland. I fancied that my wahine must dwell in a cave somewhere among that jungled heap of lava floes.

I did explore several caves there, but I never did find the one I was seeking.

CHAPTER XI

COASTING

I had taken little advice from anyone, for I had a right to my own opinions in matters pertaining to the sea.

– From *Sailing Alone Around the World*
by Joshua Slocum

South Atlantic: November 28, 1895

'Admit it, you stiff-necked Spaniard, there be no more beautiful city in this whole world than this one. Turn round and look back at the sheer glory of it, God damn you! With the morning sun shining on the Sugarloaf just so, Rio de Janeiro fairly takes your breath away!'

'May your cajones roast like chestnuts in hell, Inglés! It's not enough that you drag me through that pox-ridden Pernambuco, but no, you must drag me down here to this pig-sty as well! How could you stand to stay in a city that has treated you so shamefully?'

'It's true that I've had extremely bad luck here in the past, my friend, but you've brought me good luck. Because of you I'm disposed to adopt a new attitude where this great country is concerned. Our affairs are coming along just fine this time around.'

'Si, señor, at least this time they did not steal or sink your vessel. You do not have to build yourself a big canoe to paddle yourself back home.'

'Don't be so uncharitable, Francisco! By and large, I take these Brazilians to be a warmhearted people.'

'Warmhearted? You best put on your hat, compadre. I think your poor bald head has been out in the sun too long. Did not the collector of customs at Pernambuco charge your little vessel commercial tonnage dues? Did not the Brazilian admiralty refuse to meet your claims for bringing them the steel ship *Destroyer?* Two thousand leagues across the seas you sailed her at risk of your life for them. And all they did was sink her for your troubles. Warmhearted people, indeed!'

'What you say is true as far as it goes, Francisco, but do not forget that it was Brazilians who lent me enough cruzeiros to clear port and to meet our other necessities. And just have a look at this excellent anchor and cable our friends gave us! Not to mention all this mahogany for my new jigger brace.'

'Mere trifles, señor capitán. These Brazilians are true spawn of the Portuguese, a people I loathe more than even the Moors. Do you forget so easily how these Brazilians lost you your last true sailing ship – what was her outlandish name?'

The Aquidneck. Aye, you are my witness, Virginia, that of all man's handiwork she was nearest to perfection in beauty. In speed, she asked no quarter of steamers when the wind blew. She'd been a coffee clipper running from here to Baltimore before Captain Cheeseborough rerigged her into a little bark. That in itself I should have taken for a bad omen, but I bought her anyway with the last of our money from the Pato. She'd been laid up a long time, so I changed her aged hemp for steel wire, re-caulked and re-coppered her. Then I took on a cargo of flour bound for Pernambuco and telegraphed you to come down to me at Baltimore.

And down you came from Boston with all four children in tow. I noticed for the first time how fast they were growing up. You were looking better than I'd seen you since before our last voyage on Morning Light. How your cheeks glowed and your eyes and hair shone when you set eyes on her! Lord, we did love our little ship! And Victor and Ben and Garfield and Jessie all took to her as much as we did. That voyage south was our second honeymoon. We must have known we were clinging to something that was about to be lost forever.

Aye, our Aquidneck was a perfect yacht fit for royalty to live aboard. Why, she even sported a little library where I'd hide away among my books, listening to you play the square piano bolted to the deck in her cozy saloon. Aye, I loved that ship as much as I love Spray.

Alas, she sailed us much too swiftly to Pernambuco and Buenos Aires, for you and I, we both knew deep down our time together was ending, though I would not admit it, even when you asked me to find a cargo bound for your home in Australia. Aquidneck was never the same once you were gone. Ah, my dear Virginia, what did I ever do to make you leave me?

'Señor capitán, where are you? Do you not see? Far out to sea there is a devil of a gale making up.'

'Well, my friend, what would you have us do, turn back to Rio?'

'A pox on that, mi capitán! I'll gladly brace a full hurricane first.'

'Then head her up into the wind, sir. I'll have that main topsail hoisted this instant, if you please.'

'We already carry too much sail, señor!'

'She can handle it, Francisco!'

Into just such a gale as this I drove Aquidneck after we carried you up the River Plate and laid you to rest. Aye, I stranded her in my drunken grief, for I was never the same man after you left me, Ginny. By rights I deserved to lose her that very night, but I've always had more than my share from Lady Luck. It took some awfully hard work next morning, but we kedged her off that bar not much the worse for wear.

Then nineteen days we spent driving furiously back to New York from Maceio with a full cargo. Even steamships could not equal that run, so the newspapers said, but the truth is, I no longer cared whether I lived or died. I lay in our berth between watches and prayed for the sea to take me. I took risks with Aquidneck no proper sailing master should ever take. Aye, I took terrible risks, Ginny, even though your children sailed aboard her. Can you forgive me that there were times I could not even remember their names? It was well for them that I packed them off to their aunts in Boston, all except for Victor, that is. He was old enough to go for a sailor and still young enough to mistake his father for a god of the sea.

Aye, Ginny, three more times I drove that little ship down to Pernambuco and back again, but I could not drive the loss of you from my soul. My own crew began to hate me for driving so hard, and all the while I blamed what I did to them on my pressing need for enough money to survive. There was more than some truth in that, for the stinkpots were snatching up every cargo in sight. Woe on the sailing ship that came late into port, for it would go a begging for its next cargo.

Riding the Gulf Stream that third time, I flogged her back to New York for all she was worth. So it came as no real surprise to come on deck one morning and find the mainmast head asway with the heel of the topmast down on the trestle-trees. Ginny, can you believe I'd fallen so low as to let our ship be partially dismasted while I slept? No choice but to bring the whole tangled and broken mess crashing down to the deck. How close I came to losing her again that day! If not for your son and his unshaken faith in me, I might have allowed my prayers to come true.

Aye, it was Victor who saw me through that terrible time. Though half dismasted, Aquidneck survived that savage storm, for I'm not an easy man to turn aside once my mind is set and I put my head down. Who would know that better than you, my love? Trying to stay abreast of me while bearing our children, isn't that what finally laid you low?

For ten days we clawed our way to windward, for the truth is, we'd not enough sail left to forereach in a heavy sea. What the Lord gave us one day he took away the next. He meant it as punishment for my hardheartedness, I know, but I still couldn't forgive Him for taking you from me so young. We might still be drifting around out there if that tug hadn't come along.

After that, it was clear even to me that changes had to be made. Well, my love, the urge to live on can be a compelling habit even for the shadow of a man that I had become. So I let my relatives in Boston persuade me to take another wife. I think perhaps you'll forgive me for that, Ginny; it never used to bother you that I always had an eye for a jaunty jib or a graceful stern. Was there ever a woman who understood a man as well as you did me?

Our children needed a mother, Ginny, and aye, your husband needed a lover.

Henrietta Elliot, my own cousin from Nova Scotia she was. Her hardscrabble family thought me a rich and famous sea-captain, so they were glad enough to take me for a son-in-law, even if I were old enough to be the poor girl's father. Little Hettie has proven herself a good mother to your children, Virginia – that much I will give her.

But she tried her best to make me bide by her side on land. 'My proper home is the deck of a sailing ship, Hettie.' I was not above quoting to her that same Marlowe poem I whispered into your ear so long ago in Sydney Town. 'Come live with me and be my love.'

107

Oh, she came aboard Aquidneck and took over your berth, my love, but she would not all our pleasures prove. But who can blame her? I became an old man the night you died. Cold comfort I was for a hot-blooded young woman like her. And her maiden voyage was bad enough to have tested even your mettle, Ginny.

Not that we haven't been through much worse, you and I. Remember Pato and the typhoon we slipped past on our way to fish off Kamchatka? Nothing we could do but lay in each others' arms on the cabin sole and ride out the storm with the unborn twins kicking between us. Aye, our poor dead twins. I know what you thought in your heart but never put into words: that I never gave them a chance in this world. Oh Ginny, I was so young and foolish!

So I haven't learned much over the years, have I? Else I'd never have left port on the tail of a hurricane with a new wife crying and praying belowdecks. Not that riding that storm's coattails was such a bad idea, all other things considered. There was a good crew laid in by the crimps and a deadline to meet in Montevideo with a cargo of case oil. Aquidneck was up to it – if only I'd been up to my job as her master. Lord knows Victor had warned me that the deck needed recaulking after all the troubles we'd had on the previous voyage, but I gave his pleadings short shrift, telling him to go mend her planking with some pitch. Truth was, I hadn't the money anymore to keep my ship in the manner of a proper lady.

So we made our offing and went scudding off under nothing but a reefed foresail. Then we turned south running before heavy following seas that flooded over the rails and broke the deck-seams open. For thirty-six hours we manned the pumps like fiends, for we knew that otherwise our tomorrow would not come.

Hettie was born a Bluenose, but she wasn't a daughter of the sea like you, Ginny. Can you even begin to imagine her terror in the midst of that great storm? Exhausted men pumping till they dropped around her? Feeling the ship going down under us till the hold was half-filled with water?

I remember her; standing there in the companionway, vomit on her cheek, holding your little Garfield against her skirts. 'Joshua, if you want to kill yourself, go right ahead. But me and this child of yours, you've no right doing this to us!'

The last thing I needed right then was an hysterical woman aboard. All I could think was, if only Ginny were here to help me through this. You'd have found those leaks even if the crew couldn't. How many times did you come through when all else around me failed? Afterwards when all was set to rights, you'd turn on me with a laugh. 'Oh, well, Joshua, you never could find things. But then, you're only a man. To really get things done in this world, it takes a woman.'

Not that it would have ever come to such desperate straits if you'd been there to watch over me. You'd have made me re-caulk those decks straight off before we ever cleared Baltimore. You'd have never let me put our children at such risk, even if you had to walk the streets to find the money.

Oh Ginny, if you could have seen how those cruel waves came crashing down onto Aquidneck's stern! It wasn't long till she started going 'loggy' on us. I knew soon she'd lose stability, and we'd have to cut the masts away to keep her from capsizing. Not that she could ever sink with an unballasted cargo of case-oil, but there's no worse hell on earth than a waterlogged hulk. I called the steward aside and ordered him to get the lifeboats ready.

Hettie must have read the reproach in my eyes. She stopped weeping, and then she gathered up her sodden skirts and dragged herself down into the hold. She was gone so long that I finally gave the wheel over to Victor and went below.

Somehow she'd crept along the dark crawlspace above the shifting cargo. You can imagine what it was like with the terrified rats squeaking and the flooded bilge splashing and sloshing up through it all. It's a small miracle of God she wasn't drowned or buried alive. I found her lying on her back, ripping her petticoats into strips and stuffing them overhead into the streaming deck-seams. 'Well, Joshua, here are your leaks!'

I could see Hettie's face shining from the light streaming through cracks along the break of the poop, they had opened that wide. Water was pouring down over her so hard and fast, I couldn't tell whether she was still crying. She wasn't making much headway with the torn petticoats, but she'd found the cracks for us, that was the main thing. The crew of the Aquidneck wasn't long finishing her job with hemp and sailcloth, I can tell you.

Aye, what a wonderful sound it is when finally you hear the pumps start sucking air. I took Hettie in my arms and tried to tell her how proud I was of her, that she'd done as good a job as you could have done, Ginny. Too late I saw her anger flare at my foolish words. 'I'm tired to death, Joshua. But at least I understand now why you took a new wife. Now leave me be.'

After that, the sun came out and the seas went down and all our other troubles passed away for a time. But some things are never mended. Little Hettie from Nova Scotia sits all alone in Boston, stitching petticoats and frocks to feed your children, Ginny.

CHAPTER XII

SEAHORSES

Under great excitement one thinks fast, and in a few seconds one may think a great deal of one's past life. Not only did the past with electric speed flash before me, but I had time while in my hazardous position for resolution for the future that would take a long time to fulfill.

– From *Sailing Alone Around the World*
by Joshua Slocum

South Atlantic, December 11, 1895

'Don Jèsu, wake up! Don't tell me I've managed to catch *Spray's* master napping once again!'

'Aye, you have that. What's worrying you this time, Francisco?'

'I think we hug this coast much too close for the comfort of our mortal bodies, mi capitán!'

'My friend, how many times do I have to spell it out for you? There's a swift current setting north a mile or two offshore. We must stay close in or else be carried sternwards.'

'Si, compadre, but it will get us nowhere fast to run aground!'

'You're a born worrier, Francisco. Just keep abeam of that line of sand hills off to starboard there, and I promise you all shall go well.'

'If you say so, mi capitán, but this moon, she is so bright this night. I think maybe she plays tricks on us.'

'Steady as she goes, Francisco. In an hour comes the dawn.'

'Si, mi capitán, doubtless you have the right of it as usual, but it's a pilot's duty to worry. I remember once cruising off Tunis. Three fast *galleys* we were, all hot as a bitch in heat to snap up some fat infidel dhow. A full moon sailed across a cloudless sky that night as well. I was just telling our capitán we should steer for deeper water when ... Caramba!'

'Aye, Francisco, what is it this time?'

'She does not answer the helm! Madre de dios! We've gone soft aground, mi capitán!'

'Impossible!'

'Look, mi capitán, the sails, they are backing! She's going to jibe! Watch your bald head!'

'Devil take you, sirrah. What kind of a pilot are you anyway to pull such a trick? Quick! Hard a-lee!'

'Too late, señor capitán! She's heeling over! You were right to say your luck is always bad in Brazil.'

'This is the coast of Uruguay, you papist Spaniard! Quick, let fly the sheets before she beaches herself!'

'Too late for that, you heretic Inglés! Can you not see that the wind and surf are pounding us ashore!'

'Look, see you how that perfidious moon deserts us after luring us onto this bar? I can feel *Spray* sewing her foot in the sand! We must kedge ourselves off! Quick, help me launch the dinghy, Francisco!'

'Don Jèsu, that dinghy of yours is not worthy of the name. I pray you, do not trust your life to so perilous a vessel with this heavy sea running and the wind rising out of the east.'

'There'll be nothing left for us to lose if we lose *Spray*, my friend. Here, bend this rode on the anchor, quickly now! I will row it out and set it. Where in God's name did you stow the oars?'

'Lashed handily against the toe-rail, Don Jèsu.'

'Aye, just where I always trip over them. Hand them down to me, will you?

'Ave Maria. Madre de Dios...'

'Francisco, you pirate dog, this dinghy leaks!'

'Si, capitán, it's been cracking open in the sun since we left Gibraltar. Bail it out with your hat.'

'My hat? I'll have you know that this good hat of mine was not made for bailing sea-water, you carping Andalusian.'

'Carping Andalusian, am I? Well, have it your way, you stubborn Yankee! I just pray you are good and thirsty. Presently you'll be sitting in salt-water up to your bald pate!'

'Oh very well, but I hate abusing a good hat. I've owned this one since the *Liberdade.*'

'Do tell, señor capitán! I thought perhaps you pirated it off Noah's ark.'

'Oh, you're a fine one to talk, my friend. You stole that old cockbill you sport from poor old Adam himself, I'm sure. There now, that should about do it. Hand me down the anchor, step lively now!'

'Be careful, mi capitán, or this mother of an anchor, she will swamp you!'

'There, I've got it!'

'You are sinking again under all that weight! Row, Don Jèsu, row as though the devil himself were after you! Row!'

'Just here should do it.'

'Si, it must. You're at the end of your rode, señor. Do not stand up for the love of God! The water, she is rising over your gunwales!'

'I must throw it clear, Francisco! There!'

'Look out! Madre di Dios! You've capsized her. Don Jèsu, I swear you are the most reckless man in all the world! Are there sharks in these waters? Do not let go the dinghy for the love of God!'

'I keep meaning to learn to swim, Francisco, but somehow I never get around to it. I almost drowned once in Tahiti – but never mind Tahiti! I have all I can do to keep from drowning this time around.'

'We sailors are like that, Don Jèsu. Why put off drowning till tomorrow when you can get it over with today? But I take your point. If only I myself had learned to swim, I might not be here in this salty pickle with you now.'

'We've no time for gaming, Francisco. I must somehow right this dinghy. Arghhh! Damnation, but you're heavy, Madame!'

'Your Madame kept going right on over, señor, and ducked you under again!'

'Francisco, must you forever be stating the obvious!'

'Well, Don Jèsu, a good pilot feels the need to keep his captain posted at all times. Try it again!'

'Aye, what's there left to lose? Arghh! God's blood! I'm sorry, my friend, but I simply haven't the strength left to do it!'

'Do you mean thus to deliver up your unshriven soul to the Devil like a lamb going to the slaughter, compadre?'

'In God's name, what choice have I?'

'Very well, Don Jèsu. I will say a prayer for you, though much good it will do coming from a soul suffering in purgatory!'

'No, damn your papist prayers to hell! Letting myself drown like this would only give those prophets of doom in Fairhaven leave to say: I told you that old fart Slocum was a fool!'

'Ole! By the blood of the Christ, you almost did it that time, Don Jèsu! Come, give it one more try for the sake of your sinful soul! You have only to remember whence you sprang, I swear, and the deed is good as done!'

'Aye, this water's as cold as the Bay of Fundy, my friend. One, two, three, heave!'

'Muy bueno! I think you did it, mi capitán!'

'Aye, Francisco, but now for the hard part of hauling myself over her side. What are you braying at, you jack-ass?'

'It's just that you so remind me of the proverbial Berber who got seasick riding his camel to market.'

'And well I might get seasick! I've swallowed half this Atlantic Ocean so far!'

'Don Jèsu, hook the anchor cable with an oar and pull yourself back to me!'

'I've not the strength left for it, my friend. I do not think I could even climb aboard, assuming I did make it so far. Will the rode take a turn or two round the windlass, Francisco?'

'Si, but with not so much as an inch to spare! The Blessed Virgin has answered our prayers!'

'That's right! Give the damned virgin all the credit, you papist dog!'

'Caramba, what a miserable heretic you are, Don Jèsu.'

'Stow your gaff and heave her taut, will you? I'm as weak as a hooked cod.'

'There, mi capitán, that's got her! She cannot flinch so much as an inch if only the anchor holds.'

'Then let me go ashore, Francisco. A vessel on her beam's end is no fit place to rest for a man still living.'

'Si, compadre, drift ashore and take another nap. I will stand watch at *Spray's* helm this night.'

'Thank you, Francisco. You are a friend in need.'

'I wish you sweet dreams, compadre. Look, dawn breaks in the east.'

Better take shelter from the wind behind this sand-ridge. I can't help shivering, but soon the warm sun will beat down upon my back. I must sleep and gather strength enough to kedge *Spray* off in the morning. Ah, I never thought to feel sand so welcome between my toes and fingers.

Do you remember, Virginia? How we rode your wild ponies down along the beaches south of Sydney? All to ourselves we had those white windrows of sand stretching on forever. Teaching me how to swim, I swear you almost succeeded in drowning me! So you became a vengeful Siren taunting me into the deep till we bobbled on our toes. Holding hands, we'd catch and ride a curling wave till it crashed upon the strand. Surfing, you gaily called it, but I died a little each time to keep from seeming a coward in your eyes ... and to see your blue bathing-chemise cling to your skin and creep into the mysterious space between your thighs.

Aye, I was a lucky man in those days and knew it. But I was luckier even than I knew.

Then the god of the sea himself caught us unawares. He lifted us twenty feet high, tumbled us end over end and flung us, a pair of rag dolls upon the sand. You lay sprawled on your face, gasping for breath. Knight errant, I rushed to aid my damsel in distress, but erect on my elbows I became a satyr glutting on your naked charms. That lustful old Neptune had stripped the chemise to a mere garland about your ankles. Sand frosted your budding nipples as you rose upon your knees. Too late you tried to cover yourself, for my eyes had already violated the rhyming curves of your belly and thighs, the perfect moon-fullness of your breasts and hips.

So you let me have my way with you upon the sand, knowing I must have taken you by force otherwise, for the madness of you was upon me. After all, we were to wed

116

*the very next day in a proper church, so it was no very
great sin. Then you kissed your family and the Australian
ponies goodbye, and you moved into Washington's master
cabin, never once looking back.*

*Aye, Ginny, I remember the way we were as though it
were yesterday!*

There, the pitter-patter of your ponies still cantering
up the beach! No, wake up, you doddering old fool – you
have stranded yourself on the wild coast of Uruguay,
remember? Why, not to worry! It's only a stripling riding
among the dunes. Listen, that's Spanish he's speaking to
his horse. Oh-ho, he's after pirating my *Spray,* by God!
What's he doing with the lariat?

I say, you must be the son of a real gaucho to lasso
Spray's bobstay with a single cast like that. So you think
she's yours if you can drag her home as salvage, eh?
Well, one such nag will not serve your purpose, I can tell
you! You'll need a whole posse of horses for that. Wait
now, my dinghy's another matter. You can't have that!
Here I am, gaucho! 'Ahoy there!'

'Buenos dias, señor, I thought perhaps you had
drowned yourself.'

'Buenos dias, muchacho! Sorry to disappoint you.'

'I like your ship well enough, but I am very glad you
are still alive. Where do you come from, señor? How
many days were you in sailing here? What are you doing
ashore so early in the morning?'

'Your questions are easily answered, muchacho. My
ship is a slave-ship from the moon. She's been a whole
month sailing to get her here. Tis the early slaver who
catches a full cargo of boys, *quien sabe?*'

'A cargo of boys, did you say? Si, I've heard of slavers
such as you! Stand clear, señor, or I'll ride you down!'

Caramba, as Francisco would say! He means to drag
me home across the campo by the neck! 'Belay your
lasso, muchacho! I make a joke! I am not a slaver from
the moon. Let us be friends!'

117

'And what will you give me in token of your friend-ship, señor?'

'Why, I'm only a poor sailor as you can plainly see, muchacho, but there's some fresh-baked biscuit aboard my vessel.'

'Biscuit, you say? Bueno! I like biscuit very much, señor!'

'Help me kedge off my vessel, muchacho, and I'll give you all the biscuit you can eat!'

'Your ship, she is much too heavy, señor. My horse cannot drag her into the sea, but I will fetch you butter and milk in trade for the biscuit.'

'Bueno! It's a deal! And perhaps some eggs as well? I'd give a ton of biscuit for a good fresh egg to suck right now. My ship-biscuits are good and hard as rocks, muchacho.'

'Muy bueno! My mother's geese give eggs as big as my fists, señor. I will ride home like the wind and fetch you some goose eggs!'

'Muy bueno, muchacho, but wait! See how the tide is flooding in? Can you fetch me some grown men with horses as well?'

'Si, señor, but do not forget the ship-biscuit you promised me!'

'Si, muchacho, only bring me some friends to aid me, and you shall have all the biscuit you can eat!'

CHAPTER XIII

SPELLBOUND

One day, however, coming to an island [in the river], one that was inhabited only by birds, we came to a stand, as if it were impossible to go further on the voyage; a spell seemed to hang over us. I recognized the place as one I knew well; a very dear friend had stood by me on deck, looking at this island some years before. It was the last land my friend ever saw.

– From *Sailing Alone Around the World*
by Joshua Slocum

Rio Plata Estuary: December 29, 1895

'The jib, Don Jèsu, she is luffing in the wind like a Neapolitan whore. Tighten the sheet a half-turn, if it so pleases you.'

'It pleases me to please you, Don Francisco Pinzón. There, how does that suit you?'

'Well enough, compadre, but why pull such a long face on me? We've a half-gale of wind and a favorable current pushing us along.'

'Nothing that need worry you, my friend. It's just that our stranding has stirred up some bad memories in me. Twice before I've run ships of mine aground in

119

these waters. Each time something was taken from me more precious than life itself.'

'Take it from me, Don Jèsu: nothing is more precious than life. You could not grieve for your losses if you were not still alive. So count yourself lucky to be sailing up this great river tonight. *Spray's* old bones would still be pounding hard on that sandbar, I think, if it were not for that wild Uruguayan boy bringing his family back to save her! And where would we be this night if your friends in Montevideo hadn't insisted on recaulking her?'

'Aye, my friend, and do not forget to mention the new shoe and the false keel as well. Aye, I'm grateful to them all, but I still find a beggar's lot a hard one to bear.'

'As for that, Don Cristóbal Colón himself hounded Their Most Catholic Majesties all over Spain till they gave him money to be rid of him. You only take what your good friends freely give you. Consider it the due of a superior man to receive such things from the hands of lesser men, Don Jèsu. We sail free of all else, you and I. What matters gold to free-living hidalgos like us?'

'Hah! The world must be turning on it's head for a Spaniard to even say such a thing!'

'Need I remind you once again, Inglés, that we Pinzóns are Andalusian born? We are not so fond of gold as the Castilians. Nevertheless, I do think much on what you have told me of what came of our ill-starred voyage to the Indies. How sad that all the gold in the world did no more for my countrymen than to make them lose their way! It would have gone much better for us to have remained humble in spirit and to have let God provide for our wants.'

'So you say, my friend, so you say. I am no gold-hungry Castilian, but I must admit my faith in God's Providence would wax greater if good Spanish doubloons were wearing holes in my pockets right now. I mean to overhaul *Spray's* rig when we reach Buenos

Aires. I would have done it at Pernambuco or Rio if want of ready coin had not kept me from it.'

'Spare yourself the trouble, mi capitán. What more can you ask from a sloop built to fish oysters on a pond?'

'She'll handle far better once we shorten her boom and turn her into a yawl. It must be done, my friend, for my mind's eye already sees Cape Horn looming over us.'

'Think you to frighten the pilot of the Pinta with rantings about this terrible Cape Horn of yours. Tis nothing but a wretched spit of land some homesick Dutchman named for his port of call.'

'Francisco, listen to me well! In all these Seven Seas, there is nothing sailors fear more than Cape Horn. And for good reason! Hundreds of ships have perished there, many of their crews served up to feed the native savages, so they say. Aye, don't laugh! It is said the Fuegians would starve otherwise for want of fresh meat so poor and wretched is their land. Ask Captain Howard, he can tell you all about Cape Horn.'

'Fortunately, your superstitious friend cannot see me, let alone hear me. By the by, what keeps him so long down below?'

'He is making his famous chowder on our wonderful new cooker. He brought a mess of fine rockfish aboard. A nice change from flying fish, eh?'

'I dare not partake lest he jump overboard in fright, señor capitán. You best go keep your guest company before he hears you talking to me under your breath.'

'What Go down below and leave you to navigate these shoals and sandbars all by yourself?'

'Señor capitán, do you mean to insult the first pilot to navigate his way across the Atlantic Ocean?'

'Well no, Francisco, of course not! Do carry on. I'll save you some chowder if I can.'

'Si, Don Jèsu. Just don't let the good capitán frighten you out of your wits with stories of ghosts and cannibals!'

'Ah, Captain Howard, your chowder smells fit for a king!'

'Well, Slocum, you seem in fine form for a man who sails across oceans alone. I did hear you talking to yourself up on deck, though. Not a good sign, that! I take you to be King Neptune come down to us in human form, you know. Who else but him would dare to try sailing round the world in such a cockleshell vessel as this?'

'Cockleshell? Sir, you impugn the integrity of my noble *Spray!* Do you forget this vessel has already carried me twice across the Atlantic? There's not the slightest doubt in my mind that she'll carry me safely round the Horn and back home again before she's through.'

'My dear Slocum, the poor quality of the vessel you employ makes you all the more deserving of credit for what you are doing.'

'Sir, I fear you commit an injustice of the rankest kind! All the mistakes made on the voyage so far have not been *Spray's* but mine.'

'Well, Slocum, I admit it did give me pause to sit by the binnacle and watch the compass. She holds the course so steadily that I would swear a seasoned pilot manned the helm. Not a quarter of a point did she deviate. I actually reached over several times to make sure no one was seated beside me.'

'In truth, Captain, someone was sitting there.'

'Ha ha! Very good, Slocum, but I should tell you that I've had my legs pulled near off me by Yankees before! Still, I'll be stranded on Chico Bank if ever I did see the like of it! You actually dare sit here gamming with me while your vessel sails herself up this treacherous river in a devil of a gale!'

'Look to your chowder, Captain! It's about to boil over!'

122

'Well don't just sit there, man! Help me chock up the pot on the cabin sole here before it tips over. Where do you stow your soup tureens, Slocum?'

'There, Captain, tucked under your feet.'

'Aye, battered tin cups with an inch of dust ready for planting geraniums! You could use a wife aboard this vessel, old friend.'

'I asked mine to come along, but she declined the invitation.'

'Aye, I've heard about that voyage you gave her aboard the *Aquidneck*, Slocum. After shipwrecking and then rafting her home five thousand blue water miles on that jury-rigged canoe of yours, what did you expect?'

'Nothing, Captain. I've come to expect absolutely nothing more from Hettie in this world. Lord knows she does enough for me already.'

'Aye, second wives just aren't the same as the first ones, are they? Third ones wear even worse, you may take it from me. By Jove! I remember now – you lost your first one right here at Buenos Aires, did you not? And a fine figure of a woman, she was, too. They told me your grief at losing her was a sight to behold.'

'Aye, Captain. All my life, I've been a man who never drinks to excess. But when Virgina died on me so suddenly, I got crazy on rum and ran *Aquidneck* aground just a few miles up river from here.'

'By God, show me that spot in the morning, will you? Then we'll go ashore in Buenos Aires, you and I, and pay our respects to that good wife of yours.'

'The reef I'll gladly show you, Captain. As for the English Cemetery, I'll ask you to kindly let me make that visit alone.'

'Aye, Slocum, I understand. Women, they get inside a man's skin almost as bad as the ship we sail. How's the chowder?'

'Fit for a king, Captain Howard. Fit for a king, just as you promised me it would be.'

'I also promised you more stories of the Fuegians, did I not? You best prepare yourself, for you'll probably have to shoot some of them before you make it through the Straits, Captain.'

That's the magic of our guns. They make it so easy for us to fit the deed to the murderous thought. Remember that time waiting for Prince Mori of Hawaii to arrive in San Francisco Bay, Ginny? Even with you beside me, I felt myself adrift in that dockside crowd. I felt this boyish need to stand out among that throng, to escape from being just another one of them. So I wagered a drummer a silver dollar that you could hit the loon diving off the pier head with my new Smith & Wesson revolver.

'A bobbing loon's near impossible to hit with anything less than a shotgun,' opined one of the loungers as the bird surfaced and dived like quicksilver. 'Don't even bother trying, Mrs. Slocum, or you'll waste your bullets as well as your husband's wager.'

There was something akin to scorn as you took the pistol from my hands. Womanly contempt at the ways of all men, but you were too good a wife to ever belittle your husband in public. Gold flecks were dancing in your dark eyes.

The loon resurfaced. Quicker than thought, you threw up the pistol, squeezing its hair trigger as you did so. Off came the bird's graceful head as though blown away by magic.

'It was worth the dollar to see it, Captain,' said the drummer, flipping me the silver coin amid the chorus of praise. 'I thank God it's not my neck your wife was shooting at.'

'Here's the chowder I promised you, Francisco.'

'Mucho gracias, compadre. Don't tell me you've already tucked our fine English guest into your berth?'

'Aye, Francisco, though I have my doubts that he will get much good of it this night. He delighted in telling me hair-raising stories of the Fuegians, but he did not take it so kindly when I told him that the pilot of the *Pinta* was steering *Spray* up this treacherous river.'

'I can hardly blame him for that, señor capitán. He doubtless thinks you are losing your mind. Something tells me he will not be sailing with us on the return trip to Montevideo.'

'Well, that's as it may be, Francisco. I'm past desiring any man's company for long – excepting yours, of course.'

'You are thinking tonight of your Virginia, señor capitán?'

'Aye, Francisco, I expect this will likely be the last time I visit her grave. I've not been the same since she took her leave of me. I'm like a man alone on a wrecked ship that's slowly sinking, no matter which way he steers.'

Harbor of Punta Arenas, February 18, 1896

'I cannot thank you enough, Captain Samblich. Your help and advice are worth more to me than all the guards and dogs to be had for gold in Patagonia. And these bags of good smoked venison will stand me in good stead as well. As for these ship-biscuits of yours, I fear I'd need a maul just to break them.'

'Don't neglect to eat them every day, Slocum. They're more nutritious than yours and less liable to harbor weevils. And by the by, you must allow me to trade you this compass of mine for that old one of yours.'

'I can't accept your best compass off you, Captain Samblich!'

'Think of it from my point of view, sir: Before me stands the first man with the fortitude to sail alone around the world! Should I let him sail onward with a compass not fit for rounding the Horn? If you were not to make it, I would have naugh to blame but myself. The same goes for your mains'l. Here, I'll unbend mine. God knows my sloop won't be needing it ever again.'

'Hold, Captain! I'll trade you compasses, but not sails. No sailor worthy of the name could accept such a gift from another. Besides, it's not as though I'm sailing round the Horn itself. It's the Strait of Magellan for *Spray* and me.'

'It's six of one and half a dozen of the other which is the worse, Slocum. Here then, at least help yourself to a good stake from this poke of mine.'

'Your poke of Fuegian gold-dust, Captain Samblich? Now what more can you ask of a man than that he should give you his gold?'

'Here, you'll be needing this bag of carpet-tacks, as well.'

'Carpet-tacks, Captain? What need have I of carpet-tacks where I am going?'

'Spread them on the decks before you go off watch. I lost a brother to those bare-footed savages, you know. These tacks may save you having to shoot someone. Just take care that you don't step on them yourself.'

CHAPTER XIV

BLACK PEDRO

I had not for many years been south of these regions. I will not say that I expected all fine sailing on the course for Cape Horn direct, but while I worked at the sails and rigging I thought only of onward and upward. It was when I anchored in the lonely places that a feeling of awe crept over me.

– From *Sailing Alone Around the World*
by Joshua Slocum

Strait of Magellan, February 24, 1896

'Señor capitán, here they come just as good old Captain Samblich promised us they would come!'

'Aye, Francisco, I see them. Three canoes out from Fortescue, I make it. Those Fuegian devils think they can overhaul us now that we are all but becalmed.'

'Caramba, I never thought I'd pray for more gales in this part of the world. Give her more sail, mi capitaine. Give her more sail!'

'More sail? To do that, I should have to rig another mast.'

'Is that not what you are doing, Don Jèsu?'

'Of course not! I'm fashioning a dummy helmsman from this bit of bowsprit. Complete with my jacket and sou'wester, he may be enough to fool them. I only wish they could see you in that outlandish getup, my friend. You would be enough to scare them off all by yourself.'

'Look, señor capitán, they've stopped paddling! That one with the black beard, he is standing up. Listen, what's that he's yelling at us?'

'Yammerschooner! Yammerschooner!'

'Yammerschooner. That's their begging term, Francisco.'

'Once let them get close enough to parley, señor capitán, and they'll swarm over us like rats over a cave full of Gorgonzola!'

'Ahoy there! No yammerschooner! No yammerschooner! Keep off or we'll shoot, damn you!'

'They come on again, mi capitán. You shall have to be good as your word, I think! Just look at the wretches! You'll be doing them a favor to put them out of their misery.'

'That may be, but I promised the port captain at Puntas Arenas to shoot them only if I had to. Steady as she goes, Francisco.'

'Where are you going, Don Jèsu?'

'Forward to the lookout perch via the hold. Keep moving this scarecrow about, will you? That way they'll think there's at least three of us to fight.'

'Be sure to keep your harquebus handy, compadre.'

'Aye, my friend, I'd as soon leave go my right leg right now.'

'And don't forget to change your hat.'

'Good idea. Where did I put that wool tuque that Pedro Samblich gave me?'

'In the rope locker abaft the companionway.'

'Aye, here it is.'

Aye, Virginia, remember your first voyage? It was in the old Washington. You called it our honeymoon, though we were bound for Alaska to fish a cargo of salmon. All we had to guide us was a hand-traced copy of an old Russian chart picked up for three pounds ten in Hong Kong.

As night came on, the wind began blowing the caps off the thirty-foot waves. You came across to me in my sea-berth, trembling. 'I'm not so brave as I thought I'd be, Joshua.'

Ah, you made me feel strong and fearless to hold you in my arms that night. Every part of you so perfectly formed, yet lithe as a leopardess beneath the lush soft-ness, though you were not made of iron as I so foolishly took you to be. How it delighted me to take advantage of your fear as the ship tossed. All this you read in my eyes as you bit my ear. 'You should be on deck with Thompson and the crew. Something is bound to come of what you are doing, Joshua.'

'Come live with me and be my love and we shall all our pleasures prove.' Thrusting deep, I sang that song to you for the hundredth time. Oh my darling, that was so long ago!

This is a different voyage. Now just pop your head up through the fore-scuttle like a jack-in-the-box. There's Francisco still at the wheel scowling like the hounds of hell are nipping at his heels. 'No yammer-schooner, damn you! Stand clear!'

'And still they come on, señor capitán! No good to just wave your harquebus at them! You must shoot them dead before it be too late for us!'

'Four-handed canoes can't hold this pace much longer, Francisco. I feel a breath of air. We may outrun them yet!'

'Look again, Don Jèsu! Another four scoundrels hide in the bottom of each canoe. They spell each other at the oars!'

'Damnation! Perhaps a warning shot across their bows will turn the trick. This Martini-Henry bellows like a cannon. Hah, see! That stopped them dead in the water!'

'Just for a moment, mi capitán. Look, here they come again! For the love of God, at least shoot the one with the black beard! Isn't he the villain the port captain warned you about?'

Black Pedro. Aye, it's really you I have in my sights, isn't it? The port captain gave me leave to shoot thee. A renegade mongrel and the worst murderer in Tierra del Fuego, that's what he called you. Samblich blames you for the massacre of his brother and his crew taken unawares. You cut their throats while they lay sleeping at anchor. I need but tighten this finger and consign thee to the flames of hell. Aye, Black Pedro, you might be a brother to Dangerous Jack himself, from the look of you.

'Wake up, Joshua!'

'What is it, Hettie?'

'Something is wrong on deck! The boat tackle has been let go with a great deal of noise!'

'You're just dreaming, my dear! Go back to sleep.'

'Dreaming? I certainly am not! While you've been snoring, I've not slept a single wink this whole night through!'

'Oh very well, Hettie! I'll go up on deck and have a look if that will make you feel better.'

'Joshua! Don't you dare go up on deck by the companionway. I heard creaking on the cabin steps and whispering in the forward entry! They are waiting up there for you!'

'What's that? Sailors rambling on the poop-deck between their watches? Well, we can't have that. Don't worry, Hettie, I'll soon settle their hash!'

'Joshua, something tells me they mean to harm you. That's bad enough, but far worse will happen to me and the children if they should kill you!'

Dangerous Jack and Bloody Tommy! My mind balked at picturing what such cut-throats would do once I was stretched out cold and bleeding on the deck. Cholera or not, the authorities at Rosario should have been hanged for opening the prisons and letting such murderers and rapists loose! And so should I for signing on such a crew. 'Well then, my dear, where did I lay my carbine?'

'Here it is, Joshua. Right under your pillow where you always keep it.'

'Thank ye, Hettie. Here, hold on to this pistol just in case. Shoot anyone who comes through this door, except me, of course.'

'Joshua, I'm not Virginia to be shooting people with guns.'

'No, Hettie, Viriginia you're not, but you're woman enough to do what you have to do when the chips are down.'

'I'd rather have you be man enough to keep me from having to be such a woman, Joshua.' She kissed my cheek. She must have been mighty worried, for I can count on the fingers of one hand the times she's ever done that. 'Be careful! There's at least three of them up there waiting for you! Take the aft hatchway.'

'Hettie, I didn't get to be a sea captain by being afraid of a few malcontent ruffians!'

Yet I tiptoed up the aft companionway just as she bade me do. I almost forgot to stop along the way and load eight .56 calibre ball-cartridges into the carbine's magazine. As I did it, I couldn't help thinking what a terrible mess slugs that size would make of a man.

At first I could not see my hand in front of me in the moonless dark. Then a coarse voice roared down the forward hatch. 'Come on deck like a proper ship's master and order your men forward, Captain Slocum! Don't think you can hide down there forever with your woman!'

I counted four of the crew lurking by the forward companionway. There could be no longer any doubt. I had a mutiny to face. I took a deep breath and stepped forth from the shadows. 'Very well then, you men! Get your asses forward there before I kick them till your noses bleed buttermilk!'

'So ye've skipped round behind us, have ye, Captain? May God damn me to boil in hell if I don't roast yer yellow liver on a spit before this night is through.' Aye, it was Dangerous Jack leading the others on. A bear of a man who had boasted of thrashing to a pulp all the officers of the last ship he served upon.

'I said, get forward, all of you!' I brought the awful carbine to my shoulder as menacingly as I could. Some demon held my bowels in a vice. 'I am armed, you treacherous excuses for true men! Get your tails forward while you still can, or I'll shoot you down like the sea-monkeys you are!'

'Come on, mates, this fool Yankee's got a chest of gold and a lively young wife stowed aboard.' Dangerous Jack came bounding at me, but my finger froze upon the trigger. Tis not an easy thing to shoot a man in cold blood, even if he is waving his sheath knife at you. I thought instead to club him to the deck with the butt of the heavy carbine. That blow I struck would have felled an ox, but he only shook it off and leapt inside my guard. One huge paw seized my throat, forcing me out over the taffrail. 'Now you damned fool of a captain, shoot for all I care!'

As he raised his knife to my throat, all that was about to happen to my wife and children passed clearly before me. I looked into those fierce eyes and saw that my assailant yearned for his own death more than mine. It was almost as if he gave me leave to take his life. My finger squeezed tight. The carbine spat one of its great balls in a muffled roar. Dangerous Jack sank away from me, his jacket on fire.

Nothing daunted, the others came on like hungry wolves, but the dread of dying or of killing another man had quite left me. 'Go forward, men, or I'll shoot you down just like I did him!'

'What if I don't?' *Bloody Tommy brandished a carpenter's hatchet.* *'You've killed the only friend that ever spoke fair to me, you bastard! That's only an empty gun in your hand, and I've got this for you!'*

Again the carbine spat smoke and fire. The great ball took him fair in the chest and tore a gaping hole. The remaining two mutineers jumped aside and fled forward.

They had the same look about them as you bear now, Black Pedro. No, I will not spare you the pain of living out your fate, but that's not to say that a close brush with death will do you any harm.

'Bueno jo via Isla!'

'Santa Maria, señor capitán! What a shame your shot just missed him! Oh, look at the villain rub his cathead, you made him so afraid of dying! Shoot him dead this time, for the love of Christ!'

'He's had enough strong medicine, Francisco. This old Martini-Henry made him look right into the jaws of hell! Look, he's making for yonder island, and the Fuegians follow in his wake.'

'Still, Don Jèsu, I think it was a dereliction of your Christian duty to spare a man who's murdered so many!'

'Who are we to stand in judgment over a man like him, my friend? Oh never fear, I've killed such men before, but it's not an experience I care to repeat unless they force me to it.'

'Do you fear that the killing of men might become too easy a thing for you to do, compadre?'

'Something like that, Francisco, for the shades of the men I've killed are always with me. But enough of that. Look, it grows dark quickly now. Let us see about finding some safe place to anchor for the night.'

'Caramba, señor capitán! How can you even think of dropping anchor while all these murdering savages are swarming about us?'

'It'll soon be the blackest of nights for them as well as us, Francisco. Here comes a wind! I fancy it'll be a gale before it's done. Straight ahead lies a snug anchorage called Three Island Cove. We should be safe enough lying there till morning.'

'Very well, you are the master, Don Jèsu! I will not take it amiss to lie at peace, if lie at peace we can. Till this lull came over us, I had come to think the wind never ceases here at the bottom of the world. And such waves! Madre di dios, that one monster off the Cape Virgins rose up taller than our masts. It nearly took us down, I tell you.'

'Aye, Francisco, but that is but a small taste of what lies before us in these Straits of Magellan.'

'Do you think to frighten Francisco Pinzón, the pilot of the Pinta so easily, mi capitán? Tell me, what is that arc of light off to the southwest?'

'There lies in wait for us the white terror of Cape Horn itself. Something more than your good *Pinta* ever faced, my friend.'

'Santa Maria, I begin to believe you. Let us tuck our tails into this strait as fast as we can, even if it be named for some scoundrel of a Portuguese!'

'How now, Francisco! Ferdinand Magellan may be a Portuguese, but he sailed around the world in the service of your own king. It was he who laid for Spain the foundation for an empire on which the sun never sets even to this day.'

'Paugh! He only served us because his own king would not give him a ship to sail. Why, he did not even complete the voyage, but was fool enough to get himself killed by spear-chucking natives on some faraway island!'

'Be that as it may, Francisco, I still deem him the greatest navigator who ever sailed forth upon these seas.'

'What's that you say? You name him greater than Don Cristòbal Colòn himself?'

'Aye, or Drake or Cook or Odysseus, for that matter.'

'Ah, si, I see what drives you now, señor capitán! You think to be remembered as the man who sailed this little ship in Magellan's wake around the world.'

'Tis a modest enough ambition, my friend. I hope to do alone in this little sloop what he did first with five ships and many men, albeit only a few of them lived to ever see Spain again.'

'What's this about sailing alone? You forget about having me along , Don Jèsu.'

'As for that, Francisco, I myself may never forget my excellent pilot, but the world of the living will not factor you among my ship's crew, we may be sure of that. Here now, enough of this womanish gamming! I make the best entrance to the cove two points to port.'

'Look, mi capitán, across the strait and off to the south! Lights spring up all around us!'

'Aye, Francisco, it was not for nothing that Magellan named these islands. Tierra del Fuego – the Land of Fire! Nothing much has changed here since he sailed past. Black Pedro must be alerting the neighborhood to our presence. We'll be hard put to entertain them all if this gale should die on us!'

'Perhaps we should sail onwards despite this storm, compadre.'

'Nay, my friend, fighting these constant gales since we left Puntas Arenas has done me in. I must sleep or else. Look, is that not a seal lying on that rock there? Its coat fairly glows with phosphorescence. There can be no harm from savages where such animals dare show themselves.'

'If you say so, señor capitán.'

'Aye, Francisco, I do say so. Bring her up into the wind.'

CHAPTER XV

HURRICANE

In no part of the world could a rougher sea be found than off Cape Pillar, the grim sentinel of the Horn. Farther offshore, while the sea was majestic, ... the Spray rode, now like a bird on the crest of a wave, and now like a waif deep down in the hollow between seas; and so she drove on. Whole days passed, counted as other days, but with always a thrill – yes, of delight.

– From *Sailing Alone Around the World*
by Joshua Slocum

Drake Passage, March 3, 1896

'There, Francisco! See it gleam through the mist? That dagger of a headland stabbing north! That's none other than Cape Pillar!'

'Madre di dios, it's high time we sighted it, señor capitán! I make it all of six weeks that we've been tacking back and forth through this god-forsaken strait to reach it. Between the murderous natives and the treacherous willy-waws, it's been more than once I gave us up for lost.'

'Did I not tell you that slipping through Cape Horn's back door would be no ladies' picnic? But now, give praise to God, Francisco, for here we are entering the Pacific Ocean at last!'

'Why do you call her the Ocean of Peace, señor capitán? She looks no less foreboding to me than did the Atlantic first time I set sail upon her breast. Surely no seaman worthy of the name would tempt such a mistress so.'

'On the contrary, I remember reading somewhere that Ferdinand Magellan himself performed the deed.'

'But tell me, why did he call her the Ocean of Peace?'

'Because he found her waters such a welcome change after beating for weeks through these dire straits that still bear his name. Just think, Francisco: what lies in store for us out there is more than twice the size of that mill-pond you call the Atlantic. This Pacific is truly the mother of all oceans.'

'She may be as you say, señor capitán, but I think the Portuguese might have set a better example by sailing around the Horn itself. The hurricanes raging out there can be no worse than these treacherous williwaws. Caramba, how I hate the way they come shrieking like fiends down off the mountaintops without so much as a warning!'

'There's eighty-foot seas and as many knots of wind waiting out there for us in Drake Passage, my friend. And there are other monsters far worse than the winds and waves! Icebergs the size of mountains and currents that can seize hold of vessels and make off with them. Why, full-rigged ships have been known to pitch pole out there, stern over stem. It did not matter how capable their crews might be.'

'There you go trying to frighten me again, Don Jèsu.'

'I've gone past the Horn both ways, my friend. Take it from me: navigating through these straits is less dangerous than going outside for a vessel the size of *Spray*.'

'I much doubt a vessel this size has even tried this passage before, but you are right, señor capitán. After all, we did give the Fuegians the slip. It solaces me no end to think of Black Pedro gnashing his teeth in some miserable lean-to. Still, I think you would have done better to shoot him down like the mad dog he is.'

'Nay, my friend. This lonely country puts me in mind as never before that life is a precious thing. I could not bear to cause a needless death here, not even of that little swan flying off the port bow there.'

'Methinks the evil spirits inhabiting this strait have addled your brain, Don Jèsu. That swan would make us a better dinner than your potato hash will! Indeed, I sometimes think you know how to make nothing else but hash.'

'There are worse things than my hash, Francisco. Feel that? Our nor'easter is deserting us.'

'Santa Maria pray for us! Your proverbial luck, I think it just ran out, mi capitán. I pray you, take a third reef in the mains'l while you still can see to do it!'

'There, my dear Andalusian, it is done!'

'And not a minute too soon, mi capitán! Look what comes at us! I think maybe your beloved Portuguese misnamed this ocean! "Infernal" might have suited it better.'

'Aye, Francisco, Magellan was ever a wishful thinker, but then, so am I.'

'A great storm, she is making up to the northwest, or I was pilot of the *Pinta* for nothing. Caramba, mi capitán! This one might well be a full hurricane from the look and feel of her!'

'Here comes a rain-squall dark as the ace of spades. You best steer due west, my friend. See how the darkness comes down like a shroud and blots out the land! Well, its too late to turn back now.'

'Pray, compadre, pray to God that we come through this night!'

'Aye, Francisco, we would both do well to pray! Everything for an offing, Lord!'

'All I can see are the white teeth of the waves, Don
Jèsu. This wind, she is rising fast. Perhaps you should
take another reef.'

'Nay, Francisco, *Spray* needs every inch of sail she
can carry to clear this coast. This howling wind and raging sea is less a danger to her than are those reefs and
cliffs. I've lost too many ships already on lee shores to
risk that fate again.'

*Aye, Ginny, you were there that first time it happened
in Cook Inlet. The highest tides in the world except for the
gray old Bay of Fundy that spawned me. A six-knot ebb
dragging down icebergs and giant tree trunks to war
with the tidal bore. In the end we anchored two miles offshore on the shoals and flats inside the Karluk reef among
submerged glacial boulders the size of churches.*

*Then we went ashore and camped on the beach the
better to try our luck at gillnetting king salmon. Lord
knows there were plenty of the great fish to be taken, for
we were the first Yankee ship to work those waters. That
was indeed our honeymoon, Ginny. Aye, we fished in our
punts from sunup to sundown alongside our wonderful
Aleut seafarers, but we spent our nights in glorious rut
inside our tent. Aye, we found making love to be as restful
as sleeping. How Thompson and the other sailors envied
me! But the Aleuts, they just smiled and nodded their
heads.*

*I ran my fingers along the curve of your hip and
thigh. 'Is it not a wonderful thing to be so young and full
of life, Ginny?'*

'Young?' *You tossed your long black hair at
me.* 'Actually, Joshua, we're both very old, you and I.'

*Aye, that was our sojourn in Eden. I still see you land-
ing a salmon almost as long as you were tall. Laughing
and joking with the Aleuts and my crew. Hiking along the
river and getting our feet wet. Together we faced down a
shaggy Kodiak. We quarreled when the monster reared
up on its hind legs and came shambling after us, for I did*

not share your faith in its peaceful intentions. I'd not been mauled by a salmon-fishing grizzly on the Columbia for nothing. Oh how you pounded my chest and called me a Philistine when a large-bore bullet through its brain brought it crashing down!

Ah Ginny, what your Philistine wouldn't give to have you batter him so again!

Alas, our stay in Eden ended all too soon when that nor'wester came out of nowhere. Despite all the skeleton crew I left aboard her could do, our dear old Washington dragged her anchors and stranded on the beach. So high and dry did the wind and current cast her that I gave up all hope of salving her. So we took off what we could and left her bones to bleach in the shifting sand. Our precious cargo of fish would have to reach San Francisco some other way.

It was then that you frightened me by coming down deathly ill! Lord, how you railed at me when I shipped you off alone to Kodiak on the revenue cutter that came to our rescue!

Well, Ginny, there's no one inside a hundred miles of here to rescue us now. No one on the planet would even dare to try.

'How goes it, Francisco?'

'I am saying my beads as a good Catholic should, señor capitán.'

'Surely you are not frightened by a bit of storm, my friend. Good Catholics need only die once, you know.'

'All very well for you to say, but in my present state, how can I be sure of that? In any case, compadre, I must pray for you and this little sloop. The Holy Virgin knows you both need all the praying you can get.'

'Loose the sheets and let her run before the wind, Francisco. Every league we win westward gives us a better chance of surviving this night.'

'*Spray* will not stand the strain, mi capitán! Listen to her groan!'

'Like any woman worth her salt, she dearly loves to complain. I rebuilt her to weather Cape Horn, Francisco. Believe me, she's good for it and to spare.'

'Oh I am willing to believe you, señor capitán, though all the myriads of sailors drowned at sea may say you nay.'

'Tell you what, my friend! If we make it through this night, I swear to God I shall present *Spray* with a proper mizzen at our next port of call.'

'And what has making *Spray* into a yawl have to do with surviving till morn, señor capitán?'

'Well, Francisco, shaping and rigging another mast is bound to cause us a great deal of trouble. Your Catholic God delights to see his creatures suffer, does he not? Holding me to my pledge will requite His labor watching over us through this night.'

'Don Jèsu, I swear you blaspheme worse than a Castilian! You must be an infidel or at the very least a pagan heathen to say such a thing!'

'I'm just a poor excuse for a Protestant heretic, Francisco, and to tell you the truth, I'm not even much of that. It's been many years since I've seen the inside of a church.'

'There is no worse sin than heresy, Don Jèsu, even if it be done feebly. In the eyes of God and Holy Church, witchcraft and suicide are mere trifles by comparison with heresy.'

'And speaking of suicide, my friend, is that why you have been condemned to endure this terrible voyage with me?'

'Si, compadre, I believe what you suggest may be so, though I will allow that I find you tolerable enough by times. But then, I've heard it said that even the miserable sinners roasting in hell crave each other's company.'

Twas not misery which made us love each other, was it, Ginny? Twas on the bark Czarevitch, Seattle bound

*from Alaska after losing the Washington, that you kissed
my shoulder in the fastness of our berth and told me that
you were heavy with child. 'So, Joshua, don't you dare
ever leave me again. From now on, I go wherever you
go till death do us part'.*

*'Life at sea is hard on a woman.' I cupped both your
swelling breasts in the darkness.'Especially if she be a
mother of children.'*

*'But tolerable enough if she has a good man to stand
by her.' You pulled me down upon you. 'Promise never to
send me away again, Joshua.'*

*I felt myself sinking deep. 'I swear, Ginny: right now,
you could make me promise you just about anything.'*

March 4, 1896

'Here comes the dawn at last, señor capitán.'

'Aye, Francisco, and it brings with it the northeast-
erly storm we've been dreading.'

'Mi capitán, I think we have more than enough on
our hands already! Spray cannot survive two such
storms fighting for the honor of tearing us apart.'

'It will begin soon enough, my friend. We must strip
her bare and let her run before the wind.'

'But the wind and this horrid current will drive us
southeast! If we're not careful we'll be swept back
around the Horn!'

'Just where you wanted us to go, Francisco! Keep
her before the wind! No vessel afloat could face into a
hurricane such as this and hope to survive! Drake himself in the *Golden Hind* was driven back as we are
being driven back now. Pray God we've gained enough
sea-room to round the Horn, if round it we must.'

'At least keep our storm-sail triple-reefed on her
forestay, mi capitán, or she'll stagger all over the sea
like a drunken whore.'

'Aye, but be sure to keep the sheets flat amidships, Francisco. I shall play out these two long ropes of ours to break the combers and steady her.'

'Caramba, where did you learn such a curious trick as this, Don Jèsu?'

'Sailing down Cook Inlet to Kodiak after losing the *Washington. A* savage williwaw came down off the peaks and caught our whaleboat in open water. It was swamping us till my Aleuts paid out our gill nets for a sea-anchor. Playing out such ropes as these works like a charm – you'll see!'

'I shall pray to the Virgin that it works as you say, mi capitán. These waves are grown higher than our mast-head!'

'The sea rises up in all her majesty against us, Francisco. She's determined to overwhelm us. Still, I've a trick or two up my sleeve to appease so savage a mistress.'

'There is no pity in her, Don Jèsu.'

'Aye, my friend, she might well drive me to terror if you were not here to keep me company.'

'I have never felt such a wind before, compadre! Even stripped bare, see how the mast bends!'

'My friend, it was not well done of you to belittle Cape Horn! Now we must pay the piper for your blasphemy!'

'Madre de dios, you make it sound like these are the gates of hell we enter, señor capitán! It's not so bad as all that! *Spray* no longer ships those following seas thanks to your trailing rodes. Caramba, your sea-anchor works like a saint's relic indeed! Instead of falling off the wave-crests, she hangs on to them like a *menina* back at Queen Isabella's royal court in Saragossa!'

'That's the spirit, my friend! Let us face Cape Horn together in all the thrill of delight and wonder. Aye, let us look death in the face and laugh. Why else should we bother to go on living at all if we cannot live moments like this to the full?'

'Compadre, I am already dead, but what you say is God's truth. We might as well enjoy ourselves. After all, with such a crew as us to man her, *Spray's* as game a vessel as ever sailed these waters.'

'Francisco, think you can manage her by yourself while I slip below and rustle us up some hot stew?'

'A pot of your coffee would also be in order, mi capitán, if you can manage it in such a tossing sea. I've acquired a taste for that Saracen brew of yours. Madre di dios, but these seas are marvelously high and crooked. We sail through a perfect maelstrom this morn!'

'Aye, Francisco, there are no worse seas to face than this one that rises up before us now. If we can survive this, we'll have nothing left to fear.'

Except living on without you, Ginny. Whatever made me come look for you off Cape Horn of all places? Well, I found dear old Francisco in a storm in the middle of the Atlantic, didn't I? But if the gates of heaven are closed to him for his small sin, think how tightly they must be closed to me.

Well, Ginny, just to catch a glimpse of you now and then through the lattice of pearls is all I ask.

CHAPTER XVI

THE MILKY WAY

This was the greatest sea-adventure of my life. God knows how I escaped.

– From *Sailing Alone Around the World*
by Joshua Slocum

Cockburn Channel: March 7, 1896

'I hear no snores coming from down below, señor capitán, but I hope you are truly resting in your berth. God knows you are going to need some sleep before we're through this run.'

'I've no time for sleeping now, Francisco. There'll be plenty of time to sleep after I'm dead and gone. I'm pricking off a course to the Falklands on this old Spanish chart of mine.'

'What's that? Did I hear you say you are charting a course to the Maldivas?'

'You heard me right, Francisco.'

'Señor, those wretched isles lie almost three hundred leagues back along our course!'

'We've been all of four wild days and sleepless nights running before this storm, Francisco. According to my dead reckoning, we've been driven back southeasterly into Drake Channel almost to the pitch of Cape Horn itself. Our rig, as you can plainly see, is reduced to tatters. So there's nothing for it but to make our way back to Port Stanley and refit.'

'What? Go all the way back to Port Stanley with our tail betwixt our legs? Surely you do not intend to retreat so far as that, mi capitán!'

'My dear Francisco, I fear this confounded hurricane leaves us no choice in the matter.'

'Our suffering these two months in this icy purgatory will have been all in vain, compadre! But still, what am I saying? I shall compose myself and try to look on the bright side of things. Surely if we make it back safely to the Maldivas, not even a Bluenose would be so stubborn as to try passing through these jaws of the devil a second time.'

'Francisco, how you do love to go on! You know perfectly well that no choice remains for me but to sail on around this planet till I hove to at the point from which I started.'

'The point of no return, I think you mean, Don Jèsu!'

'My friend, I don't blame you for reproaching me. You have my leave to jump ship in Port Stanley if that is your druthers. Mind you, I shall greatly miss you, for you've been a boon companion to me thus far.'

'Once again you insult me, señor capitán! You know perfectly well that I am bound over in chains to stay with you, even if it should be Almighty God's will that you spend eternity trying to sail round this Devil's Horn!'

'Then it seems neither of us have been given a choice in the matter. Try to forgive me, Francisco, for being what I am.'

'Well, Don Jèsu, who am I to presume to forgive a man such as you? For better or for worse, each of us made his own berth aboard this great ship we call the world, did we not? Madre mia! Look! A mountain rises up through the clouds!'

'A mountain, you say? A high island more like! Where?'

'There, off our port beam! I make it no more than seven leagues away, señor capitán!'

'By all the Catholic saints, that's Cape Horn itself, or else I'm lady-in-waiting to Queen Isabella!'

'Cape Horn, did you say? How can we have been driven back so far so quickly, señor capitán? Is this truly Cape Horn?'

'Who can tell for sure where we are? It's been nigh on a week since we last glimpsed the sun or a star long enough to take a sighting. Right now, I'd gladly settle for a sight of the moon just to prove there is one.'

'Caramba, we are made to endure the worst of both worlds – first we passed through those infernal straits and now we enter the abode of the devil himself.'

'Aye, it has to be Cape Horn! Hard to port, sir! The hurricane has done its damnedest and we are still afloat! With a little more luck, we shall make it back to Port Stanley and prepare ourselves to once more pass through Magellan's confounded Strait!'

'She will not answer to that course unless you bend on the mainsail, señor capitán. The forestay sail, she is too small, what's left of her.'

'Aye, our mains'l's blown to ribbons as well. If I had to do it again, I would take up dear old Captain Samblich's gift of a proper suit of sails. So much for my foolish pride, Francisco! As things stand, what rags are left will have to do.'

'What! You intend to hang that pitiful little squaresail from *Spray's* gaff?'

'I'm afraid it can't be helped, Francisco. Head her up into the wind till I hoist it off the deck.'

'Caramba, señor capitán, I am glad the crew of the *Pinta* cannot see us now flying such a sail! They would laugh me to shame!'

'Well, Francisco, I'll say it again: we beggars can't be choosers if we wish to make it out of here. I hope at least that these last four days have given you a proper respect for cruising off the Horn!'

'Si, Don Jèsu, though I truly think Magellan mistook the strait of Scylla and Charybis for his own. Think you that the old Greek Odysseus might have cruised this far?'

'He was gone a 'voyaging for ten years, was he not? Stranger things have been done under this southern sun, Francisco.'

'Caramba! Feel that, señor capitán? Each time this small patch of sail shivers by the leech, it shakes poor old *Spray* from keelson to truck.'

'Just pray she does not spring a leak about the heel of the mast. It's a proper miracle that her garboard's still sound. You're my witness she's not called upon me once to man the pump.'

'You fashioned *Spray* well indeed, mi capitán; that much I will warrant you. Even my beloved *Pinta* could do no better than this little oyster sloop has done. Father in heaven, feel her now! She tears off for the land like a mare sighting her stable!'

'Make the most of her as long as the light holds, Francisco, but do not let her trip while cresting these waves! They must be seventy feet high if they're an inch! If we were to fall off, there'd be no righting us!'

'Señor capitán, what does it profit us to hurry? We can't hope to reach land before night closes down upon us.'

'Aye, Francisco, I take your point. So get ready to wear ship. We must stand guard offshore all through this long night. God snug in his heaven permits no rest for damned heretics and good Catholics alike.'

Remember the Constitution, Ginny? She went down in such a storm as this, but that was off Samoa long after we left her. A good ship she was, too. We sailed her back and forth on the San Francisco to Honolulu run for several

150

months, but she was already too small for regular packet duty on that busy route. And I soon grew bored with the 'coconut milk run', as we called it. So we sailed her down to Mexico for the sake of adventure, then on to Valparaiso, wasn't it? Aye, Victor was born on the next leg to Nukahiva, but that didn't keep you from wheedling me to water at Easter Island on the way back.

The truth is that I only humored your wish to see the giant stone heads some forgotten people had left behind. I'd no time myself for such womanish whims while driving our crew at replenishing our water stores out of the crater called Rano Raraku. God knows rousting those casks was work enough for our gang of men, but inside we found an immense unfinished statue that measured sixty-eight feet from its crown to its base. Its crown of red tuff alone weighed many tons.

'How did mere men ever manage such a thing, Joshua?'

'Manage what, Ginny?'

'How did those primitive people carve these colossal heads? You say they had no metal implements! And once built, how did they ever hope to move them down to the sea? Where did such a marvelous people come from and where did they go?'

'Ginny, you might as well ask me where did we come from! Or what are we? Or where are we going?'

Holding Victor in your arms, you cocked your fine head at me in wide-eyed surprise. 'Why Joshua, I never dreamed you gave thought to such things!'

So you are here with me after all, Virginia. I feel your hand guiding me through this wind and sea gone wild. You are still part of my becoming, Ginny. You still do what a good woman always does for her man: act as his porthole on the universe. Without you I would still be as dead blind as I was before. Aye, you were my best chance to discover the meaning of this life I've led, but you had me dead to rights right from the beginning. I had my gaze fixed on the deck and not on the stars. Ungrateful wretch that I was, you were taken from me before I caught more than a gleam of eternity in the corner of your eye. So now I must make this voyage alone in search of all that was lost. Aye, the last laugh is on me, isn't it?

'Señor capitán, here comes that terrible roar again! Can you hear it over the screeching of the wind?'

'Aye, Francisco, I'm not yet stone-deaf. Odd, there should be broken water off our port beam as well as off our starboard. Twice we've worn ship, and thrice we've run into tremendous breakers.'

'Si, this witch of a sea, she is breaking all around us, mi capitán. Whichever way I turn the wheel the crashing waves threaten us. Their roar sent shivers up and down my spine all night.'

'Well, my friend, here comes the dawn and then we shall see at last what we shall see. One thing for sure, we are not at all where I took us to be. So much for my famous dead reckoning.'

'Do you mean to say that this is not the Devil's Horn looming in the distance, señor capitán?'

'Nay, Francisco, I only wish it were.'

'Finally, here comes the first rays of dawn! I can see blood trickling down your face, Don Jèsu.'

'Aye, the hail and sleet in that last squall cut up the flesh around my eyes a bit. But now's hardly the time to complain of a little broken skin, my friend.'

'Just where are we, señor capitán?'

'I hate to name it, Francisco, but there's only one place this side of hell we could be.'

'Hell, you say? Have we somehow slipped out of purgatory and through the infernal gates during the night, Don Jèsu?'

'In a manner of speaking, Francisco. Unless I'm dead wrong yet again, we're square in the middle of the Milky Way.'

152

'Milky Way? The name has a pleasant enough ring to it, señor capitán, but I can tell from the tone of your voice that you're not happy to be here.'

'A man would need to be suffering from a death wish to boldly venture here, Francisco. See that island over there, the one that lured us into this trap? That's Fury Island with the false Cape Horn towering above.'

'Madre mia! Such huge seas! I see breakers crashing at all points of the compass, compadre!'

'Aye, my friend, they break on hidden rocks into a white foaming froth as far as the eye can reach. That is why this place is called the Milky Way.'

'Caramba! How did we make it safe across such a hellish sea in the pitch darkness, señor capitán?'

'The Virgin must have been listening to your prayers, Francisco. Now the question remains: in the light of day can we make it out of here?'

'Only set me a course to follow, mi capitán, and the pilot of the *Pinta*, he will dog it till hell itself freezes over!'

'An apt turn of phrase given our present location! There, see you that ragged line of deeper green against the light? Dog it as you say, Francisco, dog it for all you're worth. Our very lives depend on it!'

'Si, mi capitán, but may I tell you something while you are still breathing here beside me?'

'Have your say, Francisco, but do make it brief.'

'I just want to say that I reckon this a greater adventure even than crossing the Unknown Sea with Don Cristóbal Colón!'

'Why thank you, Francisco! My hands and nose are numb, but you are right! We should set ourselves to enjoy this last merry ride as best we may!'

'Si, mi capitán, you state my own sentiments exactly! Let us go lighthearted wherever this channel leads us. Speak of the Devil! A wall of rock opens up before us, señor capitán!'

'There, Francisco! Hard a lee, sir! Head her up between those two great gnashing rocks!'

'We must surely scrape the barnacles off if we make it through at all! Holy Father in heaven, excuse me, poor miserable sinner that I am! I know I should properly ask your Virgin Mother's intercession on our behalf, but as you can plainly see, there's no time left us for doing that! Our Father, who art in heaven, keep these great waves from dashing us to pieces on these terrible rocks. Deliver your servants from evil in the name of your son, Jèsu Christe.'

'There, Francisco, we've made it through, by God! You can leave off that praying now. You make me feel like I'm at a funeral.'

'Where have we got to now, señor? Is this the devil's vestibule? Madre mia, it is suddenly so quiet in here.'

'We sit in the lee of the Milky Way's inner reefs, Francisco. Look, I believe that's Cockburn Channel lying off to the northeast of us. It's still uncharted, but I think it will take us back into the Strait of Magellan if we carefully follow it.'

'Have we any choice, señor capitán? Certainly it is better to head into the unknown and fall off the edge of the world than to retreat across this Milky Way. God will not suffer us to tempt him with our lives a second time. Indeed, let us take this respite as a sign of his mercy upon us. Throw down the anchor in this quiet place and get yourself some sleep, I implore you.'

'In good time, Francisco. But first I shall climb the mast and have a look at what we have come through. Darwin the great naturalist came this way, you know. It comes to me now what he said about this desolate place. 'Any landsman seeing the Milky Way would have nightmares for a week.'

'Do you know what I think, señor capitán?'

'No, Francisco, what do you think?'

'I think your Darwin need not have set us seamen aside from suffering such nightmares!'

CHAPTER XVII

CARPET TACKS

The air of depression was about the place, and I hurried back to the sloop to forget myself again in the voyage.

– From *Sailing Alone Around the World*
by Joshua Slocum

Thieves Bay: March 8, 1896

'Tis a lucky vessel you pilot through these narrow seas, Francisco!'

'You've told me so many times already, señor capitán!'

'Then permit me to affirm it once again, my friend. First *Spray* weathers a Cape Horn hurricane, then she navigates the Milky Way in pitch darkness. And last but not least, she passes through Cockburn Channel with all its uncharted shoals and rocks without so much as scraping her keel. More than that, I believe we may be the first vessel ever to make this passage!'

'Si, señor capitán, you dare to brag now, but our passage was not accomplished without human cost. Madre de dios, but I'm sick of groping our way from rock to reef through this labyrinth of isles! I've not suffered from so choleric a humor since the night the *Santa Maria* went down!'

'You did well at the helm for a Spaniard, if I do say so. Aye, sir, how would I have ever managed to get through all this without you along to pilot us?'

'As for you, Inglés, I swear you have become a true likeness of your namesake come down from the Cross!'

'Do be careful, my friend! I fear your sojourn in purgatory may be prolonged for uttering such blasphemy!'

'I but speak the truth! You have worn yourself thin as a rail, and your face and hands still bleed as though from the stigmata and the crown of thorns.'

'Oh I'm just a bit peevish from lying about, that's all. *Spray* and you did all the work. You both deserve to curl up for the night in the snug cove lying just ahead. From the lay of the land, I take it to be Thieves' Bay.'

'Thieves' Bay? Esto es La Hostia! The very name puts me in mind of Black Pedro and his band of savages, señor capitán.'

'Don't worry your head about Black Pedro. I know how to handle the likes of him. I've not been a captain over hard and brutal men these many years for nothing. Here, try some of my hot venison stew. It will settle your nerves.'

'Douse me in olive oil and serve me up with sardines and artichokes if you like, Don Jèsu, but nothing you say or do will make me stand watch on *Spray's* deck this night. You must do it yourself.'

'So it's come down to mutiny, has it? Very well then, where's my bag of carpet tacks?'

'Those great huge carpet tacks you had of Captain Samblich? I believe you stowed them in the locker beside you.'

'Aye, here they are.'

'But tell me, why for the love of the Virgin do you call for carpet tacks now?'

'Did you not mark when those two canoes fell into our wake as we came out of Cockburn Sound into the Strait? Those devils know very well that *Spray* sails shorthanded, Francisco. I've no mind to broil on a Fuegian spit tonight.'

'Señor capitán, did I not beg you to shoot the villain down when God sent you the chance?'

'And did I not tell you, Francisco, that I would not kill again unless forced to it? There now, that should do the trick quite nicely.'

'What's this? You've scattered carpet tacks all over the deck! Caramba! Do take care not to step on those sharp points, compadre! You tickled my ears enough with heretic oaths during the hurricane!'

'Let us both get some sleep, my friend.'

'Si, señor capitán, let us count our blessings while we may! Tomorrow we have to pass through the strait of that turncoat Portuguese once more. Just like that pitiful old Greek, we are condemned to push our stone up the mountain again and again, only to have it roll back down on top of us!'

Aye, let me leave off struggling to survive for a little bit, Lord. Anything for a respite from this vile wind! But wait, what palm-treed isle floating off the starboard bow do I see? Why, the sea's turned blue and smooth as glass. This warm deck beneath my feet, 'tis the bonny B. Aymar by the feel of her. And those hands backing the main topsail up there look familiar enough. By God, if that's not my old first mate Shure driving them on!

'Father, are those pirates rowing out to catch us in that boat?'

I looked down. There you were in your sailor's ducks, scampering out from under your mother's skirts for the first time. You couldn't have been more than three years old, but you were always a precocious child. 'Aye, Victor, I suspect you're not that wide off the mark.'

'Joshua, who are they?' Your mother left off setting the gimballed deck-table. She shaded her eyes at the six-oared yawl as it shot out from a leeward harbor in answer to our signal. 'Oh, what fine oarsmen they are!'

I reached down and hoisted you up from the deck, but you baulked and kicked to be set free. You did not want Tunku, our tattooed Malay helmsman, to see you held in my arms like a baby. 'Those native fishermen we met with yesterday spoke of some foreign sailors marooned here on Oulau. They begged us to come rescue them before they devour all the chickens and pigs on the island.'

'Joshua, their gear is something outlandish.' A quick flick of your mother's fingertips assured us both that the .32 calibre revolver nestled close to her hand in the sash of her gown.

'Aye, keep an eye peeled on them for me, will you?' I sat you down all flailing arms and legs on the deck. 'Especially the big broad-shouldered one standing in the stern with his arms crossed.'

'Father, he looks way too old for a pirate. Shouldn't he be hanged or made to walk the plank by now?'

'You're right, Victor.' Your mother chuckled as she winked at me. 'He looks like he just stepped out of that color-plate of the three patriarchs in your new Bible, doesn't he?'

'It's Abraham himself, Father!'

'More like it's Jonah, my son.' I tousled your shining hair.

You stamped your foot at me. 'No, no, Father. Jonah is only a prophet.'

My first mate ambled aft from dousing the jib. 'Mr. Shure, do you know that gent steering in the stern?'

'Aye, that I do!' Shure spat his brown gob over the leeward rail. 'That's Bully Hayes hisself. You best stand by fer trouble, capt'in. Don't turn your back on 'im, whate'er you do!'

158

The most notorious scoundrel in all the South Seas climbed as nimble as you please over my stern rail, his ragtag crew of beachcombers at his rope-sandaled heels. 'You be the capt'in of this vessel, I presume, sir.'

Old Shure shook his head at me, but I've never been one to refuse another man's extended hand. 'At your service, sir. What can I do for you?'

'Well now, Capt'in, it be more a question of what I can do for you!' Hayes propped the roll of matting he carried on its end and wrung my hand with both of his. 'This island's desperate short of swine and poultry, but I did my best for you.'

'I see that, and what will you take for your boatload of bananas, sir?'

'I see you're a man who gets right down to business, Capt'in sir.' The old freebooter spread his arms wide as his men mingled with my fore-hands. 'As for obliging me in return, I must tell you that the only copy of the Holy Scriptures on the island is worn out from heavy use. And my natives sit in darkness waiting for the reading of His Word. You wouldn't have an extry copy on board by any chance? There's no telling how many souls you'll be savin'.'

'A Bible, Mr. Hayes?' At my naming of him, the old pirate sent Mr. Shure a sidelong glance of recognition. I could tell it brought the old scoundrel little joy to find a man aboard who knew all the Pacific between Kamchatka and New Zealand like the back of his hand.

'To be sure, you've the advantage of me, Capt'in.'

'Slocum's the name. Your reputation precedes you, sir. Considering the thriving trade in pipes and tobacco your men are doing with my crew, I'm thinkin' it's more than Bibles you may be after.'

'Well, now that you mention it, there are a few more things we do need on the island. What's yer general cargo, Capt'in Slocum? You wouldn't be heading for Hong Kong by any chance?'

'*Two hundred and fifty ton of coal bound for Shanghai, Mr. Hayes.*'

'*Well, the island looks cozy enough right now, capt'in, but you'd be surprised how cold it gets when that norwester blows. A few sacks of Newcastle would surely warm things up a bit fer us till we find us a ship bound for Hong Kong.*'

The first mate could bite his tongue no longer. '*You and your lot soon won't be needing coal to keep warm. You just wait a few years more, and the devil will stoke you up all the red-hot coals you can handle! Aye, I know you from way back, Bully Hayes!*'

'*Brother Shure, we should all save coal in the hereafter if we would only mend our ways in this life! Judge not that ye be not judged!*' Bully Hayes looked down at you staring up at him with big round eyes. '*Is this your son, Capt'in? My, he's a likely lookin' lad if ever I laid these peepers on one! Eyes as big as saucers! And this lovely lady come out to greet us must be his mother, Mrs. Capt'in Slocum herself!*'

'*Mr. Hayes, you're just in time to breakfast with us.*' Your mother extended him a slim gracious hand. '*It's not everyday we meet up with such a godly man.*'

Doffing his pilgrim's hat, Hayes stooped down from his great height and brushed her hand with his flowing white beard. '*Ma'am, I'd be honored to break bread with you and your husband. To be sure, it's not every capt'in's lady who'd allow a shipwrecked sailor to dine at her table.*'

'*Shipwrecked sailor, Captain Hayes? Did you lose your ship here on Oulau?*'

'*Aye, ma'am, that we did. As we speak, we're drifting past the harbor where my Leonora lies bleachin' her bones in the sand. If you look sharp you can see her final resting place.*'

'*By God, Captain, I know that rig!*' Shure turned upon me with utter amazement writ large upon his *windblown features. 'That's the John Williams II, as sure as God makes cocoanuts to grow on these trees!'*

'The missionary ship, Mr. Shure?'

'The same, Capt'in.' Bully Hayes sighed in helping your mother to be seated. 'We found her abandoned on a reef and floated her clear, but God's blessing had deserted her. She foundered in a typhoon more than a month back, though we saved all hands, doubtless due to the prayers we all offered up to God!'

'And so you and your poor crew have been marooned here on Oulau ever since, Mr. Hayes!'

'Aye, that we have, ma'am, waiting for a ship bound for Hong Kong. Not that the islanders haven't been good to us. As you can see, good old King Mongo even lends us his yawl.'

'I'm sure he has a choice in the matter.' Old Shure stood foursquare, his hands on his hips, confronting the freebooter.

'Old King Mongo's got a heart of gold!' The old reprobate began untying the roll of matting he had brought aboard. 'But it'd have been desperate drear, capt'in, I can tell you, if it hadn't been for the Reverend Snow. He's the one who turned my heart to religion. He calls me the crowning work of his mission to the islands. Poor old soul, he's desperate ill right now, or he'd have come along with us to welcome you to Oulau. He asked us to bring you this gift, Mrs. Slocum.'

'Why, Captain Hayes, this woven mat is simply splendid! Such wonderful colors! These are native girls frolicking in the surf, aren't they?'

'Ah yes, that they are, ma'am. The Reverend Snow judges them too wicked for minds just emerging from darkness, but he thought a Christian lady like yourself would be able to value it for what it is.'

'Why it's a splendid work of art!' Your mother unscrolled the roll of matting for all to see. 'Joshua, you must give Captain Hayes all the coal he can carry!'

'*Thank you kindly, ma'am.*'

'*Won't you say grace for us, Captain Hayes?*' Your mother directed the old pirate to sit in my place at the head of the table. '*My husband's not the praying type, at least not in public.*'

'*Certainly, ma'am, though I'll gladly defer such a holy office to a proper Christian such as your first mate's become. He was busy last I seen him blackbirding these isles for the squatters of Queensland.*'

'*God's blood!*' Mr. Shure shook his head in total chagrin as he seated himself at the far end of the table.

At a smile from your mother, Bully Hayes began praying.

'*Our Father who art looking down on the Benjamin Aymar, we pray*

That You soften the heart of those who take thy name in vain

That You bless Your humble servants' efforts to spread Thy Word among the savages and sinners of these islands,

And we thank You for these fine stewed pork cutlets and boiled eggs which Capt'in Slocum's good lady Virginia hath served us up in your name,

And Lord, we beseech You to deliver us from those who set themselves up in judgment of others,

And to forgive us our sins as we forgive those who sin so grievously against us, (here an eloquent gesture of forgiveness was directed at Shure)

For thou art captain over us all, forever and ever, amen.

'*Why Captain Hayes, I've seldom heard men of the cloth pray better!*' Your mother looked round at the rest of us in genuine wonderment. '*I'm sure my husband and Mr. Shure would like to apologize for doubting your need of a Bible.*'

'*Your good husband needs no forgiveness from me, ma'am. After all, a capt'in of such a fine vessel as this must needs always guard against allowing riffraff on board. There's no telling what you may run up against in these Southern Seas these days, ma'am!'*

'Truer words were never spoken, Mr. Hayes.' I cast Mr. Shure a sympathetic glance, but my vanquished first mate would not even look up from his steaming pork cutlet.

We hadn't yet finished breakfast when a dugout canoe came dashing out from shore. An islander clambered up the taffrail like a monkey and began screeching at us. 'Cappah Hayes! Preecha Snow, he sayee you come quick to the village. The Dutchmon, he cuttee off his wife's ear with beard-knife, so she spearee him in leg, then she hack-ee his shoulder half off. Cappah Hayes! He sayee you come quick or there be nothing left of Dutchmon or his wife.'

The old scoundrel sighed and rose up from the head of the table. 'Capt'in and Mrs. Slocum, would you be so kind as to have your crew dinghy me ashore? As you have heard, my people need me. I'll just leave my crew to pick up that load of coal, if I may. Mrs. Slocum, your son's gone below, pray bid him goodbye for me.'

'Of course, Captain Hayes, we understand.' Your mother graciously let her hand be kissed. Bully Hayes was just about to spring down into the canoe when you reappeared from below decks, lugging your Christmas gift. You were barely big enough to tote it along. 'Captain Hayes, wait! You'll be needing this!'

The old pirate halted astraddle the rail and looked down. For a moment your big luminous eyes seemed to transfix him like a bug on a pin. Finally he stole a sidelong glance at your mother. She nodded and smiled. Solemnly, he took up the Bible from your hands. 'Thankee, Victor. Each time it saves some poor soul, I'll say a prayer for thee.'

'Eei-owhh!'

'Eei-owhh!'

'What's that? Francisco, that's not you howling, is it?'

'Eei-owhh!'

'Madre di dios, Don Jèsu, we've been boarded by pirates!'

'Eei-owhh!'

'Francisco, where's my good old Martini-Henry?'

'Eei-owhh!'

'Here where it always is, beneath your head, mi capitán! Many feet dance on the deck over our heads!'

'Well now, we'll just let these merry rascals know we're at home and receiving company!'

'Boom! Boom!'

'Eei-owhh!'

'Eei-owhh!'

'Dear God in heaven, señor capitán, they howl up there like a pack of dogs from hell!'

'Boom! Boom!'

'Eei-owhh!'

''Por los clavos de Cristo!'

'Señor capitán, listen! Do you hear that? Someone up there is swearing in good Castilian!'

'Eei-owhh!'

'Me cago en San Isidore!'

'Did you hear that splash, Francisco? That sounds like "man overboard!" to me!'

'Eei-owhh!'

'There goes another into the drink! Light the lantern.'

'Eei-owhh!'

'Boom! Boom!'

'Caramba! Your gun deafens me in this tiny cabin, señor! And all this smoke! The swearing and screaming has stopped! They're all cooling off in the Bay of Thieves, I think!'

'Aye, Francisco. Let's go on deck and have us a look.'

'First you must put on your boots, Don Jèsu! Or you also will be needing to go for a swim and a swear!'

'Aye, Francisco! Samblich's carpet tacks came in right handy, did they not?'

'Si, señor capitán! I've never heard swearing done better in my entire life! Black Pedro is a true Spaniard if one may judge by his choice of saints.'

'Dear God, but it's dark out there! Is that one of their canoes drifting away? Listen, there he is again!'

'Me cago en Dios y los santos del año!'

'He sounds very cold and wet this time, Francisco!'

'Boom! Boom! Boom!'

'I'm glad you did not kill the scoundrel after all, Don Jèsu. It would have been such a pity for him to have missed so Christian a baptism!'

'Boom! Boom! Boom!'

'No need to waste more powder, Don Jèsu. We shall not be disturbed any more by guests who take their leave of us in so great a hurry.'

'I suspect you're right, Francisco. I think now we may turn in and sleep soundly in our berths. Good night, my friend.'

'Buenas noches, amigo! Sleep well!'

Ah, Black Pedro, what a sorry comedown you are from the pirates of yesteryear!

CHAPTER XVIII

YAMMERSCHOONER

I turned the prow of the Spray westward once more to the Pacific, to traverse a second time the second half of my first course through the strait.

– From *Sailing Alone Around the World*
by Joshua Slocum

Famine Reach: March 10, 1896

'By all the saints, Don Jèsu, our little square sail, she grows up to be a most serviceable main. You gave her a new peak yesterday, but now here's a clew and a leech besides! You missed your calling as a quilter, I think!'

'I sew on another piece with my palm and needle every chance I get, Francisco. *Spray* may not sport the best-setting mains'l afloat, but she'll weather a hard blow under this coat of many colors, that much I'll warrant you.'

'Forsooth, I rate her an improved sailing design, señor capitán. She's brought us a good three leagues today already. That's a good long run for this little vessel against a wind and current such as courses through this devil's strait.'

'Aye, Francisco, and lucky we are to find such a good anchorage as this, though there's a bit too much kelp afloat in here for my liking.'

'Doubtless that's why the mariners who first passed this way called it Snug Bay, señor capitán! We should get ourselves a good night's sleep in here for a change. I only hope this fair weather holds steady for the morrow.'

'It's already too fair for my liking, Francisco! I've grown to prefer the gales. In boisterous weather, the Fuegians do not stray far from home. I'd far sooner trust *Spray* to the vagaries of wind and sea than to the cunning of savage men. Sooner or later the Fuegians are sure to outsmart us.'

'Speak of the devil, señor! Here come those two canoes again! Look, see them sneaking along there in the shadow of the headland?'

'Aye, Francisco, and they are crammed to the gunnels with Fuegian rascals, if this spyglass be not lying to me. To brave a sea such as this in such a miserable craft suggests they are better seamen than we take them for. And maybe better pirates than we take them for as well.'

'As for that, señor, I see spears and bows sprouting amongst them aplenty!'

'Aye, Francisco, desperate they are for plunder. Let's see what such men make of a shot fired across their bows!'

'Boom!'

'Hah! My old Martini-Henry brought them smartly to attention, did she not?'

'For all the good it may do us! They are pulling into that little creek that runs back behind us, señor capitán.'

'Aye, Francisco, and passing just out of rifle range. There's nothing for it but to pull up the anchor and make across the strait as fast as we can.'

'But we've just stowed the sails! You are all in, señor capitán! I make it two more hard leagues of tacking to the other shore!'

'There's no help for it, Francisco. If we stay here, they'll sneak around behind us. Then they can shower down arrows and spears from the bluff onto our deck! Look, see the grass parting up there along the ridge?'

'Caramba, you are right! Quick, mi capitán! Up with the anchor! Already I feel their arrows tickling our ribs!'

'Damnation!'

'What's the matter now, señor capitán?'

'I can't budge the anchor for love nor money. Something's gone wrong with the windlass!'

'Listen, Don Jèsu, did you hear that sound?'

'Aye, Francisco, it reminds me of the hissing of a snake!'

'Forsooth, it brings back old memories enough to me, compadre. That's the sound an arrow makes gliding passed one's ear!'

'May the devil rack them over red hot coals in hell! Why, some of those rascals were already on the bluff waiting for us to anchor! Francisco, we must get our tails out of here as best we can!'

'Si, señor, but what are you doing?'

'Setting all the sails! There's more than one way to break out an anchor. Now head her up into the wind while I haul her short by hand.'

'Si, mi capitán. Caramba, but what a rough and ready sailor you are! I'm glad my shipmates aboard the *Pinta* cannot see me now.'

'There, that's the best I can do with these two arms for want of a dozen able-bodied seamen and a capstan. Fill her away, Francisco. Let's see if the new sail's as good as you just gave her credit for.'

'Madre de dios! This is no proper way for a master to handle his vessel, señor capitán!'

'It's no wonder you fell overboard on the way home from the Indies, Spaniard. It's clear to me that voyage had gone far too smoothly for you. I'm sure this one is far more to your liking!'

'Oh, you're a hard man, Inglés. No wonder God makes you sail around the world alone.'

'I'll warrant you're not the first man to ever tell me as much, my friend!'

'Madre di dios! *Spray* just pulled herself free! She sails along as though she thinks an anchor a thing that is meant to be towed beneath her belly!'

'Aye, but we've fished a ton of kelp loose from that reef as well! Head out into the strait, Francisco, I shall have to clear this mess away as best I can. May God take mercy on any Indian who dares to show himself now, for I shall take the mere sight of him for a declaration of war.'

'Speaking of war, mi capitán! There's an arrow quivering in the mast beside your head.'

'Aye, Francisco, a Fuegian calling card of sorts. The murdering devils must be hiding behind the bushes on the point abaft us.'

'Boom! Boom!'

'Father in heaven, señor capitán, look at them caper out from behind that bush! A regular Fuegian jig they are dancing. Now shoot them down like the treacherous dogs they are!'

'Nay, Francisco, a few shots beneath their feet to encourage their progress should do the trick!'

'Boom! Boom!'

'You're as turning of your cheek as was your holy namesake, Don Jèsu! If you weren't such an unrepentant heretic, I warrant there'd be certain salvation awaiting your soul! Ah, just look at your poor hands, they are bleeding again!'

'Aye, Francisco, they'll look worse yet before this night is out!'

Aye, I do miss being young at times like these, Ginny. Oh, you'd still recognize this rail-hard body as mine, but it takes it longer and longer to recover from the slings and arrows of a seaman's fortune. So these days I try to avoid trouble whenever I can rather than running to embrace it the way I used to do. Aye, I've come down a long way from how we were back on Subiq Bay. Remember how it was after our owners sold the B. Aymar out from under us? It didn't faze us one bit. I just went out and got us a contract to build a steamship in the Philippines. Carted you and the children off into the jungle with never a by-your-leave. Nothing seemed beyond my powers back when we were living in our nipa hut at Olongapo.

To keep out the snakes and other crawling things, we built it high off the ground on four great molave corner-posts. They had to be skidded to the site through swamp and jungle by Lapu-Lapu and his amphibious carabao. The big brute of a creature would let Victor and Jessie ride on its back or Ben hang from its tail, but I had only to get upwind to provoke a stampede. How Lapu-Lapu would shout and cast his arms about! 'Vamoose, patrone, vamoose! Want you Raja to trample your house down!'

The monster was especially gentle with you, Ginny. Not that you drew much comfort from such things in the midst of the unrelenting heat.

Even lying naked on our bed, we sweltered in a pool of perspiration. 'You don't like it here, do you, Ginny?'

'I'm not partial to being steamed alive in this palm-leaf hut, Joshua. I'd rather be aboard ship with a cool breeze blowing through the sails.'

'Just give me a couple more months to finish this steam vessel for Jackson.' I stroked your bare shoulder soothingly with my rough hands. 'You've seen Pato. You know what a beautiful schooner she is. Once she's ours, we'll go fishing way up high in the cool North Pacific.'

171

'It's just that we have small children to think of, Joshua. They could catch fever here at Olongapo. And the snakes, have you seen the one I shot this morning? I looked up and there it was coiled on a limb of the flowering jacaranda overhanging the path. It kept darting its tongue at me. I half expected it to speak to me like it did to Eve. Oh Joshua, I swear it was big enough to swallow Victor or the baby whole. Miguel's skinning it for a pair of fiesta boots. It'll make a dozen pairs of boots, I told him. Oh how I do hate snakes!'

'You suffer from girlish fantasies, Ginny, that's all.'

'Girlish fancies? How dare you accuse me of such a thing? For our honeymoon, you took me fishing in Alaska and shipwrecked me! Have I once said die to you since the day we married?'

'Well no, Virginia. Actually, you've got more grit in your craw than any man I ever met. Once we have our own ship, I promise I'll never strand you in some backwater hole like this again.'

'Don't go making me promises you've no intention of keeping, Joshua.'

'That's a hard thing to say to your very own husband, Virginia! May God strike me dead this instant if I don't mean it!'

'Remember the little gnome I told you about? The one who keeps house inside my head? He warned me the moment I first laid eyes on you. You were walking along the Bondi boardwalk, your captain's hat tucked under your arm. You still had your full head of hair back then, and he said to me: "Beware, Virginia! This man you're setting your cap for, there's nothing he isn't capable of doing." But I was so sure of myself, Joshua, and so full of you! So I told the little gnome that all I needed was such a man to become capable of doing anything as well. Oh, I didn't stop even for a moment to think about what bearing you children would mean.'

172

*'I know it's not exactly worked out the way I promised
you it would, Virginia.'*

*You nibbled my ear and put your arm around me. 'I
swear you'll be the death of me in the end, Joshua.'*

*So I went away to see about supplies for the steamship
hull we were building. You were alone with Victor and
Ben the night the Tagals came. Armed with torches and
axes, they lit fires and formed a cordon around our home.
You waited in the dark, a loaded pistol ready in either
hand for what might come next, not knowing who was
your friend and who was your foe.*

*It turned out that our Chinese shipwrights were set to
murder us 'foreign devils' in revenge for taking the shipbuilding contract that would otherwise have gone to
them. Somehow the Tagals caught wind of the plot and
acted to foil it. At least that's how we explained to ourselves what happened that night, but I think now there
was much more to the story than met our unslanted eyes.
Maybe that gang of Chinese did turn their hand to piracy
at times, but no one ever did a better job of copper-fasten-
ing a teak lapstrake hull than those Chinamen who
worked for me at Olongapo. It's just that sometimes they
weren't quick enough on their feet for my liking, that's all.*

*Aye, Ginny, you used to say that I was a sonuvabitch
to work for. Certainly I wasn't above delivering a well-
aimed kick with my Brier Island cowhides if I thought
some slacker deserved it. More often than not, it worked
wonders with my crews, who considered it the natural
order of things to be bullied by their ship's officers. As for
the Tagals, they'd been kicked about by the Spanish for
centuries. They actually seemed to love me for delivering
more of the same. But not the Chinese, they were a different cup of tea altogether.*

*I could feel their hatred rolling off their bent backs as I
moved among them in the primitive shipyard they helped
me carve out of the jungle at Olongapao. Their patrone,
Liu Chow, he and his son had trouble keeping their*

hands off their long curved belt-knives at sight of me. But what did I care about how they were feeling? I was a white man and doubted not it was my rightful place to stand somewhere between them and God.

Aye, that contemptuous arrogance of mine almost cost you and the children your lives that night, Ginny.

Not to mention almost costing me the ship I was building.

Lapu-Lapu and the other Tagals had warned me that sabotage was in the offing. God knows I kept a close watch on Liu Chow and his sons after that night they came for you, but trouble came so swiftly when it came, I did not see it till it hit me between the eyes.

You screamed in girlish delight when the dog shores were knocked out and the hull lurched forward and slid down the greased slip-ways. But it did not slide far. It shuddered to a stop and stuck hard. Too late I saw that the rail timbers had been shifted out of line during the night.

Lu Chow stood there with his arms folded, inscrutable as that stone face we found on Easter Island. His son cast me a leering smile, but I would not give either of them the satisfaction of venting my rage and frustration, even though we both knew there wasn't a hydraulic jack to be had that side of Hong Kong.

Then a wonderful thing happened, born more I think of the Tagals' hatred of the Chinese than their love for me. They came with their carabao in droves, hitching them to the great hemp hawsers they fastened to either bow of the stranded vessel. Lapu-Lapu treated me to a grin and a shrug as he urged Raja into the line. 'Tis no great thing, patrone. How think you we launch our prouas? Give a Tagal enough carabao and he will move the world.'

Chanting rhythmically, the Tagals threw themselves upon their great beasts of burden. At a deafening shout they urged their mounts forward with their heels and prods. The unmovable hull yielded slowly to the irre-

sistible pull and lurched off after the Tagals and their carabao down to Subiq Bay. Lu Chow and his knot of Chinese stood out like an iceberg in that tumultuous sea of cheering, heaving flesh as the vessel righted itself. His son shook his fist, but I couldn't help laughing in his teeth. I raised my clenched fists and shouted my gratitude above the din. 'Quel nombre?'

'Tagadito! Tagadito!' The Tagals set up a deep-throated chorus in response. 'Call it the ship of the Tagals, patrone, for did we not save it for you?'

It was then that Lu Chow's eldest son made his play. That was something I knew well how to deal with, having dealt with his kind many times before. One fist got inside his guard and knocked him senseless, his great long knife still upraised. Lu Chow bowed down in acknowledgment of defeat, but even so it was all I could do to keep the Tagals from tearing him and his Chinese to pieces.

I remember well how you shook your head at my vainglory, Ginny. Well, I hope to do a lot better this time around.

March 12, 1896

'I understand now why they called this benighted land Tierra del Fuego, señor capitán!'

'Aye, Francisco, there be at least a dozen bonfires blazing all around us, but I can't say I consider it a great honor to be at the center of the festivities. Tis like being a missionary in the cannibals' pot.'

'Si, Don Jèsu, but the gale out there in the strait, she is whipping herself into a storm. It would be so good to anchor here in the lee of this big island and rest ourselves till morning, no?'

'Simply not advisable, my friend. There's too many would-be Fuegian pirates gathering here for even old

Martini-Henry to face down, and the anchorage lies hard up against the wooded shore. Anyway, here comes rosy-fingered dawn, as Homer would have it.'

'And with it will surely come more canoes, señor capitán, but these will not be Greek.'

'Aye, Francisco, like death and taxes, there are certain things in life one may always count upon.'

'This time there will be too many of them for us to dare hope they will break for cover at sight of your harquebus, compadre. I fear they will not let us slip so easily through their fingers a second time.'

'How great minds do think alike, Francisco!'

'This time I think you will have no choice but to kill some of them, Don Jèsu.'

'Not if I can help it, my friend. Not if I can help it.'

'Yammerschooner! Yammerschooner!'

'There, six canoes coming out of that mist off our starboard bow! Señor capitán, put the harquebus-that-keeps-on-shooting where they can see it well. Caramba, what are you doing?'

'Signaling the whaleboat with the two squaws to come closer. Maybe they'll rest content if we offer them a little trade.'

'Señor, you're playing with fire!'

'You've a way of putting your finger on things, Francisco. I can see a slow-match smoldering in the bottom of each boat. I fear fire more than all their arrows and spears. Keep an eye on the other canoes for me, will you? Hear me: they're not to come within bow-shot come hell or high water.'

'Si, mi capitán.'

'Look at Black Pedro standing there athwart the boat with his arms crossed like a king. He's huge and there's not a spare ounce of flesh on him! He's the only one sporting a beard, you'll notice.'

'Si, señor capitán, and he's wearing sea-boots this time. Stolen off the corpse of some poor sailor, you can be sure of that. Samblich's carpet tacks won't stop him this time! That's Black Pedro himself, or Queen Isabella never commissioned me pilot of the *Pinta*.'

'Those squaws rowing him along – have you ever seen harder specimens of humanity, Francisco?'

'Madre di dios, think what kind of life they must lead with him as their lord and master!'

'Yammerschooner! Yammerschooner!'

'They're begging us for food, señor capitán.'

'I'll just get them that jerked beef and biscuit I've been saving up for such an occasion.'

'Look out behind you, mi capitán!'

'What? Well, sirrah, I don't remember inviting you aboard.'

'Si, amigo. We met when you sailed through here before, so please point your gun the other way.'

'Aye, sirrah, we've made each other's acquaintance all right. As I remember, it was over the barrel of my gun that time as well.'

'Si, amigo, you fired your gun at me. That was muy malo of you. Where are the rest of your crew? When we last met, there were three men aboard.'

'The same crew is still aboard, sirrah. What are the squaws up to, Francisco?'

'Behind his back, they signal you to be careful, Don Jèsu. All that stands between you and death is that little pistol you hold in your hand.'

'It shall suffice me, Francisco, it shall suffice. I only wish Virginia were here to wield it.'

'Hombre valiente, why do not the others help you sail this vessel? They must be lazy slackers, those two!'

'I do not need them during the day, sirrah. My crew sleep now so as to be fresh for standing watch during the night. We were told in Puntas Arenas that is when these Fuegians become most dangerous.'

'So you come from Puntas Arenas, amigo! It was once my home, did you know?'

'Keep off, sirrah. I've no mind to try your bear hug for size. Your home, you say? Then you must know old Captain Samblich?'

'Si, amigo! Very well! He is a good friend of mine!'

'Is he now?'

'He lies through his teeth, señor capitán! This is the very man who murdered the kinsman of good Samblich. I can feel the blood-guilt roiling within him!'

'I do not doubt it, Francisco!'

'Your rifle there, amigo. How many times will it fire? Cuantos?'

'As many times as I pull the trigger, sirrah.'

'That is a truly amazing weapon! Lend it to me, amigo, and I will hunt guanaco for you.'

'Mañana, sirrah. Now, you'll be doing both of us a favor if you get back in the canoe. Here, I've some gifts for your womenfolk.'

'Senor capitán, the gap-toothed squaw wishes to make you a gift in return. Some lumps of tallow by the look of them. See how she grins as she holds up the biggest lump of all! I think she likes you!'

'She's a good-hearted soul. A proper Christian could show no more charitable smile than hers. Here's another packet of jerky for her!'

'Amigo, these squaws are just the lowest of savages. What about me?'

'Here's some sulphur matches, will that suit you? Nay, sirrah, I'll not set them on the tip of your spear. Here! Take them off the muzzle of my rifle if you want them.'

'Be careful where you point that terrible gun, señor!'

'Quedao!'

'Eei-owl!'

'You frightened him, Don Jèsu! Now he slinks away like a dog with his tail between his legs. See how the women laugh at his fear! I think perhaps the villain clubbed them this morning for not gathering mussels enough for his breakfast, poor benighted savages that they are.'

'And yet I'm much taken with that gap-toothed one, my friend. She may be the lowest of savages as you say, but somehow the milk of human kindness still flows in her breast.'

'How is that possible, compadre? To live like she does would overwhelm the Christianity of my name-saint himself.'

'Who can say, Francisco, who can say? Certainly there are stranger things under this sun than a man can dream of!'

CHAPTER XIX

DELIVERANCE

Difficulties, however, multiplied all about in so strange a manner that had I been given to superstitious fears I should not have persisted in sailing on a thirteenth day, notwithstanding that a fair wind blew in the offing.

– From *Sailing Alone Around the World*
by Joshua Slocum

Strait of Magellan: April 13, 1896

'Zounds, what a silly old boat you're getting to be! Now you've gone and tangled your rigging in these branches! Didn't Francisco ever tell you that an oyster sloop has no business climbing trees?'

'You've no one to blame but yourself for that, señor capitán. You've made poor *Spray* do just about everything else during this voyage, so why shouldn't she think to climb a tree?'

'There, that's got it. We're away and not much the worse for wear! Do try to be more careful where you point us, Francisco.'

'Si, mi capitán, but you've loaded this poor sloop down with deck cargo till I cannot see to steer!'

'Speak of the devil! There's another cask floating dead in the water! Hard to port, Francisco.'

'Enough is enough, señor! The last cask you hauled aboard split wide open. Poor *Spray*, she be greased from keelson to truck, and so are we!'

'An old trader's habits die hard, Francisco! You may be sure that somewhere along the way we'll do a brisk business with all this tallow!'

'Who would want so much of this rank stuff, Don Jèsu?'

'Good pure tallow like this has many uses, Francisco, as you will see soon enough, God willing.'

'I only know it smells to high heaven, señor. *Madre di dios*, how I wish we had never come upon all this wreckage!'

'Oh very well, we'll quit salving right now if that's the way you feel.'

'Bueno! Muchos gracias, señor capitán! I thought you would never have enough!'

'After all, this cask we've just fetched alongside is not tallow anyway.'

'What? Not more tallow? What in the name of God is it then?'

'Wine, Francisco. It's only a cask of useless wine.'

'Santa Maria! Did you say "wine", compadre?'

'Look at the stamp on the barrel-head if you don't believe me.'

'Madre di dios! A whole cask of Amontillado! The elixir of life itself!'

'Amontillado? That's a kind of cheap Spanish sherry, isn't it?'

'Cheap sherry! It's the elixir of the gods! Oh, it's been so long since a drop of Amontillado has passed my lips! And now to find a whole cask drifting abandoned past the gates of hell itself!'

'God's blood, this cask weighs a quarter of a ton if it weighs a pound!'

'Be careful how you hoist it aboard, señor capitán, lest you stave it in before my thirsty eyes!'

'Never fear, Francisco. I have the matter well in hand. I only pray that the crew of the wrecked ship have fared as well as has their cask of Amontillado.'

'But who is there in these godforsaken waters to rescue those desperate men, even if they did survive the storm that wrecked them – Black Pedro and his Fuegian pirates perhaps?'

'Aye, Francisco, I fear you are right. I much doubt that those poor souls still partake of our earthly blessings!'

'Pray, what blessings are you talking about, Don Jèsu? Six times we've tried to clear these straits, and six times we've failed. Three times already we've drifted round this island this unlucky day, even though it's shown as a headland on your precious chart. But now we have earned a good claim to have discovered it. You are doubtless the first person to ever set foot upon its rocky shore!'

'Indeed, Francisco! In exercise of my rights as its first explorer, I've already christened it after an old friend of mine! I trust you noticed the sign I posted there on the beach?'

'I wondered about that, señor! You have a friend who calls himself "Keep Off the Grass"?'

'No, no, my friend's name is Alan Erric. You'll have to come back to Boston with me to appreciate the joke.'

'Ha! Ha! Returning to Boston with you, that would be the joke, señor capitán! I do not think we ourselves shall ever escape this hell on Earth.'

'Don't look so glum, Francisco. You're forgetting this fine cask of Amontillado we just found.'

'Si, it's muy bueno to think on the Amontillado. Gracias, Santa Maria! Ho there, do you feel that brisk wind on your cheek, compadre?'

'Aye, my friend. A fair sou'wester is setting in! Head us up into it, and I'll hoist up the jib.'

'Si, mi capitán, let's get our tails out of here while we can!'

That's how all five of us felt pulling out from Olongapo's jungle landing aboard our new schooner.

Aye, Pato, I swear you were the most intrepid of all the vessels I ever mastered, present company excepted, of course. You could fly into the wind like no ship I've sailed before or since. Virginia and I, we never lived through happier times than while sailing you around the rim of this immense ocean.

We first took you to Manila looking for a cargo bound for Hong Kong or Shanghai. That's where the old Scottish captain hired us to salve his China Rose. She was a British bark outward bound from Canton with the usual cargo. Chased by pirates across the South China Sea till she was driven onto North Danger Reef by a storm. MacGregor and his crew managed to cut away the fore and main masts before being rescued by a passing ship.

We found her still hanging in the mild trade wind on the coral teeth that had ripped her open. We rafted alongside the abandoned hulk on a sea smooth as glass and began filling your hold, cabins and decks with teas, silks and camphor. MacGregor steadied himself by holding onto the China Rose's lonesome mizzen. A tear trickled down his white bearded cheek. 'God damn their slanted eyes!'

'You would do better to give thanks that they missed you in the storm, Captain MacGregor.'

'Aye, Captain Slocum, you are right. I shall cease my cursing! This sight of your crew salving the cargo ought to be cause enough for an old sea-dog at the end of his tether to offer thanksgiving.'

'Gentlemen, how do you think I would look in a gown cut from this?' Though heavy with child, Virginia draped a bolt of figured Cantonese silk from her shoulder and

struck a coquettish pose. 'I've never seen anything quite so fine in all my life.'

'Aye, ye'll look blithe and bonny in that, me lassie.' MacGregor shook away his tears and hitched up his broad belt. 'Captain Slocum, let Pato's log show that the master of the China Rose signed for that bolt of silk.'

'Oh, Captain, your losses are far too great as it is!' Virginia hastily rewound the silk. 'I should feel I was taking advantage of your misfortune. Please forgive me; I was only dreaming. You know how we women are.'

'Aye, I had a wife once meself. As for the silk, one bolt more or less will make no difference to my case, lassie. I was a ruined man till yer good husband came along. Misfortune began to lift off my shoulders the moment he undertook to salve my China Rose for me.'

'You are too kind, Captain MacGregor! Others have done as much for me on occasion. And we're not out of hot water yet. Bear in mind that it will take at least four round trips to carry all your cargo to Manila. That's more than a thousand leagues still to go, if the pirates or the monsoon don't get here first.'

'I'm willing to take my chances after seeing the way ye skipper yer little schooner, Captain Slocum. There's a bottle of single malt stashed under the Pullman berth in my cabin, if ye'd care to join me in a toast to our mutual success.'

I caught Virginia's warning glance. 'I think we should save it for Manila, Captain. We need to get ourselves out of here as fast as we can.'

Three times you made it back loaded to the guardrails, Pato. Each time Virginia left off sewing her new silk dress to choke down a toast with MacGregor's Scotch. The fourth time we returned, the monsoon had driven the China Rose to the bottom of the sea. You came sadly about as though grieving the loss of a sister and carried us back to Manila.

'Captain Slocum, dinnae fret. Ye've saved enough to give me back my hold on life.' MacGregor poured the dregs of his fine old single malt into three crystal goblets rescued along with the whiskey from his cabin on the China Rose. 'Lassie, I'll consider my salvation complete if ye'll wear yer bonny new dress at dinner this evening.'

Aye, you did us proud, Pato. Yet in the end I sold you down the river for a few thousand pieces of gold so that I might rise up a notch in the world of men. Where are you now, Pato? Pounding your heart out on a reef somewhere?

As for Virginia, she wears that dress still.

April 11, 1896

'Madre di dios! That sea was cold, Don Jèsu! First it reared over us like a frozen mountain; then it dropped on us like the sky itself was falling. It drenched me to the bone!'

'Aye, Francisco, but this fine weather sea has washed away all my regrets. Look, see yon albatross winging off the starboard bow? Tis the best of all omens, that. We've left Cape Horn behind us. We've a mild voyage half way round the world stretching out before us now.'

'Bueno, compadre, you may go down to your berth and sleep now.'

'Not just yet, my friend. I'm not much for sleeping anymore.'

'You are still flesh and blood, Don Jèsu. You've stood by me here in the cockpit since Cape Pillar. That's two full days you've gone without once closing your eyes.'

'Oh very well, my friend, I'll go down and fall in my berth if that will please you. First though, I'll stretch a spread on the new jigger.'

'Si, señor capitán. This sou'wester becomes less a gale each league we sail. The angry seas are gone, I'm glad to say. These little waves, they only want to gossip with *Spray* as she sails along.'

'Aye, 'tis a song of joy they be singing in harmony, Francisco. Robinson Crusoe, here we come, and I promise you I'll be whipping up some of Virginia's famous doughnuts the minute we drop anchor at your island.'

'Who is Robinson Crusoe and what are these dough-nuts you keep raving about, señor capitán? Do they grow on trees like almonds?'

Aye, we'll make doughnuts. Though they'll not be so good as the ones you used to whip up for us, Ginny. That thousand leagues on the Pato from Hong Kong to the Sea of Okhotsk, how the children did clamor in vain for them. We dared only make them in safe haven lest the fat spill.

It was there at anchor in the harbor of Avacha under the cone of Mount Villuchinsky that you finally treated us all to your fried wonders. Flour frosted your elbows and forearms in the bright sunlight as you rolled out the dough on Pato's deck-table. Victor cut out the circles and shared the raw centres with Ben, who stood jealous guard over the bowl of sugar and cinnamon. I myself, you pressed into duty manning the whale-oil burner and the frying pot, for you could hardly move about, you'd grown so big with child. Our polyglot crew shook their heads in wonder at us from the foredeck. For all that, they liked the doughnuts well enough.

'So, Joshua.' *I can see you still, wiping back a wisp of raven-dark hair from your temples as the children ran off to serve doughnuts to the crew.* 'You should be happy now that you've dragged us here to the edge of the known world!'

'You have only to look at that volcano and this splen-did harbor to know the answer, Ginny. The light shines down on us much clearer up here.'

You sprinkled flour on a final dollop of batter; then you flattened it out with the rolling pin.

'What is it, Ginny?'

'Oh Joshua, you wouldn't understand. I have to keep reminding myself that you're only a man!'

'Now what in tarnation do you mean by that? What else would you have your husband be but a man?'

'Joshua, look at me and tell me what you see!'

'Why, I see a fine figure of a woman in her prime with a dab of flour on her uppity snoot.'

You wiped your nose solemnly on the shoulder flounce of your dress and fixed me with piercing gray eyes. 'Is that all you see when you look at me?'

I stole a quick look at Victor. Mercifully, he was busy teasing his brother. 'Well, I see my wife near term with our third child. Is that what you want me to say?'

'It's going to be twins this time, Joshua.'

'Twins? How do you know it's twins?'

'My great grandmother was a full-blooded Seneca, remember?'

'Well, that's grand, Ginny! Twins! You wanted more children, didn't you?'

'More womanish playthings, you mean? You think of our children as my toys, don't you, Joshua?'

'All I know is that I'm happy to have them if you are, Ginny. But as you say, I'm only a man, so I still don't know that much about what it takes to make a woman happy, let alone how to keep her that way.'

'Forget about making me happy! What about the children themselves, Joshua? Our children. What do they mean to you when it comes right down to it? Be honest with me, even if I am only a woman.'

'You really want me to be honest, do you? All right then: they're just creatures underfoot at the moment, but I expect they'll grow on me as they get older.' *In answer to your sigh, I lifted the last golden nugget from the boiling*

188

fat and laid it sizzling beside the others on the worn-out sailcloth covering the table. 'Virginia?'

'Yes, Joshua, what is it?'

'Can you tell when the twins will come? We should sail tomorrow for the fishing banks. Always before we've kept a woman aboard to help out when your time comes. Maybe we should stay here near Petropavlovsk till you're ready. There's bound to be a physician or a mid-wife of some sort in the village.'

'No, Joshua. We came here to fish cod, remember?'

'But who will help you get through this birthing, Ginny?'

'You will, Joshua.'

'Me?'

'It's you who got me into this condition, so you're the one to get me out of it!'

'Ginny, I don't know if I can do it! You said it yourself: I'm just a man!'

'Don't worry, Joshua! The truth is, I don't need much help. There's an old Indian tradition among the women in my family to uphold, and so-called civilized women tend to get in my way. As for those college-trained doctors, why they're an even worse nuisance. When my time comes, just stand ready to take orders from me the way Pato's crew takes orders from you.'

Two days out from Avacha, the twins came to us in the fog of an early gray morning. I tried to make you lie back quietly in our berth, but you insisted on squatting in your shift on the sole of our master cabin. You did let me cover the bare oak beneath your trembling thighs with a pillow and a flannel blanket.

'Cut the cord, Joshua. But first hold the blade in the steam of the kettle.'

'Ginny, I don't think I can do it.'

'Then hand me the knife, damn you.'

When Billy came, you were already nursing Jamie, so I cut the birth cord as you had done before with a quick flick of my wrist. I swaddled him in a clean flannel shift and coddled him to your other breast. You looked up at me and smiled. 'Now you can go fishing, Joshua.'

Four days later we started taking in cod.

CHAPTER XX

MAROONED

I let pass many ducks that would have made a good stew, for I had no mind ... to take the life of any living thing.

– From *Sailing Alone Around the World*
by Joshua Slocum

Juan Fernández Islands: April 27, 1896

'I told you these islanders would be friendly, didn't I, Francisco? A far cry from what we left behind us in Tierra del Fuego, eh?'

'Si, señor capitán, but permitting this king of the island to pilot *Spray* is taking friendship a bit too far! He rattles the helm so badly that I fear I shall never persuade *Spray* to follow a true course again!'

'After standing off these dangerous reefs all night, you ought to be grateful to these good people for towing us in. Look how they put their backs into their oars! Our worst travails will soon be over, Francisco. See, there's their little clapboard settlement off to starboard, and that must be the safe anchorage the king promised us straight ahead. Aye, snug as a tick in the proverbial ram's ear we'll soon be. I best go melt us some tallow.'

'Don Jèsu, how can you be so sure these islanders will want your doughnuts anyway? They look quite well fed to me. For aught we know, their womenfolk fry them up delicious pastries each morning of the year.'

'Where would they get enough grease for that? Did you not hear the king say the governor's daughter rides about on a goat because they are the only livestock kept on the island? Goats are lean beasts at best, Francisco. Not much tallow to be rendered from goats!'

'So, you doubloon-chasing Inglés, you plan to ply these innocent people with your greasy doughnuts so that they will relieve you of all this disgusting tallow?'

'What else? No wonder you Spaniards have all but lost your empire on which the sun never sets! You suffer from lack of enterprise!'

'Do be careful, Don Jèsu; this king of the island, he looks at you as though he suspects you're as loco as he is!'

'Captain, do I be disturbing your prayers?'

'Nay, Your Majesty, I was only talking to myself. It comes of sailing these empty seas alone. I suspect poor old Selkirk must have done a great deal of talking to himself.'

'Selkirk? You be speaking of the Scotchman marooned here long time ago?'

'Aye, Your Majesty. You know of him, of course?'

'Oh indeed! Soon after I be coming here, British navy ship *Topaz* also be coming. So I be guiding Commodore Powell all around the island. Strange men, those British be. First, they be naming our Bay after some stranger who never be living man at all. But next thing I be knowing, these British be posting a stone tablet outside Selkirk's cave. If you it be pleasing, the children be taking you up there some day.'

'That would be very kind of them, Your Majesty.'

'Captain, be a good man and pick up this buoy on our port bow.'

'Got it, Your Majesty! Ah, smell that warm perfumed air wafting off the land! I swear, it feels like we've arrived in Paradise! Seems only fitting, for God is our witness that we came through hell to get here!'

The king sends me a quizzical look from the corner of his eye, and I suddenly realize he's a much more intelligent man than I have given him credit for. 'We, Captain? Who be you speaking of?'

'Oh, it's just that I think of this good sloop as my companion, Your Majesty! We've come through so much together these last few months, this old oyster sloop and I. Living on this island, you must know how it is for a sailor at sea a long time alone. In truth, I feel a sudden urge to do something crazy like bow down my forehead to this deck and salaam Allah for delivering us.'

'Then do be bowing down your head, Captain. No one here be saying you nay or be thinking the worse of you for salaaming. That be why some thirty years ago I be marooning myself off a New Bedford whaler while it be stopping here for water.'

'So, you came to be here much in the same manner as Selkirk came before you, Your Majesty – only you did him one better by staying on and becoming king of the island.'

'You may be calling me Manuel, Captain. The others, they be calling me King Manuel in – how do you say – courtesy because I be first man to be making this island me home. But all of them be living here with me free as the wind. All be doing what be pleasing them. All be kings and queens here.'

'Pray what does the Chilean governor think of that?'

'His Excellency? He be after coming to this island straight from Sweden, Captain. Axel be wanting to live free as a bird himself. He be having noble blood in his veins, so he be educated man of the world, but for all that, we be counting the baron as one of us. We only be letting him be our governor so as to be keeping the world from bothering us. The only rule he be bidding us obey be the one laid down by our Lord Jesus Christ.'

'Hmmm, your governor sounds like a most extraordinary man, Manuel. But tell me, what does he do whenever someone breaks the golden rule?'

'Whenever old Diablo be paying visit to this island, a word from the governor or the king be chasing him away. More often than not, a word or two passing between us all we be needing.'

'I'm afraid I don't quite understand, Manuel.'

'The governor and I, we be keeping each other from paying heed to Old Diablo, that's all.'

'Oh, I see! The devil always starts making mischief at the top, is that it? Sounds like you've got a rather good scheme going. Too bad the rest of the world is not governed in as proper a manner as these islands. Your Majesty, would you be so kind as to convey their Excellencies my compliments and invite them to a tasting of my doughnuts?'

'So sorry, but Axel and his good Baroness, they be away at Valparaiso just now. They be seeing to schooling of their children. So sorry they be missing your wonderful doughnuts, Captain.'

'Not to worry, Manuel! I can tell that you yourself appreciate a good doughnut when you taste one. I shall set you up so you can fry the governor up a splendid batch when he gets back to Juan Fernandez. Look, see how fine and clear this tallow is!'

'Captain, you be hoping to be selling us islanders all these casks and lumps of tallow, no?'

'Aye, Manuel. Not to put too fine a point on it, I need to make some money to continue on my way.'

'Captain, I be so sorry for to be telling you this. Among us be only some coins swept ashore from wreck of old Spanish galleon. So little money as we be having not a fair trade for your wondrous boatload of tallow, I be thinking.'

'Then what do you say we take it out in trade, Manuel? As an old whaler like you can plainly see, Spray needs many repairs after rounding the Horn. Is there someone among you who could tailor her a new flying jib?'

'Be you seeing the damisela standing on the dock, the one who be waiting for us with the children?'

'Aye, and a fine figure of a woman she is, Manuel. A natural beauty, no doubt about it. I warrant she would be accounted a regular belle back in Boston town.'

'That be our Joanna. She be sewing cloth better than any other woman on the island.'

'Bueno, Manuel! We understand one another very well, you and I. Here come your little ones down to welcome us. They'll be looking for my doughnuts, no doubt. Help me give them a hand aboard, will you?'

Life's always a question of finding a market, eh Virginia? As with the catch we hauled aboard in the Sea of Okhotsk. Victor caught the first and biggest cod of all before I even so much as told him to start fishing. It near yanked him overboard. Lord, how those waters teemed with fish. I suspect there's a lot less of them now. You weren't back to being yourself after birthing yet, but even so you often hand-lined with the rest of us, the twins' cradle swinging from a yardarm in the gentle breeze. I tried not to notice how thin and pale all three of you were.

'If this keeps up, Ginny, there'll be too many fish for a quick run back to Manila. It's four thousand miles to the West Coast, but we could be sure of making a killing there with all this cod. Ah, if only we had enough salt to keep it from spoiling!'

'Well, Joshua, you always find a way.'

And find a way I did. Our old Constitution hove into sight loaded to the gunnels with cod for San Francisco, and she still carried tons of salt to spare. Instead of dumping it overboard, I talked her captain into shoveling it all into Pato's hold.

It wasn't long till we had twenty-five thousand cod salted down. Then Pato spread her white wings and flew west along the great arc of the Aleutians.

April 30, 1896

'El capitán, una higuera, si?'

'Aye, Miguel, it's a wild fig-tree all right, and these fruit, I call them figs.'

'Figgies? Ha, ha, ha! Figgies! Ha, ha, ha! Olé, el capitán! Figgies!'

'Well, now, I didn't know my native tongue could make you children all roll around on the ground and split your sides like this. Umm, they're good and ripe, these higos of yours. Si, Pedro, fill up your basket with higos for me. I'll eat higos and remember you fondly while crossing the ocean.'

'El capitán, un cabra, si?'

'Aye, Imela, we call it a goat, and a stringy old billy of a goat he is at that.'

'Goat? Ha, ha, ha! Goatee! Ha, ha, ha! Olé, el capitán! Muy hombre! Goatee! Ha, ha, ha!'

'Aye, I grant you it is a bit funny to be calling a cabra a goat. Honestly, I can't remember when I've had such a good time, muchachos, but we shall have to quit this game lest you all die of laughing. Tell me, Arturo, is that cueva up there on the hill the one I seek?'

The urchin followed my pointing finger to the mountainside. 'Si, el capitán. La cueva del Alisander Selkiro!'

'Let's go up and take a look, shall we? No, Arturo? You look as if you're afraid of seeing a ghost, Maria. Bueno! You muchachos stay here and pick figs for me while I go up and visit with the old mutineer. Entendido?'

'Si, el capitán! Figgies! Ha, ha, ha! Olé! Goatees! ha, ha, ha! Muy hombre!'

You have to give him credit for one thing; old Selkirk picked a fine sheltered nook to maroon himself in. Ouch! What's this stone doing here among the thorns? Must be the memorial tablet the British navy lugged all the way up here.'

'In memory of Alexander Selkirk, mariner, who lived on this island alone for four years and four months. He was landed from Cinque Ports, galley, 96 tons, 18 guns, AD 1704, and was taken off in the Duke, privateer, 12th February, 1709. He died Lieutenant of H.M.S. Weymouth, AD 1721.'

A dry wind full of portent came sweeping down off the mountain as I approached the cave entrance. 'Well, Lieutenant Selkirk, I think you might have lived longer and happier if you had rested content on this island with your good man Friday.'

'I suspect you'd be right, Captain – if I'd had a man Friday to keep me company, that is. It was Christian of old Defoe to supply my lack. If I had only thought to invent him myself, I might indeed have stayed on this island.'

'You were lonely here, and yet you've come back, why?'

'This island's the only real home I ever knew, Captain. I went to sea as a lad, and a hard and an empty life I made of it.'

'Was old Dampier really such a monster that you asked to be cast ashore?'

'Aye, Captain, a monster he was to those who sailed with him. At the end of that voyage, the crew of the *Cinque Ports* charged him with being a brutal coward and a drunkard. He never received another command.'

'And yet he came back here for you in the end.'

'Expecting to exhibit my bones as proof of having already sailed these waters. If he'd been master of the *Duke*, I'd never have let them rescue me.'

'Even so, Lieutenant Selkirk, he must have been a man of parts, else he could not have sailed these seas for years on end and mapped unexplored stretches of the world so skillfully.'

'He was lacking in humanity, Captain, but I must give Dampier his due. I doubt that ever a better navigator set foot on a quarterdeck. Do you follow in his wake?'

'Aye, Lieutenant, and the wake of Magellan and Drake, but I sail alone.'

'You sail alone around the world, Captain? A seasoned mariner like yourself ought to know better! Who steers while you sleep?'

'No living man at all, Lieutenant, but I stand before you as living proof it can be done. Already I've crossed the Atlantic Ocean twice and weathered Cape Horn. Only three more oceans to go, and I shall have made it home.'

'Incredible! If you make it, Captain, you'll have proven yourself a greater navigator than any who went down to the sea before you.'

'I make no claim to greatness, Lieutenant. I am able to do what I do because better men have gone before me and charted the way.'

'Your modesty becomes you, Captain. Forgive me for keeping you standing outside my humble abode. The few visitors here seldom take heed of my presence, so I'm at pains not to frighten them away. One does get lonely, as you say. I've neither rum nor tea to offer you, I'm afraid, but do come in.'

'Thank you, Lieutenant. Lord, but it's pitch dark in here after all the bright sunlight!'

'Tarry just here by the entrance, Captain, till your eyes grow used to the dimness.'

'Why, sir, your cave feels dry as a bone with just enough draft flowing through for a fire! You must live quite cozy here. Did you open that smoke hole yourself?'

'Actually, I nearly fell down it while walking along the cliffs above. That's how I first found the cave.'

'What's this, Lieutenant? It feels like the stub of a candle stuck here in the wall.'

'Aye, Captain, I swiped a bundle off the old *Cinque Ports* before bidding her adieu. They helped pass the evenings reading my books at first, but I ran out of them after a couple of years. I'd not the heart to burn that last bit of tallow.'

'You're in luck, Lieutenant Selkirk! I can provide all the tallow you'll ever need, and at a good price, too.'

'Captain, as you can see, I'm long past the burning of candles.'

'Forgive me, Lieutenant! Once a trader, you know, always a trader. Do not forget that I was born in New Scotland.'

'No offense taken, Captain. I was born in old Scotland myself.'

All that ever mattered to me in those days was finding the best price, Ginny. You wanted to stop over on Vancouver Island because the children were sick, but I only tarried long enough at Victoria to register Pato under the British flag. Yankee ships were fair game for pirates, but everyone gives the Union Jack a wide berth for fear of bringing down the British navy.

The price quoted in the newspapers for fish in Portland caught my eye. So we dashed down to Oregon, and I hired a sternwheeler to tow us up the Columbia. And then it was just a simple question of persuading the good Portlanders to buy our salt cod. You even bought yourself a sewing machine with your share of the profits from the fishing. I never had so much spare money in all my life, before or since. How was it I never thought to ask the price I was making you pay?

199

May 1, 1896

'What's this? New spuds for old, Manuel?'

'We be trading you two sacks of new potatoes for your one sack of old ones, Captain. Already they be sprouting for planting, see? Our island soil be very thin and rocky. We be badly needing to be changing the seed.'

'Entendido, Manuel. I see your wife kneeling there in the churchyard. Did you lose a child?'

'Si, Captain, our only child. Juanita be seven years old when she died. She be lying there among the lava stones these sixteen years. Juana and I, we be grieving for her still.'

The night Billy died, I looked first in that same dark mirror but turned away in fear. But the night Jamie passed on I looked again and glimpsed what I had done. So I fled to Honolulu and sold our schooner. I tossed the bag of gold Pato fetched in Ginny's lap as if that could make losing the twins up to her. Then I boarded a train and left her sick and grieving in San Francisco. I came home to you in that poor shack in Westport, Nova Scotia.

'So you made your dream come true, brother. You do look handsome in your captain's coat and braided hat.'

'I'm losing my hair, Elizabeth.'

'I see that, Joshua, but at least you still have your lungs. You've much to be grateful for.'

'I've bought myself a full-rigger, sister. Oh, the Amethyst's no virgin maiden of the sea, but she's still as sound as a dollar. Come and live aboard her with us. Ingram and Ella are coming back with me.'

'You'll soon take the whole Slocum clan for your crew, Joshua. Well, I thank you for thinking of me, but a ship's no place for an invalid who spends her days coughing up her lungs. Do you remember, I once dreamed I saw you at the helm of a great sailing ship? A strange dark-haired woman was standing at your side.'

'That would be my Virginia. She herself told me to bring you back with me, Elizabeth. She knows how much you mean to me.'

'Give my love to her and the children, Joshua.'

'Elizabeth, I can't just go off and abandon you the way Father did.'

'Yes you can. You passed out of my life a long time ago, Joshua. As for our poor Father, the linen-draper's widow he married is the first chance he's ever had for something more than making boots. I forgave you both for taking your chances a long time ago.'

'Life's not been fair to you, Elizabeth. Life's just not fair!'

'We must leave it in God's hands, Joshua. He must've had some reason for breathing so little life into me.'

I made the necessary arrangements before I headed back to San Francisco. They lie ten thousand miles apart, but this island headland reminds me of the churchyard where they laid you.

'Did Juana come from the Azores to join you, Manuel?'

'No, Captain, I be after going all the way to Rio in search of a Portuguese-speaking wife.'

'And she followed you from that great city all the way around Cape Horn to this lonely island?'

'Si, Captain. As Juana be saying to her family before we be leaving her home: A good husband all a woman be needing to be making a good life anywhere.'

'Does she still believe that's true after all these years?'

'When I be asking her that question after losing Juanita, she be telling me she has no regrets.'

'And what regrets do you have, Manuel? A man's fate is lived out differently from that of a woman.'

'Too few of them to be naming. If a man be doing the best he can, I think his God and his woman will be forgiving him his faults and mistakes. And what about you, Captain Joshua Slocum? You be leaving Juan Fernandez tomorrow?'

'Aye, Manuel, we break anchor at the break of dawn. *Spray* be as shipshape as we can make her here. We've still a long way to go. So I bid you farewell, my good friend. I don't suppose we shall ever see each other again.'

'As for that, Captain. Men like us be needing to be meeting only once in this life. We be frying doughnuts in your honor for many a year, I think.'

CHAPTER XXI

NAVIGATION

I will never be able to explain how it is done – The one thing most certain about my sea-reckonings: they are not kept with any slavish application at all and I have been right every time and seemed to know that I was right.

– Joshua Slocum from 'Letter to Joseph P. Gilder (first critic to appreciate his literary potential)'

Southeast Pacific: May 5, 1896

'May God in heaven have mercy on our souls, señor capitán! Must you keep pointing that infernal machine of yours at the sun? If you only knew how it makes my blood run cold to see you commit such sacrilege!'

'I'm sorry, Francisco, but I simply have to double-check my sun-sights. Something has gone badly amiss with my celestial navigation. It doesn't agree with my dead reckoning at all.'

'But perhaps it is your dead reckoning that is off, Don Jèsu. Even the great Don Cristóbal himself mistook where we were on occasion. This ocean, she is as wide and as full of guile as a Sevillian whore.'

'Perhaps, Francisco, but Columbus never made a mistake so big as this one. My last sun-sight sets our latitude several hundred miles west of where I've dead reckoned us to be. Sorry, but I'm going to have to do it all again.'

'Santa Maria, please ask Your Son to forgive this man! He was born a benighted heretic, and so he cannot know what mortal sins he may be committing!'

'Zounds, you do well to pray for me, Francisco! How in God's name can this possibly be? I've just obtained the very same reading a second time!'

'Caramba, what a sad way for two old seadogs to end! Lost here in the middle of a vast ocean that my brothers and I never even knew existed!'

'Nay, Francisco, I assure you we're still a long way from being lost. We're sailing due west at twelve degrees south latitude – on that much I'll stake my life. See here on the ocean chart? If all else fails, we can always run down the longitude to the northern tip of Australia.'

'But compadre, such a course will take us halfway around the world without so much as a single sighting of land!'

'Not quite so far as that, my friend, but I do confess that I'd be far happier crossing the Pacific in easier stages. A swing up to a landfall in the Marquesas and then straight across to Samoa, that's more what I have in mind. I'd hate to come so far and miss what I really came for.'

'Don Jèsu, did you not tell me soon after I came aboard that all you cared about doing in this old world was just to sail around it one last time?'

'Well, never you mind what I care about, Francisco, but there's one thing you may take from me as gospel truth.'

'And pray what is that, Don Jèsu?'

'Come storm or high water, I intend to let nothing keep me from going where I want to go and doing what I came to do.'

'But señor capitán, this ocean's too big by half for our little boat to navigate. One could sail onward forever and never get where one is going. Twice bigger than the Atlantic, did you not say this sea was?'

'Aye, Francisco, bigger than the Atlantic and the Indian and the Arctic all poured together into one.'

'I have a bad feeling about this in the pit of my stomach, Don Jèsu. Surely there is more to our situation than meets the eye. Perhaps some demon from hell, he has set a charm working against us.'

'Hmm, now there's a thought worth pondering on, Francisco! The last thing one would suspect is a gremlin in these Admiralty tables, but one never knows. Here, let's take another look at them.'

'Caramba! No wonder we are lost! Your magic incantations, they are all spelled out in Moorish numerals! In my time we used proper dead reckoning to tell us our location. Every ringing of the bell in strange waters, we'd sink a lead marked out with Christian numerals and station a fresh lookout high above.'

'The wise mariner does so still, Francisco. Right now though, there's at least a thousand fathoms of water beneath our keel and no land to be sighted for as many miles in any direction. So we need something more than dead reckoning and lead soundings to navigate ourselves through this voyage. Ahoy there, what's this?'

'Have you found the demon, señor capitán?

'Aye, by George, you were right, Francisco! There is a demon working mischief in these tables!'

'A veritable demon, señor capitán?'

'A mathematical one, more like, so there's no point in crossing yourself so feverishly, Francisco. These

tables are all based on pure science, so do calm yourself and try to understand what I'm doing! What are
you, anyway: a superstitious heathen or a proper
Christian pilot?'

'First and foremost, Don Jèsu, I am a proper Catholic.'

'Well, put that mumble-jumble aside for now, all
right? Here, take a gander! The way it's supposed to
work, all I need do is select the logarithm I need from
this particular column.'

'Si?'

'There's an obvious discontinuity between its fig-
ures and those in the flanking columns, but only someone plying these remote waters is liable to pick up on
it. Damnation, I'll have to recalculate all these entries
one by one – if I can remember enough of old Norie to
do it, that is.'

*Aye, Ginny, Spray's cramped cockpit is a far cry from
Amethyst's gracious quarterdeck. You and Victor standing at my elbows with your sextants at the ready.
Remember? I'd jot down our latitude and longitude right
off the top of my head. You'd both try to peek but I'd fold
up my result on a piece of paper and stow it inside my
hat. Nor would I let you off the hook till your sightings
had come near what I had jotted down. Backwards
thinking, you called it, and it made you spitting mad
that my dead reckoning never proved to be more than a
half minute off the mark. How you'd rail at me! 'Oh fie
on you, Joshua! Remember, pride goeth before a fall!'*

*Aye, navigation was the one place where your judg-
ment always yielded to mine, Ginny. I believe you and
the children would have felt that God was not in his
heaven if Manila or Honolulu or Hong Kong had not
arisen on the horizon where and when I commanded
them to appear. Dead shot markmanship, I'd brag, like
you being able to hit whatever you aim a pistol at. You
once told me that it was more like having perfect pitch,
whatever that is.*

'There, that's got it, Francisco. And just in the nick of time: the hand of our old tin clock's made it up to the mark again. One more sunsight, and I'll tell you our longitude to within a mile.'

'Ha! You pull my generative organ, compadre! You will only be guessing where we are, nothing more.'

'It's you that's wide of the mark, my friend. I already know exactly where we are, if the plain truth be told.'

'May our Lord and Savior pardon your pride and presumption, Don Jèsu!'

'As for that, Francisco, I'm afraid I exceeded the limits of His forgiveness a long time ago.'

That last voyage made in the Amethyst, we ran a gauntlet of pirate junks all the way from Shanghai to the island of Formosa. Virginia pleaded in vain against such a risky venture, but it would have begged my nature to pass up the fat fee that old Sun Chow, the Chinese governor, offered me for carrying six hundred kegs of gunpowder to the Imperial forces in the rebel-sieged city of Tainin.

The muddy Yangtze oozed past like quicksand, and the sun was burning off the thick yellow haze that clung to the sandbars and Amethyst's luffing sails. Virginia came on deck, and I saw at a glance she was cleared for action. Together we watched the river pilot and a boy not much older than our eldest son climb on deck from a sampan. 'God, but these slant-eyes do like dragging their asses!'

'You promised me you'd try to be more civil to them, Joshua. No name-calling this time around, you promised.'

'But why should I be nice to them, Ginny? I've never yet seen a speck of true civility displayed by subjects of the Celestial Empire.'

'No wonder, dear husband! You make it clear right from the word go that you doubt their humanity.'

'No more than they doubt mine.' She swept me from the wheel as though brushing away a fly. 'Well, Mrs. Slocum, just what do you think you're doing?'

'I'm going to steer this vessel till we reach the open sea, Captain Slocum.' She tossed her glorious raven hair, which was her way of challenging me to gainsay her if I dared. 'I know you must have your fill of fun, Joshua, but I've three children to think about.'

Victor, you circled the pilot, sizing up his pigtail and the long scar on his cheek from every angle. You signed that you would like to help his boy carry the lead and coiled lines forward to the bow, but your offer was summarily refused. You hitched up your half-britches the way I do my trousers and sidled up close to me lest Ginny overhear the colorful language you were learning from the crew. 'Jumpin' Jehoshophat, Father, did you ever see such an ugly brute? This time you've landed us a real pirate!'

I put my hands on your shoulders and met you eye to eye. 'A pirate, you say? What makes you think so, Victor?'

'He's a bully fer one thing, father. That poor boy he brought along is covered with bruises from head to toe. Can't we do something to help that boy out of his trouble, Father?'

'We've got enough trouble of our own, lad, without trying to right all the wrongs in China.' I tousled your shiny curls and gave you a playful slap on your little stern. 'Go relieve Mr. Sykes on look-out and keep an eye peeled. Any sail comes over the horizon, I want to know it the moment before you do.'

Your mother wasn't missing a trick that morning. She watched you climb the ratlines to the crow's nest. Her long sweet legs were braced against the drag of the river current on the rudder, and her tawny eyes could have scorched dragons as they swept over me.

I took myself forward where the pilot had his young helper sounding lead. Something about the scrawny boy reminded me of boots and soaking vats. 'You catchee plenty water, honorable sir?'

208

The pilot favored me with a shake of his pigtail and a reluctant bow. 'Me catchee plenty water this morning, honorable Captain.'

At least these slant-eyes usually know their business, I thought to myself. Well, I'll just leave him to it. I'm a fair enough man with people who get on with their work. Virginia's got me figured all wrong.

When I came back on the quarterdeck, Sykes was looking more than his usual worried self. He was not a bad first mate, but a couple of nights boozing and whoring in Chinkjang had left him pale about the gills.

'I do believe the weather is clearing, Mr. Sykes.'

'Aye, Captain, that it is, but there's something amiss this morning. I can smell it in the air.'

'That's rum and cheap perfume you're still smelling, Mr. Sykes.' My Virginia was never one to resist such a fine opening. The first mate sent us both a hangdog look and went about his business of checking the shrouds.

A shrill whistle sounded from the crow's nest. I looked where you pointed off our weather quarter. A three-masted junk ghosted out from behind a bamboo-covered sandbar of an island.

Only three of her crew showed on deck, but a tier of old muzzle-loaders were plainly visible. Even honest traders go well armed in those waters, but it didn't take much imagination to picture a score or two of fierce cutthroats crouched down along the scuppers. A chill of expectancy trickled up and down my spine, even though I judged it unlikely that a lone pirate would tackle a vessel flying the British flag. Chinese pirates are normally shrewd customers, or they don't stay in business for long. They know there's no percentage in taking unnecessary risks.

'You're enjoying this, aren't you, Joshua?'

'Ginny, I told you plain enough how it would be when you married me.' I applied the telescope to my best eye

and swept the rakish hull from stem to stern. It was some comfort to see that she was making no attempt to close her half-mile lead. On the other hand, she had positioned herself to come down on us at a moment's notice. Amethyst had nowhere to run, for a good junk can always sail closer to the wind than a square-rigger.

I espied what I took to be my counterpart. Standing alongside his fierce-featured helmsman, he looked every inch a proper seaman. His inscrutable expression gave nothing away, but the set of his shoulders signifies the same thing in any man's language: he was waiting for something.

I stepped below decks to rouse the off-duty watches and unlimber half a dozen large-bore rifles. Ingram's lanky frame stooped in its accustomed place over the galley stove. He looked up at me, a long pewter stirring-spoon dripping broth halfway to his drooping mustaches. I thrust a double-barreled shotgun and a handful of buckshot cartridges at him. 'Be ready to use this if I call you on deck, brother.'

He dropped the spoon in the salt horse and cabbage.

'You're absolutely right, Joshua.' Virginia made a point of ignoring the armful of rifles I dumped on the deck in front of the binnacle. 'I've no one to blame but myself for the way things stand; I just want you to hear me say that, in case worse comes to worse: God knows I wouldn't have had my life unfold any other way.'

'What you say goes doubly for me, my dear. Just make sure Ella keeps the little ones down below.' I turned my telescope from the shallow-drafted junk to the lazy ox-bow in the channel ahead. Normally the water in a river bend is deepest where the current cuts near the shore, but heavily laden Amethyst was being piloted straight down the middle of the channel. Standing there thinking, it struck me hard what the junk's captain was waiting for. I thrust a belaying pin in my belt and took off for the bow just short of a dead run.

Ginny was right: I've never been one to stand on cere-mony when it comes to foreigners. I grabbed the pilot's lead from his boy and tried to sink it deep, but it coiled over the instant after it left my hand. There was maybe less than three feet of murky water to spare under Amethyst's keel.

The pilot looked me straight in the eye and saw his jig was up. He thought to pull his belt-knife, but that's always a mistake with me. I haven't been a sea captain all those years for nothing. His frightened waif of a boy took one look at his master belayed on the deck and jumped over-board. The last I saw of him, he was dog-paddling for shore.

'Hard alee!' As Amethyst came about, Sykes and the deck watch sprang into action. Just for an instant, I thought I felt her touch bottom, but all in all, I rate that piece of sailing on the fly as the finest I've ever been called upon to manage with a square-rigger.

Except that amid all the tugging and fussing and swearing, I forgot all about the treacherous pilot. 'Father, your pirate is getting away!'

The blighter was back on his rope-sandaled feet, climbing the ratlines with that long blade clenched in his teeth. He could have followed his boy overboard, but he must have feared going back to his mates empty-handed more than me and my crew. He swung through the rig-ging like a monkey high above the heaving deck, slashing sheets and guys as he made his way toward where you stood lookout in the crow's nest. Thank God you've the presence of mind to keep out of sight, I remember think-ing. How I wished that I had used the Smith & Wesson when I had the rapscallion at my mercy on the deck. 'Here, take the wheel, Joshua!'

Virginia selected a long-barreled Winchester from the pile I had heaped at her feet. What with flapping sails and flailing yards I judged even her chances of hitting her tar-get to be on the slim side. 'Be careful, Ginny. You're as apt to hit Victor as you are the Chink.'

211

With an indignant flare of her nostrils, she slipped a cartridge into the Winchester's breech and worked the lever action. As she shouldered the rifle, the pilot scampered along the main-royal's yard and chinned himself up to the crow's nest. She'll shoot to kill the bugger for sure now that her son's life is at stake, I thought to myself as I watched her finger tighten on the trigger.

I looked aloft to see the shot take effect, but the pilot suddenly turned, his mouth agape, and fell away. We heard his ragged scream as he came plummeting down through the rigging. He managed to break his fall by bounding off yards and by banking off sails, but he never quite managed to halt his descent till he struck the deck like a sack of rice.

I'd quite forgotten about the marlinspike we always kept at hand for emergencies aloft. Mother's son that you are, you had driven it stigmata-straight through the pilot's outstretched hand as he tried to pull himself into the crow's nest.

'Quickly, Mr. Sykes.' I handed the wheel back to Virginia. 'Help me get rid of this pilot before he regains his senses.'

'God's blood, Captain!' The first mate jerked his knife from its sheath as I worked to heave the body over the railing. 'You'll not let this yellow dog get off scot-free, I'm thinking!'

'We've enough blood on our hands without you cutting his throat, Mr. Sykes. What odds would you lay me on his chances when he comes up against his ship-mates?'

Sykes grinned and helped me dump the groaning pilot into his sampan. I loosed the painter and took up my telescope again.

The junk was closing fast on us now. Her captain had spotted the havoc wrought by the pilot in the rigging. Somehow you had made your way through it all to the deck and were staring up at me expectantly. You

212

seemed perfectly composed as though driving a marlin-spike through a man's hand were all in a day's work for a ship's boy your age. 'What do you want me to do now, Father?'

'Go tell Ingram to get up here on the double with that shot-gun, and then grab one of the rifles and station yourself where you can be seen along the port rail. Don't fire it, whatever you do. It would knock you flat. Virginia, you go with him. You'll be needed there more than you are here.'

While the morning watch fought the sails high above, I doled out the rifles to the four off-duty hands and set them to make a real show beside you and Virginia. Ingram was trembling so badly that I relieved him of his shotgun and gave him the helm. My brother was a passable fair weather sailor, but he never did have much of a stomach for a good fight.

'Captain, they're starting to run out their guns.' Sykes passed me the telescope. The glance that passed between us said it all: what if a single shot should pierce Amethyst's hull and strike the gunpowder?

The captain of the junk was pacing up and down behind the gun-crews. He held his jian aloft in one hand, a slow match fizzling in the other. Obviously he was planning to personally sight the muzzle-loaders one by one and sweep Amethyst's decks with grapeshot as the two ships passed each other by. Then he would come about and board us before what was left of the crew could recover. But what if even one of those guns were loaded with roundshot? The pirate captain was going to be mighty disappointed if he succeeded in hulling us.

Or maybe not. It struck me that maybe the junk captain knew that Amethyst would go up like a Roman candle! Maybe that was all he intended to accomplish, now that his jig with the pilot was up. These Chinks were a subtle race; a body could never tell what they were going to do next.

'Joshua, she's bearing down on us!' Ingram stood white as a sheet draped across the wheel. 'We'll collide if we don't give way.'

'Steady as she goes.' I waved the shotgun at his wobbling knees as though that might serve to steady them. 'We're a whole lot stouter than he is, and I'll match Amethyst's oak against his teak any day. Make him give way, damn you, Ingram, or I'll swear on our mother's grave you're no true brother of mine. The closer we scrape by him the better!'

Virginia was leaning against the rail close beside you, Victor. Both your faces were white but neither was trembling. I handed her the telescope. 'See him, my dear, the one in the broad hat waving the sword? Shoot him through the heart just before we draw abeam.'

She looked carefully through the telescope before handing it back to me, a quirk of a smile playing about her lips. 'Aye aye, Captain,' she said and raised the rifle to her shoulder.

Of course, being a woman, she couldn't just simply follow captain's orders. Instead of his heart, she shot at the slow match. Not that your mother ever once gave me the slightest reason to complain of her, mind you. The work she did with the Winchester seemed to knock the starch plumb out of that heathen and his cutthroat crew.

We swept pass the junk close enough that I met my counterpart's startled gaze as he looked up from his mangled hand. In addition to his remaining fingers, I suppose that he must have been counting his lucky stars to still be alive.

An hour or so later Amethyst's bowsprit broke clear of the river estuary and thrust into the East China Sea. Ingram surrendered the wheel and went back to his salt horse. Virginia went off to help Ella do whatever women do with children. But you, you little scamp, you sidled near, hitching your britches as you came. 'Well, Father, I've been thinking.'

'Aye, Victor, what about?'
'Oh nothing to be bothering you with, Father, but I'd like to say thank ye for saving that poor boy from that pirate bully. I hope he makes out all right.'

CHAPTER XXII

FRIENDS

I smile at some of the comments made on my present insignificant little 'outing'. Some think I am exploring the resources of a man under great disadvantages. They are ... most all wrong as to the real object of my voyage which to tell the truth I do not think would interest ... people; so I immediately remarked before shoving off that I was going alone.

– Joshua Slocum from 'Letters to Joseph P. Gilder (first critic to appreciate his literary potential)

South Pacific: June 15, 1896

'Ahoy there! Who in God's name is trying to drown me? Francisco, are you still here?'

'Si, mi capitán, I am still here, and I'm not trying to drown you!'

'What was that then, a rogue wave? Look at me, damn you, I'm soaked! What's making that snorting sound?'

'Go back to sleep, señor capitán. It's only a whale sounding off our starboard quarter.'

'Only a whale, he says! My God, look at the size of the creature! He's covered in phosphorescence from snout to tail, and I'll swear on a stack of Bibles that he's half again as long as we are!'

'Yet I think he's more frightened of us than we are of him. Go back to sleep, señor capitán.'

'Go back to sleep, the Spaniard says! Those great flukes could thrash us into kindling. He could break *Spray's* back with just one flick of that great tail!'

'Calm yourself, you crazy Inglés! This whale, he's going off to the east as fast as he can go!'

'Then head west for heaven's sake, sirrah! Head due west as fast as you can make this cockleshell sail!'

'Caramba! You are shaking in your sea-boots, compadre! You, who braved all the demons of Cape Horn without so much as once blinking an eye. How is it that such a man fears a mere whale?'

'A mere whale? Watch what you say, Francisco! I was reading a book about just such a sperm whale as this last night by the light of a candle. Tell me, did you mark that this whale was a white one?'

'I think it only seemed white because it was bathed by the light of the moon, señor capitán.'

'Aye, Francisco, perhaps you are right. Perhaps it was only a trick of the silver moon, but sight of that whale brought such a sick feeling to the pit of my stomach. How sad it is that we men have always been the most murderous of enemies to such great creatures.'

'Si, señor capitán, but then, to what living thing, including our own kind, have we not been murderous enemies? For all I'm a good Catholic, it has always been a mystery to me why God set our kind down amid his wondrous creation to wreak havoc upon it as we do.'

'Aye, Francisco, I confess I've often harbored that same thought. So perhaps it's a guilty conscience that makes me so fearful. Facing that whale is too much like facing God Himself. I'm not ready yet to answer to my maker for the things I've done in this life.'

It seemed right enough at the time to be sweeping over sea and land like a plague of locusts. We have the guns and the ships to do what we want, I said in my heart. This whole planet is up for grabs, and there's no one here to say us nay. Look on our works, ye heathen, and dismay! Let us rape, kill and rob while we may. Yea, God help any of you who gets in our way! And to the devil with those lazy backsliders who will not join in our good work.

Fur seals off the Pribilofs, whole sleeping floes of them drifting north at the mercy of our harpoons. Great fat cod in the Sea of Okhotsk, pouring in their thousands into our holds. Salmon off Alaska, they leapt into our boats and swamped our nets in their haste to pass up the rivers. I wonder, did we leave in our wake any sea otters at all?

We asked no such questions, not even of ourselves. Nor do those who follow where we led.

Aye, we little dreamed there could be an end to our raping of this world, but it will all end some day, just as sure as God made it all in the first place. My sons' sons will never see what I have seen nor be able to do what I have done. And their sons and daughters will either learn to live or else perish in the wasteland we are creating. You spoke too soon, King Louis: not after you, but after us comes the real deluge.

What will those yet to be born think of men like me when they read their history books?

Strange what you can see when you take the trouble to look. No, this voyage will never pay me good Yankee dollars. And yet it is plain to see that this is a far more profitable voyage I make now than any I have ever made before.

June 17, 1896

'Must you forever be reading books, Don Jèsu?'

'You don't know what you are missing, Francisco. The writers of my books are my friends. This is a book by Miguel de Cervantes, a fine soldier by most accounts and considered by all to be the greatest of writers to grace your native tongue. I'd not leave port without taking him along for company.'

'Miguel de Cervantes? It has a good enough Spanish ring, señor capitán, but I have never heard the family name before. Could he have been a *converso*?'

'It's possible, Francisco, though it's strange to think the greatest of Spanish writers may have had Jewish blood flowing in his veins. In any case, he was not yet born when you were lost at sea. If only I had thought to bring along his great book in the original Spanish, you could make his acquaintance yourself.'

'I lack the skill of reading learned books, señor capitán. My two years of schooling did not proceed past what was necessary for the keeping of a log.'

'That's about as much schooling as I got, Francisco, but a man can teach himself many things if he's of a mind to. I'd be happy to read you the adventures of Don Quixote and his companion Sancho Panza if you'd care to listen.'

'Thank you, compadre, but surely their story would lose something in the translation. Excuse me, I did not mean to disturb your meditations.'

'No matter, Francisco. I need to take a sighting while that ghost of a moon keeps company with the sun. My literary friends shall have to wait for the nonce.'

Aye, Robert, you're one of those friends whom I wish I could revisit in the flesh. You were a man after my own heart who knew as well how to point a sextant at Polaris as tell an exciting tale. Not a Melville or a Cervantes, not so deep a thinker as some of the other writers I treasure, but every inch a man of the world. Despite your illness, you were as much at home canoeing the rivers of Europe with titled gentry as rubbing shoulders with sourdoughs amid the gold rush camps of California. I did not get to know you half well enough before we both sailed off to the ends of the Earth.

We met only that once on San Francisco Bay, you and I. Sixteen years ago almost to the day, wasn't it? You asked permission to come aboard Amethyst. I barely tolerated your presence on my quarterdeck till I felt your manly grip as you introduced yourself in your educated Scottish burr. 'Captain Slocum, you're just the seaman I've been seeking. For my next book, I need to discover firsthand how wooden vessels were built and worked during the golden age of sail.'

Oh God, how your transparent paleness brought to mind my sister Elizabeth when last I saw her!

Perhaps the robustness of the new American wife on your arm made you seem more delicate in health than you really were. Indeed, I should have much envied you your Fanny if my Virginia were not standing tall beside me. They looked nothing alike, those two, but they might well have been sisters. Both were lovers of adventurous men, and neither willing to sit at home waiting for their return. Aye, women too much alike to have ever been fast friends to one another, I think.

'I want to write stories of sea adventure, Captain Slocum. I want to create real living characters, authentic persons modeled on men like yourself who will live forever in the hearts of my readers.'

'You are a most ambitious man, Mr. Stevenson.' It took me back a trifle to find myself a literary specimen. 'You make me feel like I'm ready to be tossed into the dustbin of history.'

'Not at all, Captain Slocum.' You smothered your cough in a stained handkerchief. 'It's just that I insist on my stories being drawn from life, don't you see? Writing good stories is easy if one brings to it real experience of living. One has only to place oneself in the thick of things, et voilà! the deed is essentially done. All the rest can be handled by a common scrivener like me if he but practices hard enough.'

You taught me with those few words how to navigate by more than the stars, Mr. Stevenson. For the power to quicken the hearts of men as you have done, I would gladly trade you my disgusting health for your fatal tuberculosis! To fight alongside Jim and David and Alan Breck against Pew and Long John, those marvelous villains you made more wonderfully human than even your heroes! Aye, despite your easy words, I've found it's a more difficult and perilous task to make people come alive in books than to navigate one's way across this ocean.

You and your Fanny were already busy planning your voyage through these Southern Seas. She spoke of making a refuge for you on Samoa that would be your salvation, that would save you from death by consumption. Well, she won you a dozen or more very good years than would otherwise have been your lot, did she not? Your obituary mentioned that she bides still at Vailima. What holds her there still, I wonder! What does she wait for?

Dear Mr. Stevenson, I must in all courtesy ask your pardon for sending your grieving widow that letter I posted from Gibraltar! I confess to you now, as one gentleman to another, that I should never have had the courage to continue this journey without the vision of your widow as a destination to be won. Now that both of us has lost our soul mates, who knows what comfort she and I may yet give one another? I hope I have your blessing to proceed.

'There, Francisco, I do believe that's finally got it right! Our present longitude by observation agrees within five miles of my dead reckoning.'

'You have wrestled hard indeed with those Arabian ciphers to make it so, señor capitán. After forty-three days without a landfall, do you actually expect to sail right up to this tiny speck of an island as though it waited just over the horizon?'

'Francisco, my sextant against your sword that lofty Nukahiva shall rise up on our port quarter in less than two hours time. I bid you fall off a point to leeward lest we run aground on a coral reef.'

'My good sword, mi capitán, she is all I have left! I do not care to wager it for love nor money. If you say Nukahiva lies just beyond the horizon, then I am prepared to take your word, much as I believe you to be a practitioner of wishful thinking.'

'There's much more to what I do than mere wishful thinking, Francisco. One must will oneself with all one's heart to arrive at a particular place. If one can truly imagine oneself already there, then voilà! it happens! It's much like writing a good book, I think. The rest is mere ciphering. Once you master the art of going places, sailing a vessel like *Spray* across a wide ocean is much like riding a magic carpet.'

'Caramba, señor capitán, now you begin to rave like a man under the moon too long! I think we should haul ourselves into port at Nukahiva after all. It's plain to see that you need the comfort of some human society. Forty-three days is far too long to fare at sea with only a lost and wandering shade like me for company.'

'Aye, Francisco, you are right in the main. It's not good for the human soul to be left so long alone as mine has been. It was such loneliness that drove me to contemplate giving up the ghost after sailing from Horta.'

'It was fortunate I chanced upon you that night, compadre.'

'That was no accident, my friend. I understand now that somehow I summoned you to be with me as I felt myself drawing near my solitary end. I had been reading the life of Don Cristóbal Colón, so I simply imagined one of his crew aboard *Spray*. Not just any member of the crew, mind you, but you, yourself, Francesco Martin Pinzón, younger brother of the Admiral's two captains, Queen Isabella's own pilot who disappeared mysteriously from the *Pinta* while returning to Spain. And behold, you rescued me and have kept me good company ever since!'

'Forsooth, we rescued each other, Don Jèsu. But now I think, we both need rescuing from this ocean that goes on forever. I'd give you even my sword for a sight of land right about now!'

'Well speak of the Devil, there she rises! Lovely Nukahiva rearing up her lovely head from the mist on our port quarter. Steady as she goes, Francisco, and you may keep your sword.'

'Gracias, mi capitán! Si, she is not a mirage. Lovely Nukahiva, she stands on the horizon exactly where you said she would appear. I take off my hat to you, black magic and all. Si, she looks like Paradise to me. Are you sure you will not tarry here a while?'

'Nay, Francisco, unfinished business awaits me in Samoa. We must get ourselves there as fast as our little *Spray* will carry us.'

CHAPTER XXIII

PARADISE

My time was all taken up those days – not by stand-ing at the helm. I did better than that; for I sat and read my books, mended my clothes, or cooked my meals and ate them in peace. I had always found that it was not good to be alone, and so I made companionship with what there was around me, sometimes with the universe and sometimes with my own insignificant self; but my books were always my friends, let fail all else. Nothing could be easier or more restful than my voyage in the trade-winds.

– From *Sailing Alone Around the World*
by Joshua Slocum

Apia Harbor: July 16, 1896

'It's not yet noon, señor capitán. Why do you spread that old tattered sail over us now? It were better done to go ashore and walk in the shade of those palm-trees and gaze upon the wahines. I make it all of seventy-two days since you last set foot on dry land.'

'Ah, but this harbor offers us such a magnificent vista, Francisco. I would fain sit here awhile gazing up at those wondrous mountains and listening to the

225

Samoans sing. Tell me now, do they not make the most beautiful sounds you've ever heard?'

'I grant you that they sing well, señor capitán, especially the young women, but a hale and hearty man so long at sea cannot survive on sweet songs alone. The truth is, you could not get here fast enough! You flogged us twenty-nine days across this endless ocean, all the way from the Marquesas without once dropping anchor. Yet now you idle on your salt-bleached deck much as the sultan of the Turks reclines on his golden divan!'

'That's because I've grown wise as old Suleiman the Magnificent himself, Francisco. My eyes have been opened along our road to Damascus; I see now that all things come to the man who waits.'

'Ah! Here comes now what you await in all your glorious wisdom, Don Jèsu!'

'What in tarnation are you raving about, you grinning Spaniard?'

'That outrigger canoe coming down the harbour, you sly Inglés. Look over your shoulder and you will see it. Caramba, how you start, compadre! But si, my eyes have been opened also. It is plain as the nose on your face why you were willing to wait so long.'

'Indeed, my friend, such a crew as this would please even a confirmed fool, would it not?'

'Si, Don Jèsu, and please a dead man, too! Madre di dios, don't look now but they rest their paddles! These angels in paradise would speak with you, you lucky dog!'

'Well then, give way, you lost sheep, and let them speak! I am all ears for such sirens of the sea.'

'Talofa lee! Talofa lee!'

'What is it they are calling to you, señor capitán?'

'It loses something in the translation, Francisco, but I make it something like: May love come to you, chief.'

'Santa Maria, Don Jèsu! What a lucky man you are to still be alive! I would gladly burn in hell a whole year to be flesh and blood again for one night in this heathen paradise!'

'Tis only the traditional Samoan greeting, Francisco. Take hold of yourself now lest we disgrace ourselves as so many who came here before us have done.'

'Si, mi capitán, for once I agree with you. Answer them as though you were a hidalgo to the manner born.'

'And may love come to you, fair wahines.'

'Schoon come Melike?'

'Aye, lovely wahines, this little ship comes from far away.'

'You man come Samoa all 'lone?'

'Aye, me come to Samoa all by meself.'

'We don't believe you, lone man. You bring other mans with you, but you eat them!'

'Oh señor! Is their laughter not the sound bells make tinkling in heaven?'

'Nay, Francisco! I'm sure the heavenly bells never pealed so sweetly as these.'

'Lone man, what for you come so long this way?'

'To hear you wahines sing, what else?'

'Señor capitán, those knowing glances they cast over their shoulders would heat the bowels of a dead man!'

'Shush, damn you! I can't hear what they're saying!'

'Lone man, here in Samoa no need to be lone man anymore. Talofa lee.'

'And love to you, too, my fair wahines.'

'How now, you imbecile? Are you going to let them paddle away without another word? Fie on you! Tis not the mark of a true gentleman to let such lovely butterflies slip through his fingers.'

'Aye, you do well to call them butterflies, you Don Juan! Their wings are made of gossamer. All it takes is one touch by the likes of you or me to ruin them. Far better to listen to them sing!'

'Madre di dios, how these sirens have bewitched you, señor capitán!'

'Aye, it wouldn't be the first time such a thing happened to me, Francisco. I dare hope it's not the last.'

227

Aye, *Virginia, it happened to me the first time on Botany Bay. Quite bereft me of my senses, you did! You were grown heavy with our last child before it happened again. I thought I had never seen anything quite so beautiful as what I beheld there in Hong Kong harbor, not even you. You warned me she was beyond my reach, but that only made me the more determined to have her.*

While you gave birth to Garfield in womanly fashion, I went off and did what a man has to do. You and the children shed some tears at leaving Amethyst for my new mistress. As for me, I did not even look back, for I had sold my soul down the river to possess Northern Light.

It was the proudest day of my life when I first strode her quarterdeck as captain. Lord, but there's no sight on Earth to match a great windjammer scudding under a cloud of canvas with a bone in her teeth.

So we tore across the South China Sea, bound for Manila and a cargo of sugar and hemp. Like a diamond set in gold, you promenaded under your parasol beside me. 'No finer ship ever put to sea, Virginia. We've made it to the top of the heap, and your husband's not yet forty years old.'

'Don't forget, husband dear: once you've reached the top, there's no way for a man to go further up from there.'

Aye, you were angry with me, but that did not keep you from coming to love Northern Light as much as I did. I hear and see you playing Chopin on the upright bolted to the deck of the main saloon. The children tightly gathered around you, sensing how determined you were to live your life to the full and wanting to share in it. As for me, I watched from a distance, somehow a stranger to it all, but happy enough to flatter myself that what I made was good. How did I miss this wounded look in your tawny eyes? God knows, it shows clearly enough in this tintype. You knew Northern Light was the beginning of the end for us, didn't you, Ginny?

'Don Jèsu, look! Another canoe, she is coming, but this one, she is full of singing men.'

'Aye, Francisco. I think they sing even better in chorus than do the women. That's the famous Samoan boat song you're hearing, I do believe. See how they beat time with their oars?'

'Si, señor capitán. Why, they're even wearing native uniforms.'

'Ahoy there, *Spray*! Talofa lee!'

'And may love also come to you, chiefs!'

'Captain Slocum, welcome to Samoa! These two months General Churchill has anxiously awaited your arrival. He feared you lost at the bottom of the world. So it is with great happiness and thanksgiving that His Excellency and Mrs. Churchill have sent us to welcome you to Apia. They also send you this basket of good things from the island with their compliments, and they invite you to dine with them at the consulate-general this evening.'

'Thank you, Chief! Please tell the general and his good lady I'd be delighted to accept their kind invitation, though you may have to carry me ashore in a litter. It's been more than ten weeks since I last set foot on solid earth.'

Of course I've made longer voyages as a sailing master. That first time out in Northern Light we headed for Manila. It took a month just to load her with sugar and hemp from the long native dugouts. Then we sailed for Liverpool with a regular chantey crew who sang with good voices and worked with a will. Through Sunda Straits we passed and stopped at Anjer Point on the coast of Java. It was our last chance to pick up fresh supplies before heading out into the Indian Ocean. Boats a'swarm around us, their crews clamoring to trade before we could even get the anchor down. Many baskets of fruit like this one and piles of yams and sweet potatoes and crates of chickens and baskets of eggs and even cages full of civet cats to keep off the rats.

And then we were off sailing again. Four months at sea with no more than a brief sighting of the Cape of Good Hope and Saint Helena on the horizon. But you were there beside me, Garfield in arms, Victor and Ben and Jessie under our feet. That magic voyage might have gone on forever for aught I cared.

On Christmas Eve we entered the Mersey and stowed the sails off the Liverpool Docks. The crew went over the side and vanished into the bars and brothels before they'd finished belting out the refrain of, 'We'll pay Paddy Doyle for his boots.' Next morning we celebrated Christmas and the end of our voyage in the master's cabin. The stockings were stuffed with gifts that year.

The children laughed and played with Ella and Ingram while we slipped on deck. The church bells began to peal as we stood looking out over the mist-shrouded city of Liverpool. 'Well, Joshua, our magic still holds.' You squeezed my arm once again. 'Thank you for bringing us safely back once again.'

'Then you do forgive me for buying Northern Light, Ginny?'

'I married you for better or for worse, didn't I? Look, Joshua, more magic! The bells are shaking the fog loose from the spires.'

July 17, 1896

'Señor capitán, another canoe, she is coming our way!'

'I see it, Francisco. If this keeps up, we're going to need a secretary to keep track of all our social engagements.'

'Si, compadre, you returned from dining at the consulate quite puffed up with yourself. Señora Churchill must have spoiled you rotten, I think. And look, this canoe brings us a great lady by the look of her.'

'Aye, Francisco, a very great lady indeed.'

'And very handsome as well, though not so young as those native girls who paddle and swim around *Spray* like bees around honey.'

'No matter her age, Francisco! This lady will stay forever young.'

'Ahoy *Spray!* Captain Slocum, is that really you?'

'Aye, it's me, Mrs. Stevenson. How kind of you to come welcome me to Samoa!'

'I confess I shouldn't have recognized you without the letter you sent me, Captain, but then we met only that once on San Francisco Bay.'

'I've lost all my hair since then, and gained all these lines and wrinkles. Time has been much kinder to you, Mrs. Stevenson. I should have known you anywhere.'

'I see you haven't lost your chivalry, Captain. How time flies! Was it really fifteen years ago we saw each other last?'

'Sixteen years almost to the day, Mrs. Stevenson. But please, you must forgive my lack of manners! Won't you come aboard *Spray?*'

'A wave of *déjà vu is* sweeping over me, Captain Slocum. As I recollect, my late husband hailed you from our cedar canoe. He asked to be shown your good ship, the *Amethyst*, and you helped me climb over the side just as you are doing now. You were kind enough to put up with us and answer all our landlubberly questions. Your good wife, Virginia – we are almost of an age, she and I – even served us lunch on your quarterdeck: lamb chops and fresh asparagus tips with a bottle of good white Burgundy, as I remember.'

'Aye, your good husband couldn't hear enough of ships and seafaring, Mrs. Stevenson. He said he needed to hear it all in order to keep his promises to you.'

'Indeed, he never did get his fill of the sea. In after years, whenever inspiration failed him at his writing, Robbie would tear his hair and exclaim: 'Where shall I find me such a genuine seafaring man as that Captain Slocum?'

'And where shall I find another such writer as your husband, Mrs. Stevenson? I keep all his books with me aboard *Spray*. Certainly I consider that he kept the promises made us all on *Amethyst's* quarterdeck.'

'Yes, Captain, I believe that he did. I can't tell you how much it means to me to have lived with him those years while he was writing *Treasure Island, Kidnapped* and the rest. His had not been a happy life, you know. He was already dying when I first met him.'

'I'm sure he was very grateful to you, Mrs. Stevenson.'

'Grateful? Why yes, I suppose Robbie was grateful to me in his way. But not so grateful as I am to him. After all, what is a good wife but one a man can take for granted? And what chance has a divorced mother of two for making a good life in this world? But oh, what a good life that man did lead me! Only a few women have ever known such marvelous adventures as I've lived through, Captain Slocum. I'm counting your Virginia among them, of course.'

'Aye, pardon me for saying it, but I feel as though Virginia and Robert are both here in this cockpit with us, Mrs. Stevenson.'

'Yes, it does feel ever so strange being here with you on your magnificent yawl! If only Robbie could see her! I've missed my husband more than I can tell you these last months. I've tried to remember just what his presence felt like, but I could not do so till just now. How lonely and miserable I've been! You must come and cheer us up at Vailima, Captain Slocum.'

'Why, I can't think of anything I'd rather do, Mrs. Stevenson.'

'Tomorrow then, you'll come? I mustn't stay longer or the Churchills and the local missionaries will be scandalized. Up at Vailima, I promise you'll find us somewhat less formal, Captain.'

CHAPTER XXIV

RENDEZVOUS

My own canoe, a small dugout, one day when it was rolled over with me, was seized by a party of fair bathers, and before I could get my breath, almost, was towed around and around the Spray, while I sat in the bottom of it, wondering what they would do next.... One of the sprites, I remember, was a young English lady who made more sport of it than any of the others.

– From *Sailing Alone Around the World*
by Joshua Slocum

Safata Bay: August 21, 1896

'The truth, he's as plain to me as the nose on your face, Don Jèsu: you do not need me to pilot *Spray* anymore. Indeed, I have my doubts whether either of you will ever leave this island.'

'Why, you old pirate, what you say is not true at all! As you are my witness, the Churchills and the others saw us off to Australia yesterday. *Spray* and I, we have two more oceans to cross! So bide with us yet awhile, I beg of you.'

'Compadre, you are my only hope of ceasing to wander on this ocean. So it is I who should be begging you, for I feel you casting me further adrift each day since we first hove in sight of Samoa.'

'Surely, my friend, you do not begrudge me the peace that coming to this island has brought me.'

'It is not the peace of this island that I begrudge you, Don Jèsu. This widow of your friend Stevenson, she is the one whom you came seeking, isn't she?'

'Aye, Francisco. As for Fanny herself, she confessed to me that all unknowing she's been waiting for me since even before she received my letter from Gibraltar.'

'How could that be? Caramba, it matters not! Tell me, do you make love to her, Inglés?'

'Avast there, Spaniard! Since when does a gentleman ask such questions of another!'

'My apologies, señor! Indeed, I would not have asked if I were not so personally concerned with your answer. I cannot help but fear you may abandon our voyage altogether for the sake of the señora, or even worse, supplant me by bringing her along.'

'You need have no fear on that score, Francisco. Fanny's course and mine were charted long ago. She must remain here, and I must go on. This one conjunction of our stars must suffice us for the rest of our two lives.'

'But this starry conjunction you speak of, Don Jèsu, she is already lasting more than a month!'

'I know, Francisco, I know! It's a hard thing to say goodbye to one another. It's a hard thing to know we shall never see each other again.'

'And so you went behind my back and arranged this secret rendezvous with her here on lonely Safata Bay?'

'Aye, Francisco. As you know, she and I were given almost no time alone together. I would hear her laugh and sing one last time.'

'I think you deceive yourself, Don Jèsu. Such a respectable lady will not dare to come. The risk is too great to her reputation. On such a small island as this, minds are also small, and everyone knows everyone else's business.'

'She will come, just as I believe my own Virginia would come if I were dead and it were Fanny's husband who was waiting. She will come, I tell you.'

236

You and Robert are gone from this world, but this one last skein must still be warped through the woof of all our lives lest the tapestry unravel. Why did we leave off weaving it in the middle, Ginny?

That voyage out of Liverpool seemed pleasant enough. I let my bucko first mate whip our crew into shape. Aye, Black Taylor made sure our masts were scraped and slushed down, our deck-houses and bulwarks fresh painted, our standing rigging tarred and our decks holystoned to perfect whiteness. Thanks to him, we sailed into New York Harbor handsome as any millionaire's yacht.

I confess I should have examined his methods more closely. You told me so, but I was too full of myself, too drunk on the heady spirits of success, to stop and wonder why the crew couldn't wait to scramble over the side and fall back into the hands of the crimps.

Did you feel our world beginning to fall apart as you gathered us all on deck to view the new bridge spanning the Hudson? You stood with one hand shading your eyes, the other resting lightly on Victor's shoulder. 'It's just a tiny line against the sky, Father.'

'Ye'll not think so, lad, when we come under it. That bridge rises one hundred and thirty-two feet clear of the river.'

'One hundred and thirty-two feet! But that's not as high as our mains'l, Father! Northern Light will never make it under that bridge and into the harbor!'

'Right ye are, Victor. We must strike her topgallant masts to reach our appointed berth.'

Aye, I saw what that Brooklyn Bridge portended as clearly as did our son, but I would not give way so much as an inch to the changing times. I commanded the greatest windjammer plying the Seven Seas, did I not? How the newspapers loved to tell stories of the "famous and intrepid Captain Slocum!" The French doors of the Carnegies and Vanderbilts swung open to me whenever I came to port.

You and the children were part and parcel of my blindness, Ginny. What a smart crew you turned out on the quarterdeck like a graduating class of midshipmen at Annapolis. Aye, here you stand before me now, nervously adjusting Garfield's starched sailor. 'Well, dear husband, do you think there's a chance at all we'll pass your father's inspection?'

I had sent off the cable via the skipper of the tugboat that towed us into the harbor. 'Dear Father. Come to New York soonest. Return fare follows. Your Prodigal Son, Joshua.'

I hardly expected you to take me at my word. It wasn't at all like the man I had known as a child to come all the way from Nova Scotia to eat humble pie. Yet come you did wearing a pair of the coarse boots you still cobbled in the little shop on the harbor. Still reeking of the soaking-vats despite marriage to the opulent widow. I swear, you must have gone to your grave smelling of tanned cowhide.

'Well, Joshua, I see you've done quite well for yourself, but tell me, what will it all add up to in the end?'

'Add up to, Father? What do you mean?'

'I refer to religious faith, of course, without which there is no meaning. You don't appear to follow any religion at all, my son.'

'I follow the sea, Father, and today you are my witness how well it has served me.'

'I am witness that you are setting yourself up to be tested even as Job was tested. Alas, you lack the faith needed to endure the outcome as he did. What will you do when all this be taken from you and you stand before God's Judgment Seat, stripped naked as the day you were born?'

How I wish I had thought to tell him that when that time came, I would go off sailing around the world, naked as a jaybird or not. It shames me to think what a feeble jibe I couched at him! 'Life is what you make of it, Father, nothing less and nothing more.'

He did not even blink. 'You take too much on yourself,
Joshua. May God forgive me for not breaking you of your
pride, and may He have mercy on your good wife and lit-
tle ones when you take your final fall.'

'Father, can you think of nothing else to say to me
after all these years?'

'What more is there to say till life teaches you humility,
my son? Alas, an inner voice tells me that I shall not live to
see that day.'

You were quite right, of course. But even if I had
known then what a true prophet you were, it would not
have changed what passed between us that last time we
ever spoke with one another. Your way is not my way,
Father, and I will sail off the world's edge before I submit
to the will of the narrow God you worship.

'Don Jèsu, look! Is that not Senora Stevenson's horse
tethered there under the palms?'

'Aye, that is her dun mare all right. Head *Spray* up
into the wind till I douse the sail, Francisco.'

'And look, there's Señora Stevenson on the beach!
She waves her hat at us, señor capitán.'

'Anchor's away, Francisco! Back her into the wind!
Ahoy there, Mrs. Stevenson! I'm coming to fetch you!'

'In this rotten half-dory of yours, señor capitán?
Madre di dios, you will drown her for sure!'

'She swims as well as any tapo girl, Francisco. It's me
you should worry about.'

'Bueno! Have her teach you how swimming is done,
señor capitán, lest you end up drowning as I did.'

'You know you can't teach an old sea-dog like me
such fancy new tricks, my friend.'

'Si, compadre, I know it well enough not to even try,
but then, I'm not a beautiful *señora*.'

Aye, thou art fair, Fanny! Standing there, arms akim-
bo under your panama hat. Did Robert know that he
brought to this island a treasure greater than Pew's
pirate gold? Or are women like Virginia and you always

fated to be taken for granted till it's too late to assay your true value? 'Good gracious me! What a lovely pea-green boat you have, Captain Slocum!'

'Newly painted the better to ferry you aboard my *Spray*, Mrs. Stevenson. No, don't wade out. You'll ruin your boots and riding-skirt. Let me just step ashore and carry you aboard.'

'Avast there! Stay right where you are, sir! I shall pull off my boots and hike up my skirt.'

'It would be no trouble for me to carry you, Mrs. Stevenson. I may look past my prime, but when push comes to shove, I'm still an able-bodied seaman!'

'I doubt it not, but I won't have you taking me for a helpless woman, Captain Slocum! I trust you've seen a lady's knees before now!'

'Aye, Mrs. Stevenson, that I have, but I swear I've never laid eyes on a lovelier pair than these.'

'What's that you say? I can hardly credit such gallantry from an old pirate like you. Make way, sir, for I'm coming aboard!'

'Whoa! Steady as she goes, Mrs. Stevenson.'

'Don't rock the boat, sir! There now, that was easy enough, wasn't it?'

'Aye, but I'm afraid we've run aground!'

'Then hand me an oar! Don't dither, sir! Oh, I swear, you men would spend your entire lives caught up on snags if it weren't for us women constantly rescuing you! I poled Robbie's outrigger off many a coral reef in these Southern Seas, I'll have you know!'

'There, by George, you did it!'

'Certainly, I did it! Oops! Sorry! I didn't mean to strike you with the butt of the oar. Are you all right, Captain?'

'Aye, I reckon I'll live a while yet, ma'am. I didn't much fancy that bald spot on my head anyway.'

'Oh dear, you may call me Fanny now that we're pitched in solitude together, Captain. You can't expect any woman who'd run off sailing with a pirate to stand on ceremony.'

'Well, Fanny, now that we've come to blows, I guess you'd better call me Joshua as well.'

'My poor dear Joshua! Oh, forgive me, Joshua, I can't help laughing at you! What is there about causing injury to a man that always makes a woman want to laugh? How I do like shouting your name to the palm trees, Joshua! It makes a fine echo off these cliffs, does it not? Would singing you a song make your poor head feel any better?'

'That depends on how well you sing, ma'am.'

'Robbie used to tell me that I sing like a nightingale, and he was never one to humor a woman by telling her lies.'

'Well then, Fanny, I'm willing to take his word for it.'

'Rub a dub dub

In a pea-green tub,

Lost on the ocean blue.

Joshua the pi' rate

and Fanny his first mate,

They got lost those two,

Rub a dub dub

In a pea-green tub

Lost on the ocean blue.

'Oh Joshua, I wish we could stay lost like this forever, just you and I!'

'Fanny, if there's one thing I've learned in this life so far, it's that a man should never let worry about tomorrow keep him from living to the full what's set before him today.'

'I suspect what you say is even more true for us women. Certainly our brief time together would have no point if we failed to live it to the full. And yet, if it were any more than brief, my intuition tells me our happiness would fall apart despite all we could do. Ho, here's *Spray* upon us already! Ye old oyster sloop, I'm too much a woman not to be a bit jealous of you, even if you are all made of wood. You are your captain's first love, you know.'

'Now that's not true, Fanny!'

'Oh yes it is. I lived with Robbie long enough to understand that sailing ships and writing books are to men like you as raising children and managing families are to women like me. *Spray's* your true mistress, Joshua. My, you clamber up her side like you were still just a boy! This time I'll let you help me aboard if you've a mind to. We've got to know each other well enough for that while you were rowing me about in your pea green dinghy.'

'Easy does it! There, you've made it, Fanny! Welcome aboard *Spray.'*

'Yes, I must keep reminding myself that this is your real home. You'd best beware of me, Joshua. We women are never more dangerous than when we enter bachelors' quarters.'

'Aye, Fanny, I've noticed as much from time to time, though the fact is: I'm a married man.'

'Married man, indeed! No, I don't think you're really anything of the kind. You had the definite air of a married man when we first met on San Francisco Bay, but you've decidedly turned bachelor now. Fair game, I should say for any woman on the loose. Poor Hettie has lost you, if she may be said to have ever had you in the first place.'

'Fanny, Fanny, we mustn't speak of Hettie so lightly. She's a good woman, for all that I'm here with you.'

'Sorry, but I can't help it. We women can be kind to one another, but we have no mercy when men enter the picture. Hello there! Whatever is this? There's something strange here, Joshua Slocum ... someone strange, I should say, here in the cockpit with us. I can almost see someone sitting there at the wheel. There's a shadow hanging there like a cloud. A good thing for you it's the shadow of a man and not that of a woman.'

'Well, Fanny, you know how it is from living with Robert Louis. A solitary mariner has to make his own company or else go crazy.'

'Yes, of course! Your shadowy companion's a creature of your imagination, isn't he! A literary character, no less! My very favorite kind of person, you know. They never let you down in Robert's books, do they? Well, aren't you going to introduce me to your shipmate, Joshua?'

'Well now, Fanny, I think that would be taking things a bit too far, don't you?'

'Not at all, I insist! Robbie introduced me to all his characters. He once said that I helped make them come alive by chatting with them and sounding them out. I'd say your friend's feeling somewhat slighted by us. It's rude carrying on like this as though he weren't here with us.'

'Oh very well! Ah, Mrs. Robert Louis Stevenson, er Fanny, that is, I'd like you to meet Señor Francisco Martin Pinzón, pilot of the Pinta by the grace of Her Most Catholic Majesty, Queen Isabella of Spain.'

'Pilot of the Pinta, no less? I'm pleased to make so distinguished an acquaintance, Señor Pinzón.'

'Encanto, señora.'

'He speaks Spanish, of course? I'm afraid my Spanish isn't very good. You'll have to translate till I get the hang of him, Joshua.'

'He says he's enchanted by your fair presence aboard our humble vessel, Fanny.'

'Is he now? How fine it is to find myself surrounded by chivalrous caballeros of the sea! You are too kind, señor. Joshua, do reassure him that I do not intend to wear out my welcome.'

'He says that would not be possible aboard this vessel, señora.'

'So, he's a liar to boot like all men. I'm beginning to take the measure of the rogue now, but it would help if you'd describe him for me.'

'Francisco's a tall lanky fellow in a red cocked hat and ferocious black whiskers. He looks a bit like those pictures of Elizabethan seamen your husband kept in his study.'

'You forgot to mention my sword to her, señor capitán!'

'And he wears a sword of the finest Toledo steel, Fanny.'

'Yes, thank you! I can make him out clearly now. What a true and faithful friend he's been to you, Joshua!'

'Aye, that he has. There's been many a time on this voyage when I would not have made it through without him.'

'Yes, I can feel how necessary he's been to you! Señor Pinzón, I do hope you'll pardon my intrusion. I know how we women do tend to disturb male company. Lend me this old pirate of yours just for today and tomorrow, what do you say?'

'Señora, I will quit this vessel for as long as you desire.'

'No, no, señor, we would have you come sailing with us, wouldn't we, Captain Slocum? After all, Don Francisco, who's to steer *Spray* while the captain and I commune? He and I, we've much to say to one another tonight and tomorrow, for it must needs last us a lifetime.'

'Madre di dios, what are we waiting for, señora? Pull up the anchor, mi capitán, and let us go sailing!'

CHAPTER XXV

PLAIN SAILING

One more gale of wind came down upon the Spray after she passed Cape Agulhas, but that one she dodged by getting into Simons Bay. When it moderated she beat around the Cape of Good Hope, where they say the Flying Dutchman is still sailing. The voyage then seemed as good as finished; from this point on I knew that all, or nearly all, would be plain sailing.

– From *Sailing Alone Around the World*
by Joshua Slocum

Tasman Sea near Australia: September 21, 1896

'Wake up, señor capitán, wake up for the love of God!'

'Damn you to hell, Francisco!'

'Why bother damning me to hell, Don Jèsu? I am already serving my time in purgatory, remember?'

'It's no more than you deserve for dashing my splendid dream to pieces, you sinner!'

'So sorry, señor capitán, but you were ranting on so horribly that you quite frightened me. Of what terrible monster were you dreaming?'

'I was back at Vailima, if you must know, taking ava with the Stevensons. Fanny called upon me to pour the traditional libation over my shoulder. For the life of me, I could not recall the Samoan for "Let the Gods drink"! Instead, all the languages I've ever heard came flooding through my head. It was as though some evil spirit were forcing me to speak in tongues.'

'Ah, señor capitán, some evil spirit indeed! Here we are forty days out from Samoa and almost in sight of Australia, but still all you think of is Señora Stevenson. No matter how hard I try, I cannot bring you back to your old cheerful self. Sometimes I almost wish we were back still beating our way around the Horn.'

'Well, Francisco, you've been around this world long enough to know how it is with a man's heart. Even the best of shipmates can never take the place of the woman he loves.'

'Si, Don Jèsu, especially if she be so much woman as your Señora Stevenson, no?'

'Do not be cruel, Francisco. Señora Stevenson and I know we shall never see each other again. Aye, sweet lady, I must let go of you once and for all. Tofah, Fanny!'

'Si, it is the beginning of wisdom to accept that all things, even the love of a man for a woman, must come to an end. And yet, compadre, the most precious things in this fleeting life do not end. They pass beyond place and time, if you take my meaning.'

'There, your philosophy has succeeded in lightening my spirits, Francisco! Now let me return the favor. What are you brooding about?'

'Only that I myself must soon be taking leave of you, as I told you before. Now that the antipodes are almost in sight, I think it will soon be time for me to go.'

'Not so fast, you old pirate! Your penance with me is not yet served. We may be entering Australian waters, but there are still two oceans to cross before we bid each other farewell.'

'We shall see, mi capitán, we shall see!'

Mid-Indian Ocean: July 15, 1897

'I think we are close to losing our trade wind for good, señor.'

'We are twenty-two days out from Christmas Island, Francisco, so your news comes as no great surprise. See those anti-trade clouds? They're flying up high from the southwest.'

'Si, señor capitán, I see them all right. And this swell, she is heavier and more sullen than usual. It cannot mean us any good.'

'Not to worry, Francisco. It's only a big winter gale blowing off the Cape of Good Hope. That's more than a thousand leagues away. Steer a bit higher to windward, allow say twenty miles a day for shift of current till it blows itself out, and we'll do just fine.'

'Caramba, señor capitán! How can you know to do such things in the middle of an empty ocean?'

'It's far from empty, Francisco. You know yourself there's not a breeze that stirs or a wave that tumbles that does not have some meaning out here.'

'Yet surely, señor capitán, even with all your devil's magic, you can't really expect to come upon this speck of a rock amid a sea so vast? According to your English chart, this poor excuse for an island barely raises its lowly head above the waves.'

'Ye are of little faith, Francisco. Did you not mark that tern this morning? How it fluttered over our heads ever so knowingly, then took itself off westward? I mark that a true harbinger of land ahead.'

'If a single tern so excites you, señor capitán, pray take a look off our starboard bow with your magical glass.'

'Aye, Francisco, I see a great flock of birds fishing and fighting on the water! We are drawing nigh Keeling Cocos, I tell you! Steady as she goes while I shinny up the mast and take a look.'

'Be careful, señor capitán. You are not a ship's boy anymore to be cutting capers high off the deck.'

'If I fall overboard, just be sure you bring her around and pick me up, you lazy Spaniard!'

'Caramba! You should have got the señora to teach you how to swim, but no, you had better things to be teaching *her*, you crazy Inglés! Take care! If you fall overboard, you will surely drown before I can come about!'

'Land ho! Francisco! I can see cocoanut-palms standing out of the water dead ahead!'

'Are you pulling my leg again, mi capitán? I can hardly credit such a piece of luck as finding this island, if good luck it be and not more of your black magic. What new course do you set me for the end of our long run?'

'Steady as she goes, Francisco. Steady as she goes!'

'Steady as she goes? Señor capitán, it is not humanly possible to sail right up to so small a speck of an island after twenty-seven hundred miles without once sighting land along the way!'

'We've done much better than that, my friend! The current and the heave of the sea are drawing us into the fairway of the channel on our present heading. I'll just trim the sails by the wind, and you may flog her straight on to the harbor landing.'

'What? You think to sail straight into the harbor without so much as changing course? Madre di dios, Don Cristóbal himself could not have performed such a piece of seamanship!'

'If I do say so myself, Francisco: no leg of our voyage so far has been so perfectly navigated as this last one. These days dear old *Spray* simply goes where we ask her to go.'

'Then why are those tears running down your cheeks, Don Jèsu?'

Off Port Louis, Mauritius: October 2, 1897

'Seven señoritas, señor capitán? Just count them! Seven young señoritas, no less! This time you really have been out in the sun too long without your hat!'

'What would you have had me do, Francisco? Mrs. Saunderson entertained me so royally at lunch. What could I do but invite her nieces to go sailing with us? Who'd have thought such a gaggle of young girls would actually take me up on such an offer? But not to worry, their good aunt has come along to chaperone them, and she brought a Bengali manservant with her as well. It won't even be necessary to prepare them a lunch in return.'

'Madre di dios! I didn't even see the señora amid all the bright skirts and parasols. That makes eight women all told, Inglés! Putting to sea with one woman aboard is tempting fate, but now you bring us no less than eight of them? And as if that were not bad enough, you bring along this pig of a Moorish infidel besides! Just look at them harping on the foredeck like a herd of seals!'

'The young ladies are pulling up the anchor for us. Avast your carping, you ungrateful Spaniard. You don't even need to steer, for they wish to take turns at the wheel. Don't worry, we shall run *Spray* out into rough seas. These young ladies will have *mal de mer* and their fill of the sea soon enough. Then we shall sail them home again, as simple as that. I won't even miss dinner with the harbor-master and his good lady.'

'Then I leave you to it till *Spray* returns to port. Buena sombra, you Don Juan of a sea-captain!'

'What, you dare accuse me of womanizing? Ho there, where have you taken yourself off to? This is no time to turn tail on your captain, you coward!'

'Captain Slocum, whoever are you talking to back here? Aunty says I am to take first watch at steering *Spray*.'

'Did she now? Louise, I must warn you that this old boat is used to steering herself, like any woman. Still, I daresay she won't mind so fair a hand as yours at her helm for a change. Head her up into the wind while I hoist the sails.'

'You must let us do it for you, Captain! Aunty says we may. Just show us which ropes to pull on.'

'Very well, pull on the jib halyard just by your hand, Muriel. And, Gertrude, you may work the starboard sheet. That's it, my dear! Just take a turn on the belaying pin and hold on. Now, Louise, you may bring her about, if you please. Hoist her up, Muriel. Aye, Gladys, help her. That's the way! Now, Gertrude, pull her in hard till you draw the luff from the jib.'

'If I do say so, Captain Slocum, those waves breaking at the harbor entrance look quite menacing from the deck of your little vessel. I'm used to much bigger craft.'

'Don't worry, Mrs. Saunderson. I intend turning back as soon as your young ladies cry for mercy.'

'My young ladies cry for mercy, Captain? I think not! You forget that each of them comes from a long line of seafarers. It will take more than a few breakers to make my nieces cry for mercy!'

'Then I take it that you yourself are not afraid of encountering great whales and giant squid out here, Mrs. Saunderson?'

'Why certainly not, Captain Slocum! Before the diphtheria took my beloved husband from me, he hunted whales for our living!'

'Yet sometimes they rise up from the deep and break the back of stout ships, Mrs. Saunderson. Why, giant squid have been known to entangle vessels with their long tentacles and pull them right down into the abysmal depths.'

'Captain, I fear you've been reading too much of that French writer, Jules Verne, or more likely you suffer from hunger. Indeed you look half-starved, you poor man! Where shall I have Rahman set up this picnic basket?'

'Well, here in the cockpit will do, I suppose. But first brace yourself, Mrs. Saunderson. We must break through these combers into the open sea before we turn our thoughts to eating. Hang on for your lives, dear ladies. Hurrah!'

'Oh, how lovely it is to be out here, aunty! Captain Slocum, sailing your yawl is ever so much better than riding a horse!'

'Look out, Donalda! Mind you don't get washed overboard! Here comes another big one. Hurrah!'

'How beautifully she skims over the sea, Captain! How I wish we could all go sailing around the world with you.'

'A most pleasant thought, Anastasia, but you do look rather pale. Just say the word, dear ladies, and I shall turn *Spray* about and head her for home.'

'What? Just when we're beginning to have fun, Captain? What a terrible thought! Look, see how our island stands out from a distance! I've never seen it look so beautiful before. What say you, girls? Are we ready to head for home just yet?'

'Oh do go on, Captain! Your *Spray* is ever so heavenly. Would you like us to touch up her jib just a hair? It's starting to luff a bit.'

'Very good, Gertrude. How quickly you girls do get the hang of things!'

'Yes, Captain Slocum, do take us further out into the deep! Your lovely *Spray* steers like a dream.'

'Well, Mrs. Saunderson, I find it hard to believe these girls of yours never worked a sailing vessel before!'

'Did I not tell you they were made of fine stuff, Captain? Here, would you care for a cucumber sandwich? There's also watercress, if you prefer.'

'Watercress sandwiches, Mrs Saunderson? I'd love one. Oh look, those seas tumbling aboard are soaking your nieces to the skin. Their pretty gowns will be ruined.'

'Think nothing of it, Captain Slocum. I insisted they wear their old riding outfits for this outing. Rahman, a mug of hot tea for the captain, if you please.'

'Thank you, Rahman. Oh dear, Mrs. Saunderson, I think your manservant is about to be sick!'

'Well hand him your deck-pail, Captain! Quickly now, or he'll make a mess on your deck.'

'I see you enjoy a cast-iron stomach yourself, Mrs. Saunderson.'

'My father was a missionary in India during the Sepoy Mutiny, Captain. As a young girl, I saw many terrible things. The bodies of women and children rotting in the streets. Mutineers strapped over the muzzles of cannon and blown to pieces. What's a little seasickness compared to all that?'

'My turn to steer, Captain! Aunty said I'm to be next.'

'Aye, Cordelia. We've passed almost out of sight of land. Shall we turn and head for home?'

'Oh, Captain, must we? Aunty, let's go anchor in Tombo Bay and make a real picnic of it.'

'Oh yes, aunty, let's! We can camp on the beach all night and go swim in the surf along the shore!'

'Well it does sound like it might be fun, if the good captain doesn't mind putting up with all us ladies for so long. What say you, Captain Slocum?'

'Well now, Mrs. Saunderson, what true sailor in all the world could say you nay? I confess I've a weakness for charming company.'

'Oh I say, this is really delightful, Captain. I haven't had such a good time since before my dear Walter passed on. I'd have the governor order you to stay on with us at Mauritius, if you weren't already a married man.'

Saint Helena: April 20, 1898

'Do not be frightened, Monsieur Slocum. Papa was only joking when he promised you that someone would visit you tonight.'

'Have no fear on my account, Mlle. Morilleau. Governor Sterndale intimated much the same as your father when he bedded me down in a certain room at Plantation House. Alas, the only ghosts I saw that night turned out to be draped furniture and moonlight glinting off the horseshoe nailed over the door.'

'Yet we do keep this bedchamber exactly as His Imperial Majesty left it, monsieur. Perhaps it is only a young girl's imagination, but one does feel his presence here sometimes. However, I must confess that I myself have never seen him, though I have lived here at Longwood all of my sixteen years.'

'Still, this chamber where he died seems a more likely place than any other to meet the great man face to face. I shall keep the candle burning as a kind of invitation for him to show himself.'

'My father sleeps in the valet's chamber next door. If you require anything at all or if something frightens you, just pull the bell-cord and Papa will quickly attend you.'

'I'm not a man to be easily frightened off, but please assure your father again how much I do appreciate him letting me be the first man to ever spend the night in Napoleon's death bed. Bon soir, Mademoiselle Morilleau.'

'Bon soir, monsieur.'

'Such a charming jeune fille she is! A delectable tidbit fit for wild dreams, if an old man may dare say so when all alone behind closed doors. Avast such thoughts, Slocum! The excellent Bordeaux has gone straight to your head. Lord knows this room's martial enough in spirit to keep a man on sentry duty even in his sleep, but I suppose a fighting man such as yourself would not have it any other way. You've probably gone back with your earthly remains to the Place des Invalides anyhow. Hah, why here's a canopy and all! At least, Corsican, you must have been reasonably comfortable in such a bed as this, though they say you suffered a great deal at the end from whatever killed you. Well, I'm tired enough to sleep standing, so I shan't wait up for you.'

'Did you not bring your valet along, Captain Slocum? I assure you Monsieur Percier did not design that *chaise haute* for the hanging of a pea-jacket.'

'Zounds! Is that indeed you, Your Majesty?'

'Certainly I am here. Who else would dare linger in this chamber? Did you not come here expressly to visit with me this night, monsieur le capitaine?'

'Aye, Your Majesty, that I did, but I still cannot make you out among all the shadows in this room.'

'Over here by the window. Put the candle behind you, and you will see me framed in the moonlight.'

'Aye, there you are! I mistook you for something more mundane at first, but I'd know that singular shape of yours anywhere. Mind, you're not nearly so tall as I imagined you to be.'

'What? Has the world so quickly forgotten the battle of Lodi? How I charged alone across the bridge against a regiment of Croats after my soldiers turned back? Have you not heard the story of how my soldiers in their shame returned to the charge? In the fracas that followed, I was summarily knocked into the river for my pains. You have not heard of how those rascals left me stuck safely in the mud till the battle was won? Only then did they drag me out by my epaulettes and dub me "le petit corporal."

'Pardon my ignorance, Your Majesty. Even so, I daresay no man who ever lived is less likely to be forgotten than yourself.'

'It's chivalrous of you to say so, monsieur le capitaine, but I know well enough that I do not deserve better. History gives no quarter to those who fail in what they set out to do.'

'That may be true, Your Majesty, but what man ever essayed to do so much in a single lifetime as you did?'

'I did overreach myself, but my tragic blunder had nothing to do with the scale of my ambition. Rather, mine is a sordid case of a mortal man losing his way, of failing to carry out the mission I was put on this Earth for. You have proven yourself the better navigator by far, monsieur le capitaine.'

'My humble adventures as a seaman are hardly to be compared with yours, Your Majesty.'

'Call me Buonaparte, if you please. Looking back, I see now that I ceased having true friends when men commenced calling me by my resplendent titles. Your modesty becomes you, monsieur le capitaine, but I for one have nothing but admiration and respect for the first man to sail alone around the world.'

'I've yet to complete my voyage, Monsieur Buonaparte.'

'I foresee that you will do it, monsieur le capitaine. Already you draw near to crossing your outward-bound track. And you've had to butcher not a single man to encompass your world. I butchered tens of thousands at a time trying to encompass mine. Yes, I can tell at a glance you're a man worth knowing. Indeed, I would like you for a friend, my dear Slocum. Come, it grows cold in this room. Climb into my bed while the night is still young and let us talk of what we have learned.'

EPILOGUE

What I sailed for I have got and more. I found things I did not dream of meeting with. I hoist them all in – have worked harder in port than at sea – I have now a valuable cargo – Sail homeward tomorrow.

> – Joshua Slocum from 'Letter to Joseph P. Gilder (first critic to appreciate his literary potential)'

North Atlantic off New York: October 21, 1909

'Aye, I know, old friend! I know! You badly need your reef taken in, but as you can plainly see, I'm not my old self this morning. Neither are you, eh? Well, like it or not, you must sail yourself for a spell.'

'Aye, I'm afraid these short hops down to the West Indies each autumn have been taking their toll upon us both, judging by all the Irish pennants you fly these days. God knows those little cruises were not without their charm, though pretty tame pickings after sailing you round the world. Ah *Spray*! Taken all together, that voyage was better than reading *Treasure Island* or *Kidnapped*, was it not? Tell me now, do you remember the last chapter, the final leg of our voyage home?'

Why of course you remember, Spray! How's a prime blue water vessel like you to forget your proudest moment? A perfectly delightful cruise it was, so tuned were you, Francisco and I to the ways of the sea. Have you forgiven me yet for that one fit of fretting off Tobago? Talk about trying to make bad things come true! My tomfoolery almost lost you on that imaginary coral reef. Try to understand, I couldn't shake my belief that the gods were bound to thwart us in the end from finishing off our cruise around the world. Aye, you're right, I'm fudging the truth. What weighted me down most was dread of coming back to the world of worthy men. Yet that world is neither so real nor so worthy a world, my dear Spray, as the one we shared with the pilot of the Pinta.

And then right near this very spot, we ran that gauntlet of tornados. June 25, 1898, according to your log. Churning sea-spouts and lightning bolts blasting the sea all around us. Francisco and I, we could do no more than look on as you fought to stay alive, for how can a mere man or even a ghost measure himself against a tempest like that? Only a vessel like you can perform such a miracle. How you ever weathered it, I do not know. Perhaps it was the old pirate's prayers that saw you through.

When the sea finally grew calm again, the pilot of the Pinta gravely bade us both goodbye with a salute of his hanger, and we saw no more of him from that day till this. Remember how sad we both were to see him go?

So I took your helm and hove you round from starboard to port tack and made for a quiet harbor. Under short sail you reached in for the shores of Long Island while I sat alone thinking and watching the lights of vessels coasting past. Reflections of our long voyage together near o'erwhelmed me that night.

When daylight came, I saw that the sea had changed color from dark green to light. I threw the lead off your bow and got soundings in thirteen fathoms. It wasn't long after I sighted land some miles east of Fire Island, and we made for Newport as fast as we could sail.

The weather after the gale turned remarkably fine. You rounded Montauk Point in fine style; Port Judith was off your beam at dark; you fetched in at Beavertail next. Sailing on, you had one more danger to pass.

The damned Yankees had mined Newport Harbor, giving the Spanish more credit than they deserved. I remember how glad I felt that Francisco was not there to witness that sad excuse for a war we waged against his countrymen.

So we hugged the rocks where neither friend nor foe could come at us. It was close work, but far safer than following the deep channel. We were just ghosting past the Dexter, the dear old guard ship, when the moon broke from behind a cloud and someone sang out: 'There goes a sailing craft, by God!'

As quick as a flash, I unshuttered the lantern-light on your sails and heard someone hail you.

'Hold your fire, Dexter! It's just me, Joshua Slocum! I'm on my way home to Fairhaven after three years at sea! I harbor no Spaniards aboard this vessel!'

I eased off the main sheet, and you sprang off for the lights of the inner harbor. And so I cast down your anchor at 1 a.m. on June 27, 1898, after a cruise of more than forty-six thousand miles round the world, lasting three years and two months.

And were we both not the better for it, my dear old Spray? You had turned back the dial of my life till people said, 'That old Slocum, I swear he's grown young again.' Aye, younger I was by many years though I've aged them back again since that time. I did not even mind that everyone was too delirious with war fever to notice we were back from sailing around the world – except for those two women who came down to meet us at the quay.

The one who had said 'Spray shall return', she got there first, even though she was never anything more than a friend. Just a proper hug for me and a landlubber's stroke of the taffrail for you. Be that as it may, Mabel Wagnalls is to me everything one human being

259

can ever be to another. In the beginning it was she who dredged me up from my slough of despond and turned my head to sailing round the world, though I took good care to keep my fingers crossed at the time. And there at the end it was she who fixed my courage to the sticking point and made me solemnly promise to write down the story of it all. She gave freely, asking for nothing in return, save only friendship and to shake my hand. So, Spray, it was only fitting that I should dedicate our little book to her.

The one who had thought me dead, she came next to make sure my feet were firmly planted on land again. Poor Hettie, she had aged by as much as I had grown younger, wearing out her youth sewing dresses and shirts so that the children I sired on Virginia might eat and go to school. My second wife, she had no greeting for you at all, Spray, and not much more for me. But then, what did I hold in store for her beyond a dutiful peck on her fading cheek?

'Well, Joshua, I only hope the voyage will pay you for your trouble.' I see looking back that it would have been far better for her if my life had been cut short after the publishing of my best-selling book. I'm not sure who was most surprised, her or me, when it did pay me handsomely for my trouble. Thank God it made possible some small return on all that I owe her for the rearing of Virginia's children.

Aye, I did try to stick it out with her on Martha's Vineyard. I even did my best to love her as she deserves of me, but I was no more than holding my breath away from you, Spray. I was only waiting to come up for air again.

'Ahoy there! Get up, Joshua Slocum! Get up, I say!'

'Avast there! Get your grubby hooks off my wheel, you pirate!'

'Madre di dios, don't you recognize your old shipmate, señor capitán?'

'Who goes there? Why, is that really you, Francisco? Have you come back to me after all these years?'

'Si, Don Jèsu, the Pilot of the *Pinta* has returned.'

'God's blood! I thought you long graduated from purgatory, my friend.'

'I've waited out here for you in limbo, compadre, drifting on the wind. I could not bring myself to go on alone into the great unknown without you to leather me along.'

'Good Lord, it must be all of twelve years since you last stood beside me at *Spray's* helm!'

'Si, mi capitán, going on twelve years, but what is twelve years between two friends who've sailed these seven seas as fast together as we have?'

'Aye, Francisco, I've just been lying here in the cockpit dreaming about that voyage we made. You were blithely swearing at me in your usual manner just now.'

'You were always the better for a round oath or two, señor capitán. But what is wrong with you this morning? You speak so slowly, and there are tears on your cheeks!'

'You must excuse me, old friend. More than goat's cheese and plums are at work this time, I fear. I find it hard to think aloud.'

'Compadre, the one true God knows very well that you were always a mad sailor, but you must reef in your sails this time. The god of storms, he is abroad and walking on these waters.'

'Aye, I feel him breathing down our necks, Francisco. Well, let him shake his trident and come on if he will. He cannot do more harm to us than the hurricanes of Cape Horn have already done. Dear old *Spray,* she will ride him out like a duck.'

'Are you sure of that, Don Jèsu? She is no longer so trim as when we sailed her through the Milky Way together.'

'Nor am I, Francisco. Nor am I. I cannot move this arm worth a damn.'

'Caramba! I fear you have suffered an apoplexy during the night, compadre!'

'Aye. You had best take the wheel, Francisco.'

'First I must know where you are headed, mi capitán.'

'Ha! I told all the newspapers that I was off to sail up the Orinoco, then cross over to the Amazon via the Rio Negro canal and make my way up the great river to its undiscovered source.'

'Madre di dios, señor capitán, surely you were not serious!'

'I didn't expect to return from our voyage round the world, either. Remember, you old pirate? It was you who braced me up by offering to pilot me round the world.'

'Alas, I cannot promise to do so much for you this time, mi capitán.'

'Nay, Francisco, nor do I want you to. Once around the world is enough for any man, aye? Besides, you've been waiting for me too long already. Now at last I may cease turning the pages of this book. You can't imagine how tiresome the last of them has grown! Yet the habit of fighting to stay alive dies hard in a man like me. Even so, *Spray* and I, we're as game to take on whatever comes next as you are.'

'Are all your ghosts laid to rest, then? Your wife, Hettie, what of her?'

'She'll be all right without me. I bought her the farm she dreamed of on Martha's Vineyard. And Virginia's children – Victor and Ben and Jessie and Garfield – they are all making their way in this world better than their father ever did. All our sails are set and our anchors are all away, Francisco.'

'You are quite sure you're ready to go with me?'

'Aye, pilot of the *Spray*, we've both found what we crossed these seas to find, have we not?'

'After centuries of searching, señor capitán, I finally found a comrade I could stand by.'

'Aye, and stand by him you did to hell and back, Don Francisco Pinzón, Pilot of the *Pinta*!'

'So tell me now, Don Jèsu, what was the greatest treasure you found along our way?'

'There were many treasures we found and won, Francisco, but learning how to love without minding the cost, that was by far the greatest.'

'No one knows better than I how dearly that particular pearl cost you, compadre!'

'Aye, finding that pearl cost me everything, but it was well worth it in the end. But enough of this women's talk! Belay the sheets fast, sirrah. Let us meet your god of storms head on. Give her the unreefed mainsail and the whole jib, and set her on her final course. Drive her down, Francisco, drive her straight down into the deep. *Spray* and I, we both are ready to go to hell with you, if need be.'

'Very well, you crazy Inglés, though I venture that this voyage won't take us so far as that. As you said, we've already been there and back. Take one good deep breath and look around you one last time.'

'Aye, it's been a hard life by times, but I wouldn't have missed it for the world. Ah-h, Spaniard, the women and the ships I've known!'

AGMV Marquis

MEMBRE DE SCABRINI MEDIA

Québec, Canada
2004